BY MY SIDE

DARA GIRARD

ISBN: 978-1949764550

BY MY SIDE

Published by ILORI Press Books

Cover Design and Layout Copyright © 2021 ILORI Press Books

Cover design by ILORI Press Books

Cover image copyright © sandralise/depositphotos

ILORI PRESS BOOKS, LLC

P.O. Box 10332

Silver Spring, MD 20914

www.iloripressbooks.com

Duvall Sisters

The Glass Slipper Project

Taming Mariella

A Reluctant Hero

The Black Stockings Society

Power Play

A Gentleman's Offer

Body Chemistry

Round the Clock

Return of the Black Stockings Society

Playing for Keeps

After Hours

A Private Affair

Just One Look

Private Lessons

The Main Attraction

Ladies of the Pen

Words of Seduction

Pages of Passion

Beneath the Covers

Henson Series

Table for Two

Gaining Interest

Careless Rapture

Dangerous Curves

Familiar Stranger

It Happened One Wedding

Unexpected Pleasure

Midnight Promise

Sweet Temptation

Always and Forever

Truly Yours

Say Yes

Picture Perfect

Clifton Sisters

The Sapphire Pendant

The Amber Stone

The Emerald Ring

Fortune Brothers

A Tempting Proposal

A Seductive Arrangement

An Unforgettable Moment

Novels

Honest Betrayal

The Daughters of Winston Barnett

Remember My Name

Illusive Flame

Winterwood Lane

Promise Me

This Changes Everything

Sparks

Piece of Cake

Best Laid Plans

Dear Reader,

Welcome to the eighth book in the *It Happened One Wedding* series where the best part of the story comes after "I do."

Except if it's an "I don't"

That's exactly what happens at wedding planner, Alicia Fox's, first wedding.

The ruined wedding was only the beginning of the fun surprises I'd face while writing this story.

I had no idea why Trey had ruined his best friend's wedding, what secret Jacob was hiding and why a woman named Sandra kept making an appearance, proving to be just as fascinating as the main character, Alicia.

Eventually, *By My Side*, became a story of not one, but two couples finding their way to love and happiness.

I hope you enjoy going on the journey with them.

All the best,

CHAPTER ONE

*S*he still heard the wailing. A bone chilling sound trapped in the now empty cathedral, echoing off its majestic walls. Or perhaps the sound was just trapped inside her memory like the silent scream still caged like a wild bird in her throat.

There would be no glorious celebration this autumn day in Virginia, when the brilliant yellow and red leaves on the trees outside of the church seemed to be touched by the golden rays of a sun so high in the cloudless blue sky she'd thought the day was destined for perfection.

It would have been perfect...

Instead there would be no Americanized pae-baek ceremony, piggyback rides, tossing of chestnuts, pictures of the bride cutting the wedding cake or a buffet set to host a variety of food such as white rice, ribs, kimchee and wine.

Roses scented the silence that gripped the church. Alicia Fox sighed, surprised their fragrance lingered.

But she lingered too when there was no reason to stay.

But she hadn't been able to leave. Not without answers.

Alicia shifted her gaze from one of the stained glass windows and looked at the man now bathed in a kaleidoscope of colors—reds, purples, blues—touching his broad shoulders and dark hair. He was the man at the center of it all.

At first glance he didn't look like a disaster.

She would never have suspected—she doubted anyone would—that he would not only ruin the wedding, but her entire business. For her, this wedding had been the culmination of a dream—a multicultural affair, her first. A blending of Korean and American sensibilities and traditions, which hadn't been easy since the bride didn't seem very interested in the groom's background. Having conducted an extensive study to make sure she mentioned where one could rent a hanbok (traditional Korean clothing) and a make-up artist who specialized in Asian American bridal makeup for the bridesmaids, the bride yawned and said she didn't want to do anything "too foreign" because she was going to be nervous anyway and didn't want to make a fool of herself.

Mention of a second Korean wedding ceremony (paebaek) also initially met with resistance, although Alicia suspected it was due more to price than to disinterest. Fortunately, the groom was very easygoing and didn't much care how the ceremony went, although Alicia suspected his parents had hoped for more of a say and were thrilled when she was able to suggest some Americanized changes so that the bride would be more comfortable with it. But they hadn't even made it through the first part: the cathedral wedding. The bride wore a vintage floral lace print dress with tulle sleeves, the groom handsome in a tux, the aisle adorned with roses.

It was a scene from a fairytale...until...

Alicia took a deep breath and gripped her hand into a fist. That didn't matter now. All that potential and beauty and promise had been lost in an instant.

All because of this man.

This man bathed in the light of a fading sun like a fallen angel, a man who'd forced her to accept the truth.

She was cursed.

As much as Alicia wanted to, she couldn't blame him for everything. He came at the tail end of a long list of failures. Before becoming a wedding planner, she had worked at a florist shop, a yoga practice, an art gallery, a daycare, a print shop, and had owned a web design company. Her jobs had faced the similar fate of the unfortunate wives of Henry VIII, except none survived. She'd been fired (divorced), made redundant (beheaded) and saw businesses close (died).

She'd promised herself that if this day went wrong she would quit. She'd take it as a sign that she couldn't make it on her own. That she couldn't run from fate.

Now she had to fulfill that promise. She'd poured everything into this wedding. But she'd take down her website, close all accounts and start again.

But first she had to understand why.

He didn't look like the kind of man who would sleep with the bride. Let alone the bride of his best friend. Not that a sleazebag had a certain look, but strangely she wouldn't have thought they would look like an intimidatingly handsome black man. A man who looked like he had ice in his veins and eyes like chips of granite. The suit he wore gave him an elegance that didn't match the hard jaw and too broad shoulders. Alicia preferred her men sleek like a panther—all smooth muscles and elegance. But this man reminded her of a shark—powerful, calculating, lethal.

He certainly was that. He'd killed everything today with one quick swipe. One cruel act.

At the moment when the pastor said in a bored tone, "If anyone has a reason why these two should not be joined together in holy matrimony speak now or forever hold your peace," the best man—this shark—raised his hand and the groom said, "Ignore him," and the best man said, "I was with the bride last night."

The groom said, "Shut up."

But the best man ignored his friend (former friend) and said in the same bored tone, "I have pictures if you don't believe me."

No one moved.

The bride, groom, and the pastor stood frozen. Time ticked past, the only thing that still seemed to be in motion.

Alicia remembered hearing a high pitched ringing in her ears, the sound of her breathing. She half-expected to wake from a dream.

Then everything frozen seemed to come alive at once. The cacophony of a uniform gasp from the crowd, outrage mixed with denials.

"He came on to me," the bride said.

"I told you to shut up," the groom said before he lunged at his former best friend and punched him. The best man didn't resist, he could have avoided the swing, dodged the other man's fist, but he didn't move. He let a punch settle on his hard jaw—once, twice. The enraged groom said something low that Alicia couldn't hear, probably no one could, before he shoved the best man hard, causing him to stumble back.

He crashed into a vase. A bouquet of flowers toppled to the ground. The groom stormed down the aisle, his parents racing after him.

The bride fell to her knees. Her family rushed to her. Three men sent the best man a look of rage, and the pastor immediately began an impromptu sermon about the dangers of anger, but nobody listened.

One of the men moved forward as if ready to attack as the groom had, but the best man sent him a look that caused the other man to hesitate. The best man didn't look angry, but bored. It was an unsettling expression, as if he were an elephant looking at a gnat. He didn't see them as a threat; he didn't find them very important at all. There would be no allowance for them.

Although it would be three to one, somehow he made it look like an unfair fight, as if he could destroy them with two simple moves. They sensed it too. If they wanted to fight, it would be a war, they didn't look willing and there was something in his dark gaze that let them know he was itching for blood so the men turned their attention back to the bride.

Alicia had been a little surprised the bride hadn't run

after the groom to coax him back or beg for his return. Alicia turned to the best man and her heart turned cold when he raised his hand and touched his busted lip.

Instead of a wince, she saw the hint of a smile.

But he wasn't smiling now and part of her wondered if she'd imagined it. No man would take pleasure destroying a friend's wedding day, right? It wasn't as if he'd professed his love for the bride. It all seemed so pointless.

Alicia closed her eyes and took a deep breath before she stood. She'd never see this man again. She never wanted to, but she'd get some answers first.

She sat down in front of him, resting her arm on the back of the pew. He didn't look at her, his gaze remained fixed on the pulpit.

"You had to do it this way?" she said.

He nodded. Quick, stiff, defiant.

"You couldn't have made this grand announcement last night? At the rehearsal dinner? A week ago?"

He blinked. She noticed his jaw tense before it relaxed. He shook his head, his dark gaze met hers with an intensity that made her hold her breath. His eyes were not only mesmerizing but filled with an emotion she couldn't interpret. But it was visceral, vital, real. So real that for a moment she not only held her breath, but felt her skin grow hot as she became fully aware of him. "No," he said in a soft voice. "I had to save him."

CHAPTER TWO

$\mathcal{H}$er brows shot up. The shark was delusional. Was he really trying to make himself the hero of this tragedy? "You had to save your best friend? Save him from marrying the woman he loved?"

The shark shifted his gaze and nodded.

"You still should have found another way to do it," Alicia said feeling suddenly chilled, as if without his gaze she felt the cold in the air. Although he sat in front of her he suddenly seemed far away. Distant.

"I had to stop it."

"So you stopped the wedding and lost your best friend, lost the respect of his family and yours, plus the bride's family and you still think there couldn't have been a better way to handle this?"

He looked at her. This time it was an unnerving moment because he seemed to be looking at her for the first time. His eyes were still cold, but calculating-assessing—then he looked down. "That is a good question. I tried to think of other ways. This seemed the best."

"If only you'd thought of doing this at another time. You ruined everything for me too."

His gaze flew to her face, shock briefly melting the ice there. Briefly his eyes—his face—seemed vulnerable, naive. Surprisingly kind. "I did?"

"Of course," Alicia said, unnerved by his gaze. So much so she squirmed in her seat and looked at the fallen rose petals scattered in the aisle. "This was going to launch my career and you ruined it."

"No one should blame you for this," he said, his deep voice firm. "You did nothing wrong. The ceremony was amazing. I'd hire you." He touched her hand, gave it a quick squeeze of reassurance before he drew back. "You're brilliant."

She almost believed him. Her skin felt hot again as it had been when he'd first looked at her.

She found him strangely intriguing and attractive, which didn't say much about her taste since she was constantly falling for inappropriate men. Like the one who'd told her he was separated from his wife. Translation: His wife was still in Nigeria and living with her parents after the birth of their second child.

Or the one whose tragic childhood made commitment difficult. Translation: He only felt whole when he was juggling three discreet relationships.

Then there was the one who told her he loved children. Translation: As long as they were someone else's since he'd abandoned the four he'd fathered from three different women.

So finding a man who'd slept with his best friend's bride ranked rather low on the appropriate scale. But she couldn't help herself, there was something mysteriously magnetic about him. Something that called to her to try to figure him out, she wanted to know more about him.

Alicia rubbed her hand wishing it still didn't feel warm from his touch. She'd just have to keep her distance. This was the year of change. Even though it wasn't the change she'd hoped for.

She'd hoped to live life on her terms, but life wasn't having it. After ten years of trying she was going to have to surrender and go back to the fold as everyone in her family had expected her to. She knew she was destined to live by the immigrant child creed—don't make anyone's suffering go to waste. Her great-grandparents had come to America from Jamaica and struggled to make a better life for their children, it was her duty to never squander that sacrifice. To show their loyalty and dedication, everyone in her family worked in the family business, MedForm, and every generation's goal—obligation—was to make the company better than the last. MedForm provided medical accessories and uniforms. They were uniform in more ways than one. Everyone fell in line. Her older brother and sister took interest in the business since middle school. They'd obtained the requisite university education, to show employees they'd put some effort in and weren't just being given positions without reason, although it was clear their surname was reason enough. MedForm was their life.

But Alicia lasted two years at university before leaving out of boredom. She wanted to learn about life by living it. She'd first shocked her parents by telling them she wanted to start working right out of high school, believing she could learn anything important right on the job. That was a no-no. A degree was a must.

No dice. She knew that she wasn't made for what they wanted for her, she needed to forge a different path. For three generations no one strayed from that path. Well, except for one uncle who'd tried to make it as a musician and after twenty years realized marrying money and working as an accountant was preferable to struggling.

But Alicia had wanted to struggle a little to find her place in the world.

"Why would you want to do that when you've got everything?" her friend, Deanna Marshall, had said. She'd been her college roommate and initially thought they'd had nothing in common, except disappointing their parent's expectations. Deanna's parents didn't believe in academia, their daughter was a bookworm determined to own her own business. They lived for the moment; she planned five to ten years in the future.

She and Deanna liked to joke that they must have been switched at birth, if only Deanna hadn't been white, but they liked to joke that perhaps along the gene pool there had been a mix up which years of pairings had hidden, however only a DNA analysis would uncover that. But a true affection developed and years later she was Alicia's closest friend. But Deanna's path had worked. She owned a company that sold office equipment wholesale. "You don't have to work hard to find work," she liked to remind Alicia. "You just have to walk into your father's study and say, 'Where can you use me?'"

But Alicia didn't want to do that. She didn't want to depend on her family. She'd wanted to do something unique. Finding that path had eluded her as much as finding a suitable boyfriend, possibly more so. The lies hurt, sure. Her heart got broken, fine. But failing at life...

Failing at seven jobs?

That was unheard of in the circles she travelled in. Her parents spoke about her in whispers, behind covered mouths or with an exaggerated eye roll. "Heaven knows what Alicia will be up to next," they'd say as if she were a wayward teenager instead of a woman on the verge of thirty-one.

Every failure hurt because she'd given it her all. She'd truly thought that hard work and effort would amount to something. That she'd gotten the genes of her entrepreneurial great-grandmother. But she hadn't. Not a shred.

"There is nothing wrong with continuing tradition," her father had said. "Not all of us are meant to create it."

But she hadn't wanted to fall in line with everyone else. Why? She didn't know. But she felt there was something more out there for her to try and explore.

But this wedding had proven her wrong.

It had been a hellish assignment and ended on a hellish note. She'd gotten the job because the bride's former wedding planner had cracked under the pressure of a recent divorce and decided to quit and move to Finland leaving them desperate to work with someone who could stay on deadline and was relatively cheap.

When Deanna had heard those requirements from a friend of a friend, she immediately put Alicia's name forward in an effort to help her get her fledgling new business off the ground.

Unfortunately, Alicia later wondered if the former wedding planner hadn't quit because of the divorce but because the bride's parents were tyrants. They seemed to appear at every meeting. More than once Alicia wanted to say that it was the bride and groom's day not theirs, but the couple stayed silent. Alicia felt for the groom, he wasn't going to have much leeway with his in-laws. She feared for the children that the couple would have. The parents would take over immediately.

The groom had intrigued her and she had been fascinated when she learned how the couple had met. Strangely enough, at a family function—a gallery showing of the bride's mother's work.

Somehow Alicia didn't know how the gorgeous looking 6 ft something groom, who looked like he'd be more at home with a beer in his hand and shouting at a soccer or basketball game on a flat screen, found himself at an art gallery, but perhaps he had hidden depths. Jacob Kim had luxurious black hair (that 'had to be cut before the wedding, dear' his soon to be mother-in-law had said) lovely brown eyes, a square jaw and a body...

Let's just say Alicia briefly, terribly, imagined Jacob and the best man playing basketball shirtless, sweat making their bodies glisten.

The two men were beautifully built and through a family member she'd learned Jacob played sports (mainly baseball) up until college, but they wouldn't get more specific than that.

What they were willing to be specific about was the men's friendship. They'd been close since elementary school. Inseparable. Alicia had never heard of anyone talk about such a loyal pair. It had surprised no one that popular, easygoing Jacob, a man who could charm an angry skunk if he put his mind to it, had chosen the quiet, reserved Trey DeVille as his best man.

An odd pair.

But they seemed to be more suitable as a couple than Jacob did with his bride-to-be.

It wasn't the fact that she was a petite blonde (she was a natural brunette but dyed her hair for the wedding) with a habit of wearing long false lashes and dark red lipstick and laughing nervously at the oddest times.

It was the way she looked at Trey.

A way no fiancée should look at a man she didn't plan to marry.

Alicia had thought she'd imagined the look at first. Especially since Trey came off as a statue to her. He wasn't the kind to get hot looks from women, perhaps unease or suspicion, but not the kind of interest Trey was getting from the bride-to-be and Jacob was completely unaware. Poor guy.

She certainly didn't think Trey would have acted on it. He and Jacob truly seemed like best friends. Not the typical back slapping 'this is my bro' kind of relationship, but a 'you need a kidney, I'm there' kind. True brothers.

She'd been wrong. But she'd been wrong about men before so that was no surprise.

But it was disappointing.

She'd wanted the nice guy Jacob to win in the end.

She'd wanted the statue, Trey, to really be a good friend.

She'd wanted her fledgling business to get off to a good start. None of that would happen. But she'd gotten used to not getting what she wanted.

Alicia stood and left the church and the lingering scent of roses ready to face a future she'd been avoiding for years.

CHAPTER THREE

His face burned. Throbbed. Ached. Not from the punches or even from the sight of his silver Mercedes with slashed tires. He'd expected that or something similar. Few people tried to assault him physically so his car seemed a good alternative.

No, the sight of the mutilated car didn't make his face burn. It didn't tighten his throat or cause him to blink extra fast to dispel the stinging tears behind his eyes. He had no use for tears. He didn't have much use for any emotion, but a gulf of sadness still threatened to consume him anyway and the soft touch of an autumn breeze gave him no comfort.

He'd done what he had to do, he knew the consequences, but that didn't stop the hurt. The betrayal he'd had to do in order to save his friend.

Trey heard someone swear and spun around and saw her: The wedding planner.

What was her name again?

He may not remember her name (he should remember her name, Jacob had mentioned it enough) and Jacob liked her, but Jacob liked most people so that hadn't made her especially memorable to him. However she wasn't easily forgettable with her braided hair pulled back into a bun at the nape of her neck, her purple wrap-around dress complementing her nut-brown skin and accentuating the luscious curve of her hips. Right now her beautiful brown eyes stared at his car as if she'd come upon a corpse. Horror etched on her round pretty face.

Why had he noticed that? Now wasn't the time to notice whether a woman was pretty or not, especially when she'd told him that he'd ruined her career. Trey sighed. He hadn't anticipated her being a casualty. Alicia. That was her name. Alicia. It said so right on her name tag, which he'd found interesting. He hadn't expected her to wear one that said: Alicia, At Your Service. He didn't think wedding planners did that but he also assumed that most didn't wear a big purple flower, which matched the dress, and her lipstick—she had nice lips something he also didn't want to notice—in their hair either.

"Do you need a ride?" she asked him.

He reached inside his jacket pocket for his cell phone and glanced at the text messages left by his parents. "No, I'm fine. I've got roadside assistance."

"But it might take them awhile to get here. You could be here—"

"It's okay," he interrupted. He called and made arrangements for his car to be towed to a local repair shop. He disconnected then jumped when he felt a light touch on his arm. He turned, shocked to see Alicia still standing there. "Yes?"

"Are you sure you're okay?" she said.

He blinked. Why wouldn't he be okay? The car tires were slashed, those could be easily replaced. He couldn't understand her concern. "Yes. They'll be here in twenty minutes. I'll just wait in the car until they come." He opened the driver's side.

She slammed the door closed. He stared at her in shock, but it soon turned to irritation. What was wrong with her? He made the effort to keep his voice polite. "Yes?"

"What if they planted a bomb?"

"A bomb?"

"Yes. The moment you sit inside it goes off?"

"A pressure sensor bomb?"

She nodded.

"Or perhaps one that is connected to the ignition and when I turn it on the bomb will detonate?"

She nodded again.

Trey cleared his throat. She looked serious. It probably wasn't kind but he couldn't help himself. He threw his head back and laughed.

He laughed so hard he did start crying. Tears streamed down his cheeks. He wiped his eyes, looked at her and quickly sobered.

Laughing hadn't been a good idea. She looked hurt and offended.

He waved his hand and bit his lip. "I'm sorry, but what you said makes no sense."

"You have no idea how angry—"

"I do," Trey said grim. There was no hint of the amusement that had briefly given him solace left in his tone. "I know more than you think. But I surprised them. Do you really think someone in there had the time to prepare a bomb and plant it within minutes?" He paused. "Unless you know something I don't?"

"Now you're making fun of me."

He opened the hood of the car. "No, I'm not. If you think my life is in danger I'll check it out." He cast his eye over the interior. "Nope." He got down on the gravel surface and checked underneath the carriage. "Looks clear." He stood and wiped gravel from his trousers. "But just in case I'm wrong, I'd suggest you leave before the tow truck comes."

Alicia folded her arms. "I was only trying to help."

Trey nodded, wondering why she still looked annoyed. He was doing what she'd asked. "I know. Thank you." He patted her on the shoulder. He was taught touch was a good thing and could make people trust him. "I'll make it up to you. I promise."

His words and his touch didn't seem to improve her mood however, her frown increased. "Fine. Bye."

"Bye."

She walked away, quickly as if she were suddenly in a hurry to get somewhere. He was a little sorry to see her go.

"Many thanks," he called after her.

She didn't turn but she raised her hand and flashed a rude gesture.

Trey frowned. That was strange. Why would she do that? Maybe she didn't know a raised middle finger was a curse word. He'd gotten in trouble not knowing things too. He turned from her. It had been an awful day but somehow, for a few brief minutes, she'd made it a little brighter.

He'd repay her.

Trey rested against his car and briefly closed his eyes. One... two...three.

He was no longer standing alone in a church parking lot. Instead he was in a river, no an ocean. And the ocean was still, the waves gentle. He heard the cry of a seagull and in the distance he saw an island. And he began to swim towards it, because an island meant safety. He may be alone but he wouldn't drown.

He couldn't drown.

He had to keep swimming. Even when the sun's rays pounded against his skin and the distance to the island felt both close and far away. He had to keep swimming, no matter how weary he felt. He had to reach it.

He. Must. Not. Drown.

The sound of footsteps broke through his fantasy. He didn't need to open his eyes to know who they belonged to. They were coming closer to him. Not rushed, casual but determined. He heard them stop about a foot away.

He slowly opened his eyes.

CHAPTER FOUR

He heard Jacob swear, but his words were more colorful than Alicia's gesture had been.

Trey hadn't expected Jacob to come back. He hadn't expected to see or hear from him again.

He felt Jacob's grip on his collar. He smelled cologne but not the cheap beer he knew his friend would consume later. He'd usually drink with him (cold beer with a hot pizza had been a favorite), but there would be no shared drinks between them anymore.

"Why'd you do it?" Jacob said. His voice still held anger, but Trey could take anger. He didn't like the hurt, the same hurt he'd seen in Alicia's eyes. He didn't want to hurt anyone. He only wanted to help. Jacob may not have known about Trey's plan, but he knew the reason behind his actions.

Trey kept his gaze lowered. Jacob's shoes were still shiny, but his tux's jacket was gone. He wondered where he'd left it. Jacob was always careful with his clothes. "You're not supposed to be here."

"I'll get back before they worry."

Trey nodded. "You don't want that. They've been through enough."

Jacob's tone hardened. "Answer me. Why did you do it?"

"You know why."

"Do you really understand what you've done?" Jacob's voice cracked in misery. Trey took a deep breath. He willed himself not to feel anything. Nothing mattered. He didn't regret a thing. "I can't...you not only ruined the wedding but we're over. Finished. More than twenty years of—"

"I know." Trey glanced at the large silver watch on Jacob's wrist. When would he stop talking and go away? Nothing he said could change anything. "I know."

"And still you—"

Trey nodded. "Yes."

He felt the grip on his collar tighten. Jacob was strong. He could probably strangle him with one twist of his wrist. A little more pain would be nice. Pain was better than longing for something to be different than it was.

"Why do you have dirt on your shirt?"

Trey looked up surprised by the question. "My shirt?" He glanced down and noticed oil marks on his white shirt. That's right, Jacob would notice things like that. "She wanted me to check for bombs."

"Who?"

"Alicia. Your wedding planner." The thought amused

him again and he bit his lip to keep from laughing. "She looked so serious I checked. I checked under the hood and everything."

Jacob folded his arms. "Did you laugh?"

"At first," Trey said feeling a little guilty, "but I stopped. I even thanked her twice." He rubbed his chin. "But then when she was walking away she did this to me," he mimicked the crude gesture. "Maybe she didn't hear me."

Jacob sighed. "You really are out of this world."

Trey frowned. "You know I hate when you say that."

"I'm not far from wrong." He met his eyes. "You don't know how this world works. And the worst part of all isn't that to make your plan work I can never see you again, but because you protected me, now you have no one to protect you. Now you're all alone."

Trey felt his face burn again, but this time there was no tightened throat, no threat of tears. There was no gulf to swallow him, only emptiness and a sad resignation. He heard the sound of dry leaves being pushed over the ground by the breeze. He looked up at the blue sky and saw red and yellow leaves swirl around each other and dance in the wind. He felt his heart lift. They were free. He hoped they would continue to dance before they landed somewhere far from here. "Doesn't matter. I'm used to it."

Jacob shook his head. "You shouldn't be." He tugged him forward and Trey knew he wanted to hug him as a final goodbye.

He could bear a lot of things but not that. This was a

new beginning not a goodbye. Trey stepped back. "Let go."

Jacob didn't move. His dark eyes defiant.

"I mean it. Someone could see us."

"I don't care." Jacob lowered his head and swore before he looked at him again. "I wish you hadn't—"

Trey wrapped his hand around Jacob's throat. "It's done. Now let go."

Jacob swore again before he released him. "You—"

Trey turned and opened his car door. "Go. No use wishing for what can't be changed. Just make it worth it." He closed the door to any words Jacob may have said and turned on the engine. It took him only a second to realize he was in a car that couldn't go anywhere.

CHAPTER FIVE

"Tell me again."

"I've already told you three times."

"It's funnier each time you say it."

"It's not funny at all. How can you find pleasure in someone's ruined wedding?"

Deanna laughed and shook her head, curling her feet underneath her where she sat on the couch. "No, it's not that." She adjusted her glasses and ran a hand through her curly brown hair. "It's how you tell the story. How you imitate this guy is hilarious."

Alicia wondered if inviting Deanna over to her apartment to cheer her up had been a good idea. She realized it hadn't. She didn't feel any better. A half pint of Cherry Garcia ice cream hadn't helped. Not even letting Deanna paint her nails a hot new orange hadn't worked. Usually bright colors brightened her mood, but nothing was working. All she remembered were cold, dark eyes set in the face of a handsome shark who'd laughed at her.

Of course she didn't tell Deanna about that. It hurt too much. But she should be used to people laughing at her. They always found her amusing no matter how serious she was being. Like now. She knew and loved Deanna but her friend's laughter was more cutting because of how much it echoed his.

He must have thought she was ridiculous. But she'd truly been worried about him. She wished she hadn't. Standing tall in the sunshine the shark looked even more intimidating, not only his size but the haughty look in his eyes.

Inside the church she hadn't paid much attention to what emphasized him the most. Was it the expensive cut of his suit, the Rolex on his wrist or the Italian shoes? Standing next to his Mercedes he looked like a model for an American Express card. He was the picture of wealth and success and she was a failed wedding planner.

But he hadn't only laughed at her, he'd mocked her too. He'd pretended to listen to her concerns, dramatically looking under the hood of his car and then crawling under it, getting oil on his shirt for good measure, in a cruel sarcastic manner and then...

And then the bastard thanked her. Twice!

"I wish I could meet him," she heard Deanna say.

Alicia turned to her friend alarmed. "Why would you say that? It was awful. The wedding was a disaster." She held up a finger in warning when Deanna's lip trembled in amusement. "I'm serious. It was..." Alicia shook her head. "I read them both so wrong. I truly thought they were best friends. I'd never seen two people who seemed to get on so well and everyone else thought so...Wait are you writing this down?" she said stunned when Deanna started to furiously type on her phone.

"Just keep talking. This is good stuff. Great material. This Ray—"

"Trey."

"He sounds interesting and his friend too, Jacob, right? I wish I had pictures." She wiggled her eyebrows at Alicia. "You must have pictures."

She did have pictures—ones she'd later delete—of the fabulous reception hall, the gorgeous cathedral and one which showed Trey and Jacob talking before the ceremony began. "I'm not giving you pictures."

"Doesn't matter. I'll use my imagination. I'm sure it's better than the real thing anyway. What are they? Medium height? A little pudgy?"

"They're both six foot something, fit and very good looking."

Deanna wiggled in her seat like a happy child. "Ooh even better. This sounds too good to be true." She narrowed her eyes. "Are you teasing me?"

Alicia folded her arms. "I'm having an emotional breakdown, my business is ruined and you're worried about *me* teasing *you*?"

Deanna looked properly contrite. "You're right. It's just that when you started talking about them I got this great idea for my next story. I'm sorry."

Alicia sighed ready to forgive her friend. Deanna had few faults. She was smart, driven, ambitious, successful, kind, but she had one huge weakness. She was an unwavering fan of yaoi or BL (boys' love) manga. She had rows of the books on her shelf at home, electronic versions for ready access on her phone and iPad and she not only consumed the genre, but also created fan fiction for some of her favorite series.

"Okay, I forgive you. Now I—"

Deanna held up a hand before she continued to type. "Just give me a minute. Who do you think would be the dominant one? Jacob or Trey?"

Alicia threw up her hands. "I don't know."

Deanna tapped her cheek, thoughtful. "From your description probably Jacob. Trey would be the submissive one." She licked her lips. "Oh, this is going to be so good."

"Why would you think that?" Alicia said then mentally kicked herself for asking. She didn't want to be interested in her friend's crazy obsession, especially about a man she quickly wanted to forget. But her friend's logic made her curious. "Trey doesn't look like he'd submit to anyone."

Deanna snapped her fingers then pointed at her. "Exactly and yet he let Jacob hit him. Only a submissive would do that. And then later Jacob would..."

Alicia held out her hands. "Just stop." She let her hands fall. "I'm having a career crisis I don't want to deal with your BL fantasies right now. Put the phone away."

"Just let me—"

"Now! Otherwise I'm telling Mark about the two stories you wrote about him and his mechanic."

Deanna's eyes widened at the mention of her long term boyfriend who still didn't know the extent of her BL admiration. "You wouldn't dare."

Alicia flashed a sly grinned. "I can recite their first meeting by heart."

"It was a moment of weakness. I haven't done anything since." Deanna quickly put the cell phone away. "But, you're right. I got carried away with this and I'm sorry. I'm listening." She rubbed her hands together. "So what are you going to do?"

Alicia looked down at her orange colored nails. "Go to work with my family." She glanced up when Deanna started laughing. She gritted her teeth. She was getting really annoyed at people laughing at her. "What's so funny?"

Deanna wiped her eyes then shoved her glasses back on. "It sounded like you said you were going to work for your family."

"Because that's exactly what I said."

Deanna blinked. "You're serious?"

"Yes."

"But you'll hate it."

"You've always wondered why I hadn't done it in the first place."

"That was before I got to know you. You don't belong there. MedForm isn't you."

"Maybe it is. Maybe I never really gave it a chance. All I know is that I'm tired of failing."

"You can't give up."

"I'm not giving up. I'm giving in. The signs are all there. It's time to stop dreaming." It was time to be the adult her family expected her to be.

CHAPTER SIX

Sneaking out was always easier than sneaking in, but Jacob made it back to his bedroom in the family house without anyone noticing.

He could have gone to his apartment but he knew his family would have followed him there, so he opted to stay at the family house in the meantime while he played the broken hearted groom.

He flopped back on his bed and then texted his sister, Maya, who stayed at the family house while finishing her master's degree, to let her know he was back. Moments later he heard a tapping on the door.

He used his arm to cover his eyes. "Come in."

He heard the door open then close.

"Oh my God, Jacob," she said.

He made a noncommittal sound.

"Where did you go?"

He shook his head. He wasn't going to tell her. He wasn't going to tell anyone.

He heard her sigh and knew she understood. "What the hell was that?"

He didn't want to talk about the wedding either.

As a kid he used to dream about acquiring a superpower. It used to change every couple of years. At seven he wanted to fly. At ten he wanted laser vision. Twelve it was speed. By fifteen he pretended that he didn't care, though he secretly wished he had the mind power of Professor X. Now, at thirty-two, he wished he had the ability to time travel and make sure he never said 'yes' to the hot woman flirting with him at an art gallery he shouldn't have gone to in the first place. He'd make sure not to convince himself he was in love with her, that she was in love with him. He'd definitely make sure he wouldn't convince himself that he wanted to spend the rest of his life with her.

But he didn't have a superpower so he had to deal with this present hell.

"Did that really just happen," Maya said, "or did I just drop down into some parallel universe where Trey acts completely out of character?"

Jacob ran a hand down his face and shook his head, "You—"

"No wait! What if it's some sort of alien invasion? That would be amazing. I mean Trey would never do something like that. What if they have the real Trey locked up somewhere and—"

"Enough," Jacob said with a tired sigh. He usually could take his sister's strange theories, especially when she was on a role. They usually amused him. Instead, this time, they just depressed him more.

Trey had done the unforgivable in front of everyone and all for the dumbest of reasons. But he didn't want to think about that right now.

Jacob sat up, looked at her then quickly covered his eyes. "What the hell are you wearing?"

"Grayson's got some ideas for a new painting he's working on and I'm his muse. He wanted some pictures."

"In which he needs you to wear a polka dot bikini in the middle of autumn?"

"The house isn't cold."

Jacob groped for his tuxedo jacket then threw it at her. "Put this on."

She slipped the jacket on and pulled her face into a pout. "Grayson says I look beautiful."

Maya wasn't beautiful, not in any conventional sense (his family liked to joke that he got the looks and she got what was left over). To a critical outsider's gaze her eyes were too small and her lips too thin, she wasn't elegantly petite, she was just short and stocky with brown highlights in her shoulder length black hair.

But to him, his younger sister was one of the dearest people in his life; someone he thought deserved to be respected and treasured. Not squeezed into a bikini that was too small and didn't compliment her curvy figure. But it wasn't something he'd ever say. Nor would he ever tell her that he didn't particularly like Grayson.

Maya's artist boyfriend was the reason why Jacob had ended up at said gallery where he'd met said fiancée. If he could time travel his sister wouldn't have met Grayson at the Folklife Festival in Washington DC, instead she'd fall for Trey as Jacob originally hoped and all would have been perfect.

Maya buttoned the jacket then held out her arms. "Better?"

Jacob looked at her and couldn't stop a smile. "Not by much." His jacket nearly swallowed her up, making her look like a five year old playing dress up. He pulled out his cell phone. "Trey needs to see this." He stopped before he took the shot. He sighed and let the phone fall to the bed. Trey was no longer part of his life anymore.

Maya sat on the bed and took his hand in hers. Her eyes searched his. "Where did you go? Did you see him? You've got to tell me what happened."

Jacob pulled his hand away. "You saw what happened."

"I can't believe he'd do that." She shook her head. "Not Trey."

Jacob swallowed. He couldn't tell her the truth. There was too much at stake. "What's going on downstairs?"

Maya folded her arms in surrender, giving him a chance to change the subject. "Do you want the long or short version?"

"Short."

"Appa refuses to speak. Eomma is still in a rage, crying and having a one sided conversation with God, and Halmeoni is fielding all the phone calls. But she's been giggling. I think she's the only one enjoying this. I don't think she ever liked—"

"I know." His grandmother had barely hid how she felt about Beth.

Maya fell silent then asked in a quiet voice, "What are you going to do?"

"I don't know." Jacob looked at her feeling helpless. Everything had been planned. His future, his life, had been set on a path that had been derailed. He'd never known such freedom before. It was liberating and terrifying. "What am I supposed to do?"

Maya stared at him speechless, which was a rare thing.

He swore. If she didn't have anything to say, that meant it was really bad. The family liked to joke that it would take another Ice Age to freeze her tongue in place.

Obviously not.

"Did it really just happen?" she said again and this time he knew she wasn't trying to be facetious. He felt the same way. It all felt surreal. Only six hours ago he'd been worried about the amount of bags Beth had packed for their honeymoon. He had prepared himself for his life changing. But not like this.

"I warned you," Trey had whispered before Jacob punched him. Trey didn't flinch. He took the full brunt of his anger. He didn't make any apologizes or excuses. Everyone else would see Trey in one way, but Jacob knew the truth. A truth he couldn't tell anyone. Not if he wanted to survive. Not if he wanted to make Trey's sacrifice worth it.

On the drive home, his favorite aunt and a cousin started to say horrible things about Trey, but he stopped them cold. "This is between Trey and me. If you have to say anything, don't say it within my hearing."

"That's the trouble with you," his cousin told him. "You're too nice. That's why you get taken advantage of."

Jacob's brother, the smart one, smirked. "Still going to stand up for him? Then you're dumber than we all thought."

"Shut up, Yong," Maya said, ever his protector.

Yong rolled his eyes. "How many space invasion scenarios have you come up with?"

She folded her arms and muttered something under her breath while Yong turned his attention to Jacob and said, "The truth is Trey was always jealous of you and now you know how much. Time to face the truth."

The truth was Trey had been covering for him for years. When Jacob had first come to the new elementary school, a large building cradled in a Virginia suburb, he wasn't sure what to do on the third grade history test so he copied the kid next to him.

Later, the teacher, a woman so tall that when she stood Jacob could see the dark hairs under her chin, called them both in during recess and scolded them. But that didn't bother him. He'd grown used to getting in trouble since starting school back in Georgia where he'd moved from. His family had gotten used to calls from the school but he'd also gotten used to disappointing them too.

The teacher held up the two tests, which had the exact same answers wrong and what struck him was how neat this kid wrote his name: Trey DeVille. He'd never seen handwriting that neat before, it looked like it had been done on a computer.

She frowned and pointed a long nail bitten finger at Trey. "You should apologize for cheating."

Jacob held his breath. He waited for Trey to deny the unfair charge and point to him as the cheater. He was the stupid one. The loser.

Instead, Trey looked at her and laughed.

Knee-slapping, tear wiping laughter. The sound of his laughter was so infectious Jacob had to bite his lip to keep from starting to laugh too.

The teacher glared at Trey, her cheeks sunk in so much and her red lips puckered in a way that reminded him of a fish. Jacob bit his lip harder and stared down at his shoes praying he wouldn't start laughing. He squeezed his eyes shut. *Please. Please don't make me laugh.* He took a deep breath before he looked up at her again.

"You think this is funny?"

Jacob shook his head; Trey nodded.

And then Jacob laughed.

As punishment she made them both write 'I will respect others' one hundred times.

It was only later that Jacob learned that the teacher had been a substitute and didn't know that Trey was one of the smartest kids in the class. Because the real teacher hadn't been there, Trey got in trouble because of him.

It took Jacob a couple of weeks to gain the courage to approach Trey to thank him for covering for him. Not only because he was afraid of Trey's anger, but because of what the other kids said about the kid who always played by himself at recess.

One day, trying to gain the courage to talk to him,

Jacob noticed Trey alone in the corner of the playground with his back to the rest of the kids looking at something in the dirt.

"Stay away from him," his new friend, a skinny kid with spiky black hair named Louis, warned him, "He's Haitian."

Jacob blinked feeling stupid as always. "What does that mean?" he whispered, hoping no one else would hear him.

"It means he's from Haiti."

Jacob chewed his lower lip, feeling even dumber. He still didn't understand. "Okay."

Louis moved his shoulders with impatience and said, "He'll put a voodoo curse on you."

"A whoohoo what?"

Louis laughed. "A voodoo curse. Really bad stuff. He's smart but he's also scary."

But he didn't seem scary. Just really quiet.

After Trey hadn't snitched on him about the cheating, Jacob'd kept his distance. He knew that Trey wasn't someone to fear, instead he was someone he wanted to know. How could the smartest kid in class have no friends? He didn't brag. He didn't bully. He really didn't say anything, except when he was called on in class and the teacher rarely did that.

It was a soggy spring afternoon when Jacob finally decided to talk to him. He ignored Louis' pleas and the other kids' warnings as he crossed the blacktop to where Trey knelt in the dirt.

He felt his heart pounding as he crouched down beside him. Trey didn't say anything and Jacob wondered if he'd tell him to leave him alone. Instead, after a few seconds Trey said, "Did you see that?"

"See what?"

Trey pointed to an earthworm popping its head out of the soil. "That."

He'd seen worms before and didn't find them interesting. He started to stand and Trey didn't move or ask him to stay. He began to turn then stopped. It was the way Trey was focused that intrigued him more than the worm did.

"Why do you care?"

"I didn't think it was strong enough."

"Of course it's strong enough to move dirt."

"I didn't think it could move money."

Jacob crouched beside him again, intrigued. "What?"

"Look."

Jacob looked down and then finally saw what Trey had really been looking at: the earthworm was moving a dime out of its tunnel. It was quite a feat. That day began one of many where Trey showed him things that he'd overlooked. But at eight years old he wasn't to know that the quiet kid was to become his best friend. Instead, he was a little afraid that he'd reject him when he apologized.

He moved some dirt with his thumb and said, "Thanks for not...saying anything about the test."

"Hmm."

"I'm sorry you got in trouble."

Trey shrugged. "She's stupid."

Jacob dug deeper, feeling the wet dirt under his nails. "So am I."

"No you're not."

It was the way he spoke—so certain, with such confidence—that Jacob almost believed him. Almost. Then he got a little angry. Was he making fun of him? He was only seven years old how come he sounded like an old man? And how could he say that when he didn't even know him? "But I cheated."

"You were scared. That's what people do. That's what my grandma says. But you don't have to be scared. She's not going to be here next month."

Trey thought Jacob was scared of the teacher. But in truth Jacob was scared of everything, making new friends was easy, but tests and grades always made him nervous. No, they terrified him.

And things didn't get better.

He coasted on his charm. It was better than trying when he kept disappointing his parents and he had two siblings who did amazingly well in school. He remembered his first B—sophomore year in algebra—being met with a tired sigh from his dad and a wish from his mother that he'd given his schoolwork more effort. That he should try to be like Yong and Maya.

He still remembered the feel of his nails biting into the flesh of his palm as he gripped his hand into a fist. He'd struggled for that damn B. He'd made Trey test him over and over again and yet it wasn't enough. He stopped caring about much after that.

Except his friendship with Trey.

Trey became not only his best friend but his champion. From seven years old until now he'd been by his side. The one person he could trust.

The one person who thought he was smart, though Jacob still didn't know why. Jacob wasn't the one with the master's degree in... Hell, he kept forgetting what Trey had studied—something to do with rocks. Something complicated and scientific. But Jacob never felt stupid around him. He never felt inferior. He could always be himself.

He'd lost the one person who truly saw him as he was.

Because he was too afraid to admit what he really wanted.

CHAPTER SEVEN

*I*f she didn't think, she wouldn't cry.

Alicia walked down MedForm's hallway with its dark blue carpeted floors and pristine grey walls to her office, returning from a meeting she still didn't know the purpose for (or rather pretending she was returning from a meeting, when she'd actually left the meeting and gone to her car, put on a silver and pink wig, because it always put her in character, and played a prison escape game on her cell phone before returning to the office like nothing was wrong), wishing she hadn't worn heels.

She preferred boots to heels. But in her role as production manager she was expected to wear heels with her grey, blue or black suits. It had been two months since her sister reminded her that the pink A-line skirt that worked wonderfully with her favorite pair of black boots and a matching black and pink blouse were not the kind of attire employees at MedForm wore. Especially employees who were part of the founding family —namely her.

Two months since she'd had to remove the fairy lights she'd decorated around her two foot high rubber plant. The plant could stay, the lights had to go as did her large abstract painting that her mother was convinced looked like a vagina. Her sister disagreed and thought it looked more like a vulva. Alicia had been unable to convince them otherwise so the broad colorful painting bursting with lush pinks, creams and reds had been replaced by a staid landscape of a beach scene.

She hated the beach.

She also hated having to push all her comfortable clothes to the back of her closet and 'dress like an adult' as her sister liked to tell her. No more neon blues and purples, no outrageous nail colors, no flair skirts or designer blouses, unless they were simple and as unfussy as the uniforms they sold. But at least she had a job. She didn't have any reason to complain. She only had to keep her head down, do what she was told, vacation at one of the family beach homes in the Caribbean, and invest wisely until she retired.

Alicia swallowed, suddenly feeling ill. This was the price she had to pay. She knew what the world was like and the world wasn't ready for her.

Alicia walked into her office, which looked about as grey as the sky outside her window, closed the door, and hung up her jacket on the freestanding coat rack.

She turned to walk to her desk then stopped. Her office didn't have a coat rack. And if she *did* have a coat rack it wouldn't smell like cinnamon espresso. She spun around and gaped at the tall black man removing her jacket from his face.

Him!

The statue! The shark! The reason she felt like she was slowly dying of boredom was standing in her office!

Alicia was too shocked to scream so she gasped instead in a way that caused her to choke on her own air and start coughing.

She waved away the bottled juice he offered her from off her desk. He actually looked concerned. She didn't remember his eyes being so soft and brown.

Wait, he was the jerk who'd laughed at her. What was she thinking?

She held up her hand when he opened his mouth to speak. "Excuse me." She dashed out of her office and rushed to the admin assistant's desk. Fabian was a man in his late thirties who managed to do as little work as possible while he improved his Candy Crush skills. He also happened to be a cousin, the son of her father's favorite sister, so instead of being fired he tended to be moved around every couple years to a different division. Unfortunately, it was her year to have him. Alicia planted her hands on his desk. "Is there something you forgot to tell me?"

He blinked. He sat as erect as a dancer, looking poised in a dark blue turtleneck, his tawny brown skin freshly moisturized, and looked as vacuous as an empty warehouse.

Alicia took a deep breath. "Like...There's a man in my office."

Fabian blinked again this time dawning coming over

his handsome features. "Oh. Right. Sorry. I meant to tell you about him when you got back from your meeting."

"And?" Alicia pressed when he fell silent.

"There's a man in your office."

Alicia stared at her cousin's turtleneck and briefly imagined her hands wrapped around it. "And?"

"And..." Fabian looked at his laptop. "His name is um...give me a second. I think I have it on a Post-it."

Alicia spun away. "Never mind."

"Wait," he called after her, "You might want to check your hair."

Alicia ignored him (she really didn't want style advice right now) and marched back to her office. She halted in the doorway when she saw that Trey was gone. She'd expected to find him sitting in front of her desk impatiently waiting, but he wasn't there. She didn't know why she felt a sense of loss. She closed the door and rested against it.

"Long day?" a deep voice said.

CHAPTER EIGHT

She jumped from the door and turned to see Trey, who still stood in the corner like a sentinel. "What are you doing there?"

He stared at her confused. "Standing."

"Why didn't you take a seat?" She motioned to the chair. "I'd thought you'd gone."

He frowned. "Why would I be gone? I came here to see you."

Alicia rubbed her forehead. It was no use trying to make sense of the situation. Or him. Or anything.

"Why are you here?" she finally managed, taking care to keep her words slow and modulated.

"I wanted to see you," he said in the same tone.

She folded her arms. "Are you mocking me?"

He stared at her surprised. "No."

Alicia let her hands fall to her hips. His surprise seemed sincere. "Why didn't you say anything?"

"I didn't want to scare you."

Her brows shot up. "You thought standing in the dark was a better idea?"

"I wasn't in the dark, there's plenty of light from the window," he said then paused. "And I wasn't sitting down when you first came in because I was studying your fascinating plant and then you came into the room and I thought about saying something, but then I thought that would frighten you, so I thought it would be better for you to notice me first."

Alicia stared at him for a long moment, taking in his maroon shirt and dark trousers. Even standing in the corner he looked like he was modeling men's wear or wall paint. He actually made the wall look good. She shook her head, annoyed that she'd been distracted. She had to remember that she didn't like him. He'd made fun of her. "That makes absolutely no sense."

Trey paused then said, "Perhaps I should explain it this way—"

She waved him away. "No need. I still won't understand you. But before we begin we need to take care of your hands." She went to her desk and opened a drawer.

"My hands?"

"Yes," she said, returning to him with a bottle of lotion. She squirted a quarter sized dollop into his palm. "They're dry. The cold weather is cruel to our skin. You need to take care of it. Didn't your mother teach you that? My mother made it her mission that my brother, sister and I were well lathered. So much so that I made up a song about it: *Dash that Ash.* I'd sing it after every shower. She was not amused."

Trey tentatively lifted his hand to his nose. "It smells nice."

Alicia frowned. "It shouldn't smell at all." She glanced down at the tube in her hand and realized she'd grabbed the one that smelled like roses instead of the scent-free bottle. Damn. But no need to tell him that and fortunately he didn't look bothered by it being scented, he actually looked pleased. The shark looked so pleased that Alicia looked down at his hands and saw how supple and moisture rich they looked now, emphasizing the beauty of his brown skin that she was tempted to smell his hands too.

She took a step back and folded her arms. She had to focus. "So what are you doing here?"

"I just told you."

"You wanted to see me?"

He nodded. His gaze swept her from head to toe. "You look amazing."

She rested her hands on her hips. "No, I don't."

He looked like he wanted to argue then decided against it. Instead he said, "Sorry it took me so long to get in touch, but work got in the way, I was out of the country for a bit and then it took me a while to find you after you closed down your business."

Alicia narrowed her eyes. "Why would you want to find me?"

"Because of what I did."

"And what did you do?"

"You said I ruined your career. I wanted to remedy that. In all my calculations I didn't think you'd become a casualty of my actions."

Alicia waited for him to break into a smile or laugh or something. But he only stared at her. "You're serious?"

"Absolutely. I know of three other couples who could use your services."

She gestured to the room. "As you can see, I'm not doing event planning anymore."

He blinked. "You're trying to make me feel guilty."

She shook her head with a sad smile. "No, you're not the only reason I decided to stop. I realized that career wasn't me."

"But you were excellent. Everything was amazing," he said then recited a list of all the things she'd done. Alicia stared at him stunned that he'd noticed. It made her heart swell and ache at the same time.

"Please let me make it up to you. What business are you in now?"

"I just showed you." She made another sweeping gesture, indicating her office.

His gaze darted to the beach scene on the wall. "I mean your side project."

"There is no side project. This is it."

His sharp, assessing gaze briefly met hers before darting away again but not before making her feel as if she'd been shocked by lightning. An intense energy seemed to swirl around him making the air around her feel electrified. His expression remained neutral but his eyes shifted from her desk to the window to her face then back to her desk again in a manner that was unsettling.

She'd noticed that he had a strange manner of not holding her gaze, even at the church. His brown eyes would make brief contact and then his gaze would dart away and focus on something else. Because of that she couldn't tell if he was putting her on, but she sensed he was in earnest. He really felt guilty.

Alicia felt her defenses weakening. He was strange but at least he wasn't making fun of her. She'd grown tired of that. "It's okay. Really. I'm not the one you need to apologize to anyway," she said, wondering why he'd feel guilty about her but not what he'd done to his former best friend. "The day I told you that you ruined my career I was just taking my frustration out on you."

Trey nodded. "Are you hungry?"

She glanced at the clock on the wall. It was a simple circular decoration (that had replaced her original dog shaped clock with a wagging pendulum tail) and sometimes made time feel as if it were passing so slowly.

It was four-thirty. She had another hour and a half to go since her family liked her to work until six.

But she didn't have much more to do and she was eager to get out of there even for an hour.

And he was an enigma she wanted to figure out. "Are you paying?"

"Of course."

She grinned. "Then I'm starving."

CHAPTER NINE

She hadn't run away screaming. He'd take that as a good sign. Trey followed Alicia to the elevator feeling the tension within him ease.

He had a chance to redeem himself. He'd spent a week contemplating the value of trying to find her. He'd assessed the pros and cons.

But rationality, usually his more assuring friend, abandoned him. As much as he knew, her business failure had nothing to do with him. The fact that she'd accused him of it bothered him. *She* bothered him.

In the church she'd looked so defeated and in spite of her pain she'd still tried to help him. She had a good heart. She deserved better and he'd hated the idea of an innocent bystander getting hurt by his scheme, especially when he'd planned it to affect as few people as possible. He'd studied the cancellation clause for all the vendors and paid them, including the entire cost for the honeymoon.

He hadn't thought about the wedding planner but had assumed that, since she'd been paid well, she would have a story to tell and move on to her next client. He never imagined Jacob's wedding would be her first and last.

Trey remembered the first time he'd met her when she'd stopped by Jacob's place for an appointment Jacob had forgotten about.

He and Jacob had returned to his apartment sweaty from a long jog and been attacked by a cheetah. At least that was what Beth reminded him of when she met them at the door with her teeth baring.

"Where have you been?"

Jacob grinned. "Why? You've missed me that much?"

"You're late."

"Late?"

"For our meeting with the wedding planner."

He swore. "That was today?"

"An hour ago. I called and texted you."

Jacob pulled out his cell phone and swore again. "Sorry, I put it on mute."

Beth shifted her gaze to Trey. "I even called you."

"You didn't tell me she called," Jacob said.

Trey shrugged. "I didn't notice until we were driving back and she didn't leave a message so I didn't think it was important."

Jacob groaned. "I am so sorry, hon." He bent down to kiss her but she moved away and he understood because she didn't like him when he was sweaty.

"You're lucky I got her to wait."

"Let me take a quick shower and I'll be ready." He raced into the main bedroom.

Beth's green gaze met Trey's in a look that said: This is all your fault. But Trey didn't mind, he'd gotten used to her animosity and she wasn't the first one to look at him like that. Every girlfriend Jacob had had given Trey that look. Anytime Jacob had failed them in some way—missed birthday, rescheduled anniversary, wrong gift—Trey was the one to blame. But Beth wasn't a passing girl-friend she was a fiancée and that made her more powerful than the others.

And she wielded her power well and as much as Trey admired that—she was a beautiful, smart woman who knew what she wanted—Trey worried for his friend. A worry that continued to grow. He wasn't sure Beth was the right woman for him.

Beth was the first of Jacob's girlfriends to admire Trey's new haircut by brushing her fingers along the base of his neck or the first to be unable to squeeze past him in Jacob's small kitchen without pressing her butt or breasts against him.

But Trey couldn't really blame her for that, he was a big guy and took up a lot of space. But he could blame her for the winter day when she slipped on some ice and Trey caught her arm and she held onto him longer than necessary.

Trey didn't want to believe it. Beth truly seemed to care for Jacob and made him happy when she wasn't criti-cizing him.

So he decided to test a hypothesis that he'd been tweaking over several months. What would she do if he gave her a little extra attention? What would she do if he looked at her a little longer than he should have? If he brushed his hand against her bare shoulder when they went out to eat? If his leg brushed hers when they were all relaxing on the couch?

And it was on that hot summer day that he'd learned his answer. She licked her lower lip and said a little breathless, "Did you ignore my call on purpose?"

He lightly touched her chin. "No."

Her green eyes warmed and it was at that moment Trey devised his plan.

And he would have left and not thought about the wedding planner if Alicia hadn't walked over to Beth and said, "Jacob said he wants to talk to you about something." And they all looked at a towel-clad Jacob motioning Beth over.

Beth sighed and went over to him.

Trey took a step back ready to leave when Alicia did the unthinkable.

She smiled at him.

People didn't usually do that. He'd get a tight lipped grin or nod, but for some reason people didn't feel comfortable smiling at him. "Probably because you have all the charm of a rattlesnake," Jacob used to tease him.

It didn't bother him. His friend was right. People were either fascinated or terrified of him. But she'd smiled at him and held out her hand and said, "I'm Alicia. It's a pleasure to meet you."

Trey couldn't be certain if his mouth fell open but he did stare at her for three beats as he shook her hand before he looked away. Her voice was so warm and friendly he was certain she'd confused him with someone else. "I'm Trey."

"I know," she said with laughter in her voice. "Jacob has told me a lot about you." She winked. "I hope you'll put in a good word for me with any of your friends. Anyway, I just wanted to introduce myself and let you know your friend is in good hands."

Trey felt someone tugging him and glanced down. He still held her hand. He knew he should let go, but for a moment he didn't want to. "You have nice hands."

"Liar."

He looked at her surprised. "What?"

"They're short and stubby."

"Maybe." He released her hand. "But I like them."

"Then you're really strange," she said in a teasing voice before she turned and walked away.

She was right. He was strange. Most people didn't understand him and he made a cursory effort to understand them. With effort he could be charming or glib, but most times he left that to Jacob. Those traits came easily to him.

What Trey prided himself on was being loyal. Dependable. A true friend no matter what.

And he'd lost the only friend he'd ever had. But it had been worth it to save him even if that meant he was alone.

"Where should we go?" Alicia asked him as they rode down the elevator.

He jiggled his keys in his pocket. "Depends on how long you want to wait."

"Not too long."

"You like Italian?"

"I like most food."

Trey glanced at her and saw that she was smiling. He wondered how she could smile so easily in a way that seemed genuine. Why her smile warmed his heart. Why he wanted to make her smile more.

"I'm glad to hear that because I know of a place that Ja...I know a place you'll like."

"Sounds good."

He wished he could offer her more than dinner to make up for ruining her career. But he'd stopped wishing for things a long time ago.

CHAPTER TEN

Between the Cesar salad and the fettuccini Alfredo, Alicia realized something wasn't right about him. There were few patrons in the restaurant, but the waiters bustled back and forth with courteous smiles and quickly cleared tables of plates whenever anyone left as if preparing for a sudden onslaught of hungry people.

Trey remained a mystery. What man would hurt his best friend—publicly—and then worry about a stranger?

The best man at the wedding had been callous and cold, but he hadn't been that way when she'd first met him.

Who was he really? He'd said he'd been with the bride the night before the wedding.

The bride didn't deny it.

Why hadn't Beth denied it? Wouldn't someone's first instinct be to deny such a charge? To say it wasn't true?

Wasn't that a basic survival instinct? But she'd just crumbled to her knees in defeat.

Alicia took another bite of her fettuccini and studied the man sitting across from her. It was easy to do since he wasn't much of a talker and his gaze remained focused on his plate as if he thought the neat chunks he'd cut his grilled chicken into would run away. She'd learned that professionally, he consulted on geological issues. He was quiet and reserved. She had a hard time imagining him seducing the bride.

But Beth hadn't denied they'd been together.

Alicia still couldn't figure out how.

Alicia clearly remembered when she'd first met Trey at Jacob's apartment. She'd spent nearly an hour assuring Beth that it was okay that Jacob had forgotten their meeting as the other woman frantically tried to reach him by phone. More than Beth's irritation, Alicia remembered thinking how much she liked Jacob's apartment. It was as welcoming as the man himself. She could fall asleep on his comfortable grey couch and the blue area rug felt lush under her stocking feet. Hardcover books lay scattered on his coffee table among disorderly papers, yellow and green highlighters and pens. Beth apologized for the mess.

"No, it's fine," Alicia tried to reassure her as she thought of the true mess she'd left her apartment in that morning. She'd come home to breakfast dishes in the sink, three boxes from Amazon she had yet to recycle still on her couch and empty bags of plantain chips and dried mango slices on the ground. Compared to her, Jacob was a neat freak.

Alicia lifted one of the books to see the cover: *Running a Bed and Breakfast.* "They look interesting."

Beth made a face as she closed up the books, without bookmarking them so Jacob could find his place again, and stacked them. "They're just a silly dream of his for when he retires. He talks about it all the time."

"Opening his own bed and breakfast?"

"Yes," Beth said, brushing her dark hair back from her shoulders, she'd still been a brunette then, "I don't know why it interests him. He's secured an excellent position as assistant manager at Haven Hotel. The pay is great and one day he will be a manager. Everybody thinks so."

"Does he want to be?"

Beth looked at her confused. "Why wouldn't he want to be?"

Alicia shifted in her seat, realizing she'd said the wrong thing. But after catching a glimpse of the notes and highlighted passages in one of the books, Alicia sensed that to Jacob the B&B industry seemed to be more than a passing fancy. However, their personal life and future was none of her business and not for the first time did Alicia wonder how such a laid back guy would manage with such an ambitious wife. Dressed in her designer blouse and stretched jeans, Beth seemed out of place in Jacob's apartment. Like a Tiffany bracelet being kept in a Reebok shoe.

But she'd only just met them. She didn't know everything. Perhaps Jacob really was thinking forty years into the future. "No reason." Alicia looked away from the books and glanced at a photo on the bookshelf. She saw a framed photo of Jacob smiling at the camera, dressed in a yellow T-shirt with palm trees in the background and a black guy standing next to him with his head turned looking at something out of view.

It seemed like a strange picture to keep. Alicia wondered where the photo had been taken and what the picture meant to him.

"Oh, that's Jacob and Trey," Beth said following Alicia's gaze.

She'd heard enough about Trey to know that he was Jacob's best friend and that the two men were almost inseparable but it still didn't explain the picture to her. One would have thought they'd have taken a second one with both men looking at the camera.

Jacob looked so happy...

"It's probably his fault."

Alicia looked at Beth who paced as she tried to reach Jacob again on the phone. "Fault?"

"Yes, Trey. Jacob would probably be here if it wasn't for him."

"Have you tried contacting him?"

"What do you think I'm doing right now?"

"Not Jacob," Alicia said in a patient voice. "Trey."

"I have," Beth said in a quiet voice. "He won't pick up either."

Alicia glanced at her watch. It was all pretense since she didn't have anything else scheduled for the day, but she didn't think anyone needed to know that. "Well, I can wait a little longer so it's okay. Why don't we get started?"

Fortunately, before Beth had a complete meltdown, they heard male laughter outside the front door. The door swung open and Beth rushed over to the two men with the ferocity of a guard dog. Alicia had a good viewpoint from her position on the couch and saw Jacob's face fall before he cast an apologetic look her way. Alicia smiled at him eager to let him know it was okay, but was sure he didn't notice. Few people did. She was just the wedding planner after all.

She pulled out her cell phone and glanced at the notes she'd highlighted to discuss. She scrolled through then stopped when she felt the weight of a large hand on her shoulder. Her eyes flew up and met Jacob's soft gaze. "Won't be a sec," he said, giving her shoulder a gentle squeeze, before he disappeared into his bedroom.

Alicia blinked. Surprised he'd managed to make her feel so good in an instant. She could understand Beth's certainty that Jacob would be a hotel manager one day, Alicia could imagine him owning a string of hotels if he wanted to. She put her phone away, suddenly feeling confident. She had nothing to worry about.

Alicia looked at the two people still in the doorway.

Beth and Trey DeVille in the flesh. Somehow she'd expected him to be smaller. From all she'd heard about him, he seemed to stand in Jacob's shadow. But in person she could see that he didn't stand in anyone's shadow. He was his own man.

Unlike Jacob there was no hint of apology in Trey's expression. And was it her imagination or was Beth standing closer to Trey than necessary? She didn't think too much about it when she was suddenly enveloped in the fresh scent of eucalyptus. "I'm sorry to ask you this, but I need a favor."

Alicia turned and saw Jacob, partially wet, a towel

wrapped around his waist. She knows she stared, she might have drooled, but she couldn't be sure. All she knew was that with his soft voice and beautiful brown eyes he could have asked her to shave her head and she probably would have complied. "A favor?" she said determined to keep her eyes on his face.

He nodded then sent a glance towards the front door. "Could you save Trey for me? I know Beth's probably giving him hell right now and it's not his fault. Any time I get in trouble she blames him. He's an easy scapegoat. I'll make it up to you. If you could just—"

Alicia leapt to her feet ready to jump into action. Not only would she help Jacob, she could get a chance to meet Trey and possibly get him to put in a good word for her with his friends. "Leave it to me."

Jacob smiled and Alicia melted a little before she turned and went on her mission. Coming up with a lie that Jacob wanted to speak to Beth was easy, meeting Trey, on the other hand, had been more trying.

He didn't return her smile. He briefly stared at her as if she were an alien life form, held onto her hand as if he'd forgotten it was there and then made fun of it. He was awkward and strange. She couldn't imagine what Jacob saw in him. But as odd and distant as he seemed she never got the sense that he was cold and calculating.

She still remembered the touch of his hand, his grip was solid but warm. And the longer he held her hand she felt her palm grow hot, not because of fear, but awareness. Trey had his own magnetism. His own beauty that took time to see and it was at that moment she understood why Jacob cared about him. There was a sincere kindness in his manner that drew her to him and also frightened her a little because it was a rare trait in adults. Adults had hidden agendas and artifice. This man seemed to possess none of that, but he wasn't simple, he was just different.

Jacob, Beth and Trey.

Something didn't fit...

Alicia set her fork down and took a sip of her grape juice.

"Why did you sleep with her?"

His eyes flew up to hers and she nearly gasped at the surprise and vulnerability she saw in his gaze before he lowered it again. She felt her heart beating fast, her tongue suddenly dry. He was hiding something.

But it wasn't just that. The look in his eyes shook something deep within her. A sense of certainty settled within her. She knew that he hadn't slept with Beth. Anyone who believed that he had didn't know him. That's what he was banking on, the fact that people didn't know him, that people were quick to make judgments about him, that people liked to blame him. She remembered Jacob's words: He's an easy scapegoat.

Alicia leaned forward and whispered, "You lied."

Trey shook his head. "I didn't lie and I don't—"

"You didn't sleep with her. You're not the kind of man who would do that."

A quick, secretive grin touched the corner of his mouth. "You don't know anything about me."

The grin intrigued her. It was similar to the grin that had quickly come and gone after Jacob had punched him. He was a man with no regrets and a man who wouldn't let her get close to a truth he didn't want revealed. But she was determined. "I know enough. I know that..." Alicia's words drifted away when she realized Trey was no longer listening to her. Something behind her had caught his attention.

She turned and saw Jacob.

CHAPTER ELEVEN

*N*ow this was awkward.

Jacob had just been seated at a table only four tables away and stared right at them. How had she and Trey ended up at the same restaurant as his former best friend? And what did it say about her that she was with him? She'd been Jacob's wedding planner after all. She should be loyal to him. What would he think of her? She didn't know what to do. Did she acknowledge with a nod? Pretend she didn't see him? Or…

Trey made the decision for her. He calmly switched their plates then stood, lifted her arm and gently led her to his seat then took hers. Before she could ask him what he was doing he said, "Do you want to order dessert?"

Alicia stared at him stunned. Dessert? He could eat dessert? She could hardly breathe. Sure, he now had his back facing Jacob but wasn't he disturbed even a little bit? Trey didn't appear shaken. Not as much as Jacob, who hadn't moved. Alicia quickly glanced at Jacob again and caught a look on his face: A look not of anger, but anguish.

At first she thought it was the anguish of betrayal, but there seemed to be something else in his stiff presence that shone in his eyes. The look of loss.

She turned back to Trey. He seemed a little too focused on the food, but then again he'd kept his gaze down even before Jacob had arrived. While he didn't appear as shaken as his former friend, she saw his jaw tighten then relax. Something had bothered him. Something else was going on.

"Did he know?"

Trey took a sip of his soda then put the glass down. "Did who know what?"

"Did Jacob know you were going to pull that stunt on his wedding day?"

Trey shook his head. "If he knew he would have stopped me." He frowned at her. "That's a very odd question."

True. But the look between the men seemed odd to her. Trey had said he'd saved Jacob. From what exactly?

Trey speared one of this chicken cubes. "Why do you keep staring at me?"

"I'm trying to figure you out."

"Don't try. I can hardly figure myself out."

"I just can't believe you did what you did."

His jaw twitched. "What's done, is done. I'd rather not talk about it."

"I just get this sense that you're hiding something."

He lifted his gaze, his dark eyes impaled her. He looked at her for a long moment. "So what?"

He was right. It was none of her business. So what if he was hiding something? So what if her curiosity was dying to know what it was. She was only here to have dinner with him. Let him feel less guilty about harming her business and then they'd go their separate ways. They'd remain strangers.

She cleared her throat ashamed she'd crossed the line. She didn't want him angry at her. "I'm sorry."

"No need to apologize. Do you want dessert?"

She shook her head, gripping her hand in her lap. What she wanted right now was for the dinner to end but Trey was taking a long time finishing his meal. She didn't know a man could eat so slowly. Maybe she could feign an emergency.

"Do you have any particular plans?" he asked.

"Plans?"

"Yes."

"Plans for what?"

"Your next project."

"No."

"Want one?"

"I'm sorry?"

"I'm good at planning things. Just give me a general idea of something you want and I can plan it out for you."

"No need. I plan on going on the path I should have stayed on since the beginning."

"What is that?"

"Working at my family's company."

"And you want to do that?"

"No," Alicia said with a defeated sigh. "But there's no other choice."

"That's not true. There are plenty of other choices. I can list them for you if you like."

"Are you making fun of me?"

Trey looked up at her surprised before he lowered his gaze again. "No, why would I do that?"

"It's just you sound so superior and condescending as if I'm too stupid to know what options are out there."

He shifted in his chair and rubbed his forehead. He set his fork down, picked it up, set it down, picked it up again. "I'm sorry. No, I...I want to help."

His voice sounded so cold and yet sincere. And yet he could hardly look at her.

She sighed. He looked tortured. "You've done enough. I've already told you that you don't need to feel guilty. The mess my life is, started way before you did your display at the wedding. You don't have to suffer through this dinner with me any longer."

His brows furrowed. "Suffer? You think I'm suffering?"

"Yes. I am."

An expression—startled, hurt—crossed his face. He twirled his fork. "Oh...okay. I'm sorry. I'm having a great time, but—"

"A great time?" She sniffed. "Your sense of humor is strange."

"I wasn't trying to be funny."

She sat back. "You're serious?"

He nodded.

"You've enjoyed this entire meal so far?"

He nodded then paused. "Not everything, of course.

Seeing Jacob again was difficult but the rest has been nice. Especially you."

"Me?"

He nodded. "I really like your wig."

Her body turned cold. Wig? She was wearing a wig? She was *still* wearing the pink and silver wig? She reached to take it off then stopped. Her hair probably looked a fright underneath.

She groaned. That was probably what Fabian was talking about. "This day just keeps getting worse. Why didn't you say anything?"

"I did. I said you looked amazing."

"Like a space alien."

"Invite me to your planet anytime." The corner of his mouth kicked up. "That was a joke."

"You have a strange sense of humor."

"You've already said that. Why are you wearing it anyway?"

"Sometimes I take a break and..." She covered her face. "I'm going to sound weird."

"So what?"

He was right. She let her hands fall. "There's this game I like to play on my phone and when I wear my wig I pretend I'm someone else for a while. It's a stress relief for me."

He bit his lip.

"Do you want to laugh?"

"No, I was curious if—" He shook his head before he looked around as if searching for something. "Let me call the waiter."

"Why?" Alicia asked surprised by his sudden change. "What were you going to say?"

Trey set his fork down, picked it up, set it down and picked it up again. "Doesn't matter if I'm having a good time and you're not."

She folded her arms. It wasn't entirely true. Before Jacob's appearance she'd been fine. Calm in a way she hadn't been in months. She hadn't thought about how miserable she was at work, she didn't dread the next day, and she'd enjoyed the company of a quiet man and a delicious meal.

"I changed my mind," she said.

Trey looked up at her surprised and she realized she liked seeing him surprised. She liked whenever his brown eyes met hers, they weren't as glacial as they'd first appeared, and right now they were oddly endearing. He lowered them again. "Really?"

"Surprisingly yes." She grabbed the dessert menu. "I think I will order something else," she said and to her delight he rewarded her with a quick grin before he said, "Tell me more about this game."

CHAPTER TWELVE

"Are you sure you're okay?" Maya asked.

"I'm fine," Jacob said. "Why?"

"Because you're buttering your napkin."

Jacob looked down and realized she was right. He softly swore. Trey and he used to frequent this restaurant all the time, Jacob could eat his weight in breadsticks while Trey could consume enough pasta to fill a bathtub.

"Want to go somewhere else?" Maya said.

"No."

"I know this is hard."

She didn't understand. It was hard to see Trey but that wasn't what had truly startled him. It was Trey's behavior.

Trey was with a woman.

Trey was with Jacob's wedding planner.

How had that happened? His curiosity was killing him. Trey usually spent time with his rocks or lizard. This development was strange and worrisome. It didn't look like a date; Trey was too intense for those. He looked too relaxed (by Trey standards) to be on a date. If it had been a date he'd wear his black suit. Trey always wore a black suit on a date because then he didn't have to worry about matching anything and could focus on the seven items of conversation he had programmed on his cell phone to keep the conversation from stalling. Jacob had helped him develop them when Trey had scared prospects away by discussing geological demographics and the life cycle of a gecko.

Or worse, he'd talk about Jacob. Trey had a terrible habit of telling everyone how amazing and brilliant Jacob was. Jacob still couldn't understand why Trey was so enthralled with him when Trey had accomplished so much more. Those who didn't know Trey would think he was on the autism spectrum, but he wasn't. He was just different.

"No one wants to hear about me," Trey used to say to him, "but you're interesting."

"No, you can't talk about rocks, lizards or me. Understood?"

He nodded. "Then what am I supposed to say?"

What Jacob couldn't understand was how Trey seized up when he was with others. On his own he was funny, gregarious, easy to be with, but around others it was like something was turned off. But strangely he didn't look completely turned off now.

Jacob shifted his gaze to Alicia. Women usually attracted to Trey's looks quickly lost interest within five minutes, but Alicia didn't have a strained smile on her face or glazed expression. She was really looking at him with animated interest as she showed Trey something on her cell phone.

Jacob stared, feeling as if he was witnessing a miracle. Could it be that Trey had finally found someone who understood him? That Trey would be okay so that Jacob could give up his sense of guilt? Trey had given up a lot the day he said he'd been with Beth—Jacob knew how much their friendship had meant to him—perhaps he wouldn't be alone. Over the past two months that had been his greatest fear: that Trey was alone. That he had no one to turn to.

Jacob's heart expanded with joy and ached with pain at the same time. He wanted the best for Trey and then again he felt a keen jealousy...

"You're doing it again."

He glanced down at his butter smeared napkin. He set the knife down.

Maya glanced behind her. "Do you want me to go over and talk to him?"

"And say what?"

"Oh, I don't know. I could tell him how much the family blames him for you completely losing your mind, quitting your well paying job and buying an old B&B."

"He doesn't need to know that."

"Or...um... how about 'Why are you out with the wedding planner after ruining my brother's wedding?' That could be a start."

"Shut up."

"But you're curious, right?"

"Doesn't matter."

"You may not be curious but I am." She stood.

He grabbed her arm. "Sit down."

She flopped back in the chair and narrowed her eyes. "What aren't you telling me?"

"What do you mean?"

"You should be shooting daggers at him. You should be asking the waiter to spit in his food. Instead you're curious about his love life?"

"It isn't a date."

"How do you know?"

"I just do. He's wearing the wrong clothes and he looks too relaxed."

She turned and looked at Trey's straight back, the way he gripped his knife and fork. "You call that relaxed?"

"Yes." Jacob didn't need to tell her that on a date Trey kept his hands out of view, usually in his lap where he would tap his fingers together to pace the speed and flow of the conversation, trying his best to appear relaxed even though he wasn't. That habit always made him smile.

The first time he'd seen it he'd thought Trey was being impatient with him. He'd never been with someone who couldn't seem to stay still, but Trey's father had gently said, "He likes you, so he's trying to calm himself."

But Trey wasn't trying to calm himself now, however, there was something more going on.

"Oh my God, Jacob," Maya said.

"What?"

"You're watching him like he's an ex-lover in a new relationship."

The analogy was wrong, completely wrong, but the

sentiment wasn't. He tore his gaze away. "Sorry. It's an old habit."

"You know there were times you were closer to him than anyone else."

Yes, he knew that and made no excuses for it. It had been that way as long as he could remember. There were things only he and Trey would ever know. It wasn't the first time someone didn't understand their relationship. Nor had it been the first time a woman had gotten between them or, at least, tried.

CHAPTER THIRTEEN

"You're going to have to talk to Jeannie," Trey told Jacob, while munching on an Asian pear one day during their junior year as they sat in Jacob's dining room. Trey helped him with his advanced algebra homework (Jacob had barely passed algebra, finding himself in an *advanced* algebra class was just cruel).

Jacob was bad at most subjects but for some reason math was one of his worst and no matter how much Trey tutored him, Jacob's grades didn't improve. His parents had hired other tutors and put him in special study programs but Trey was the only person who didn't make Jacob feel like an idiot.

They could study at the library or at Trey's house, but Jacob desperately wanted to show his parents that he was making an effort so they always studied at Jacob's house even when his brother would come by and say,

"Hey, Jay, still trying to figure out what two plus two is?" before laughing and walking away.

Jacob looked at the notes he'd written down, frustration giving him a headache. The formulas still didn't make sense to him. "I'm never gonna graduate."

"Of course you are. You're a smart guy. It's my fault for not explaining it better. But first...about Jeannie."

The sound of his girlfriend's name lifted Jacob's mood a bit. She was bubbly and funny. They planned to go to a big house party that weekend and then after... "What about her?"

"She's told me to stay away from you."

Jacob squeezed his eyes shut and rubbed his forehead. "Again?"

"She said it's either me or her."

Jacob tossed his pencil down and swore. He didn't need this right now.

"She was crying."

"Real tears?"

"Of course they were real tears."

"People can fake tears you know."

Trey's gaze sharpened with interest. "Really?"

Jacob waved his hand. "Never mind."

It had become almost a ritual. Jacob would start dating, his girlfriend would get jealous and tell him he was spending too much time with Trey, which wasn't true because anytime Jacob started seeing someone, Trey tried to fade into the background and be as unavailable as possible giving Jacob only a third of the time they used to spend together. Jacob knew this because Trey had even given him a chart and a calendar to show the times and the days. Little did his girlfriends know how much Trey wanted him to be happy and how much he was rooting for them. But few people understood Trey like he did.

Jacob sighed. "I'll talk to her."

But what he'd told Jeannie hadn't made her happy. He'd caught her in the hallway after homeroom and apologized before he told her there was no contest.

When her face brightened with joy, he realized he'd phrased his words wrong. "You mean you'll get rid of him?" she said.

"No."

Her face fell. "But you just said there was no contest."

"Right." He stared at her for a long time hoping he wouldn't have to spell it out for her, but since she continued to look at him confused he finally said, "Trey's not just a friend, he's a brother. If I had to choose…" Jacob shook his head. "This is stupid. I don't need to choose. I care about you both."

Her eyes filled with tears. He heard the warning bell for them to get to the next class, but Jeannie didn't look like she was ready to go anywhere. She grabbed his arm.

"I'm just worried about you."

He smiled and kissed her, hoping she'd let go. "There's nothing to worry about. Now let's get to class and I'll talk to you later."

Her grip tightened. "You don't realize how important this is. You're so nice and Trey's…" She scowled. "He's not good for your reputation. Everyone thinks so. I'm trying to look out for you."

"You don't have to. I can look after myself." He wiped her tears and kissed her again in the way that she liked. A way that would make her forget about Trey and even that they were going to be late for class. She finally let go of his arm.

"Okay," she said breathless when he finally pulled away.

But it was never really okay with her and at that weekend party she tried to make him jealous by dancing with other guys. When that didn't work he saw her laughing with two guys from the track team. Jacob eventually let her dump him one hot August day in front of a gelato stand.

He hadn't even been angry that she'd broken up with him after he'd paid for her to see one of her favorite bands in concert. He remembered trying to eat his strawberry gelato fast to keep it from melting and Jeannie telling him that he had issues and she wanted a guy without 'baggage.'

He couldn't remember what he'd said in return, but it must have upset her because the next thing he felt was something cold and wet slammed into his chest. He heard the sound of her cup of gelato hitting the pavement and the slap of her sandals as she marched away.

He felt oddly relieved. Anyone who thought of Trey as baggage wasn't right for him anyway. Since that day he made it clear to his girlfriends that his relationship with Trey was off-limits.

But he still never thought that a woman would be one of the reasons that would eventually end their friendship.

But that had been Jacob's fault not Trey's. And now

Trey had a look on his face that truly worried him. Trey could get his heart broken and Jacob could do nothing to protect him unless he exposed why Trey had done what he'd done in the first place— without spilling his own secret.

CHAPTER FOURTEEN

The shark was back.

Alicia sat back in her office chair and stared at the man who looked like Trey amazed by how happy she was to see him. Or perhaps she was hallucinating since she'd seen him only yesterday.

And after telling him all the rules of the prison game and indulging in a delicious tiramisu for dessert she'd gone home and dreamed about him.

Except it was partly a nightmare. She and Trey were locked in a prison cell together (that wasn't the scary part) he was bare-chested (that wasn't the scary part either, he looked amazing) dressed in orange slacks and helped them escape, much like the game. The terror came when they had to run and stay out of reach of the guards and hidden traps. Initially, Trey held her hand but then as the guards and traps multiplied, Trey sacrificed himself so that she could reach the freedom of the prison gates without him.

Alicia woke up in a cold sweat, her heart pounding. The nightmare had felt so vivid, the loss of him left her desolate. She sensed a real danger she couldn't name so when she saw him that afternoon she nearly leapt to her feet and said, "You're alive."

Instead she rubbed her eyes, fighting against tears. He was safe.

He closed the door behind him and said with the hint of a smile, "No wig this time."

No, she definitely wasn't dreaming. The dream Trey wouldn't say something like that.

"What are you doing here?"

He frowned as if she'd asked him a really crucial question he didn't want to reply to. "Do I really have to answer that question?"

"Yes."

He shoved his hands in his pockets, rocked on his heels. "Yesterday I told you I'd treat you to lunch. You said that was fine. I checked with your assistant to make sure your schedule was free."

"I know I agreed to lunch but I didn't think it'd be the next day."

"Why not?"

"Because we saw each other yesterday."

He blinked. Bit his lip. "So...we can't see each other today?"

"Normally you wait a couple days."

He nodded. "Right. Normally," he drew out the word before he took his hands out of his pockets, beat a rhythm against his thigh before he folded his arms. His gaze briefly rested on her face before darting away. "I shouldn't have come. I'm doing this wrong. I'm sorry."

"Where are you going?" Alicia asked startled when he turned to leave.

"I'll come back another day and—"

Now that he was here, as surprising and strange as it was, she didn't want him to go. She raced around her desk and grabbed his arm. He violently yanked free from her grasp, the force of the motion caused her to stumble backwards and she could feel herself falling so she twisted her body to brace herself against the desk and missed, instead knocking the side of her forehead against it with a thud before crashing to the ground.

She touched her fingers to her throbbing forehead and felt the wet stickiness of blood before she saw the red stain on them.

Trey rushed towards her and within minutes she felt his breath against her cheek as he mumbled something she couldn't understand. He pressed her body against his solid chest as he lifted her to her feet, the fresh scent of the coming winter clung to his dark blue wool coat but she felt anything but cold. She felt the pounding of a heart unsure if it was hers or his or both, and she sank into one of the chairs facing her desk almost bereft when he let her go.

Because she was so startled by her clumsy fall and how he'd effortlessly helped her to a chair, as if she'd weighed a lot less than she did, it took Alicia a moment to realize Trey had shed his coat and had his light blue shirt halfway off his shoulders. She stared at him alarmed. "What are you doing?"

"I need to stop the bleeding," Trey said, pressing the shirt to her forehead. For a moment, a deliciously short moment, she was engulfed in his body heat and the scent of spiced cider. She took a deep breath inhaling as much of it as she could. How could a man smell so good?

"Are you feeling faint?"

"No, why?"

"Your eyes were fluttering closed."

Alicia felt heat steal into her cheeks, she couldn't tell him the reason why. "No, I just—"

She paused at the sight of his tattoo. Somehow she'd never imagined he'd have a tattoo on his forearm. Let alone one in the shape of a lizard. Its tail seemed to move with the motion of his biceps. She didn't expect his biceps to be that defined either. She'd dreamed about him half-naked but the real life version was much better and full of exquisite detail she'd secure to memory.

The shark was well made, but anything but cold. From the warmth of his shirt, the warmth of his hand, even his eyes, when she got a chance to look at them. Trey rarely looked at her long enough for her to see their true color. Depending on the light they were sometimes darker in shade more than at other times.

He abruptly turned and surged to his feet and before she could stop him he opened the door and shouted, "I need water, now!"

CHAPTER FIFTEEN

*A*licia felt like falling through the floor. She never imagined Trey could make an embarrassing moment even worse. She could picture the poor people in their cubicles staring at Trey in shock.

Everything about MedForm was about order. On the wall was a list of how people were to behave. No loud conversations, music, be respectful of personal space etc... A big black man with a loud voice certainly didn't fit.

But whatever they thought of the shirtless man barking orders the employees went into action. Alicia heard a scurry of activity in the usually quiet surroundings. Shifting chairs, muffled voices, hurried footsteps, splashing of liquid.

Trey had such command that only seconds later, without question or hesitation, her desk was filled with glasses, a thermos and bottles of water.

Alicia inwardly groaned at the sight of their worried

faces as they left her office. She managed a smile to reassure them. "It's really nothing."

Fabian opened his mouth and she narrowed her eyes at him and mouthed, Say one word and I will kill you.

He took the threat to heart and left the room—silent.

"Thanks," she heard Trey say after the final person had left her office. He stood in the doorway, his broad back blocking her from seeing anything. "And if anyone has something soft—"

"I do," Alicia heard someone say and Trey disappeared and reappeared with a stuffed koala.

"You're going overboard," she said when he pushed the chairs together to form a makeshift cot and then forced her to lie down, placing the stuffed toy animal behind her head.

"No, I'm not. There are times it's better to be over-cautious than under cautious."

She sat up and let her hand fall. "But I don't want to lie down. I'm fine."

He raised the shirt back to her forehead. "I told you to keep applying pressure."

She tried to push his hand away. "You don't use your nice shirt—"

"It's my fault. Blood will wash out."

She was too tired to argue and his shirt smelled good, he smelled good and looked good and made her feel good. She closed her eyes.

"Are you sure you don't feel faint?"

Her eyes flew open. What was she doing? How had she let this strange man lull her into thinking everything was okay? That she was okay? "Yes. No. I mean I'm sure I don't feel faint." She let her hand fall again. "I'm okay, really."

He gently lifted her hand to her forehead. "Hold this a little while longer."

Because he had the kind of look on his face that said he wouldn't move until she said 'yes' she nodded.

Trey moved one of the chairs back and sat down in front of her. His voice remained low as well as his gaze. "I didn't mean to hurt you."

"You didn't hurt me. I slipped because I'm clumsy."

"No, you're not." His gaze met hers and held her captive. "It was me." He bit his lip. "I need to be more careful. I don't like being grabbed and I wasn't prepared. I'm sorry. Next time tell me first."

"There won't be a next time."

A brief expression, a mixture of sadness and hurt, crossed his face before it disappeared. She didn't know why it made him look young and vulnerable. Two things she knew he was not.

He stood. "Do you want me to get you something to drink?"

"Sure." She stared at the crowded desk. "It's not as if all this water is enough."

He studied her for a moment. "You're being sarcastic."

She winked at him. "You're catching on."

He shoved his hands in his pockets. "Does that mean you're still angry?"

Alicia studied him for a moment. Trey stood against the bland background of the beach scene and in the middle of winter he looked like a man advertising sunscreen.

She shook her head. "I was never angry."

He narrowed his eyes, doubtful. "But I—"

"Did nothing wrong," she said with a sigh. "I shouldn't have grabbed you."

She pulled the shirt from her head and looked at the stain with regret. She should have just let him go. Like most things in her life—dreams, ambitions—she'd tried to hold onto something that wasn't hers.

"Do you want to see a doctor?"

"No." She glanced up at him and saw he'd put on his coat, covering up his bare chest. At least that was one distraction gone.

"I've hurt you twice now," he said.

"Not really I—"

He sat down in front of her and leaned forward. "But I'd like to hire you."

She tried to focus on his words but the way he leaned forward caused her eyes to dip to his chest again. He reminded her of a partially opened chocolate bar in a blue wrapper. A column of beautiful brown skin peeking out at her in a coaxing manner that seemed to say 'eat me'. She glanced down at his soiled shirt trying to get a hold of her racing thoughts. "I'll get this dry-cleaned."

"I have an event—"

She rolled up his shirt. "No."

"You haven't let me finish. "

"I don't need you to."

"I'll pay you your going rate and it won't take long.

You can do it after work or on the weekends." He flashed a bright quick smile. "I'm flexible."

"The answer is still no. I work here now. This is what I do. Nothing else."

"I promise it will only be a couple hours. I'll pay you as a consultant and—"

Say yes. Say yes, her heart cried. Alicia bit the inside of her cheek to keep from saying anything. His words tempted her as much as the rest of him. He was more dangerous than she'd ever thought of him being before. She felt as if she were cast out in the ocean, the cold darkness above her and he was a shark circling around her.

Slowly, slowly circling...offering her his back to keep her from drowning. 'Cling to me. Hold on to me,' he said. 'I won't hurt you. You can trust me.' She needed something to trust when miles of ocean stretched out before her, birds of prey flew overhead and all she saw was darkness below her. There was nothing else to hold on to. She could only tread water for so long before she sank beneath the waves and let the ocean swallow her. The shark's offer was tempting... 'Grab my fin,' he urged her. 'Hold on to me and I won't let you drown.'

What would it hurt to hold on for just a little while? Her legs and arms were growing tired.

Alicia continued to chew the inside of her cheek as she considered Trey's offer. He said it would only be a couple hours...and wouldn't it be fun to do something else for a change? Something that was on her own and not connected to her family? The shark's calm offer and promises lulled her fears and filled her with hope. The same hope she'd had whenever she started something new—like working in the gallery or the flower shop or being a wedding planner.

No. She couldn't go back. This was where she needed to stay. Her family had finally accepted her. She had a regular salary like everyone else, and talked about investments and long term health care with them. She'd relieved her parents' fears about her and proven to her siblings that she could be responsible. She'd tried to do something on her own and failed. She wouldn't fail again. She had to make this work.

"I cannot work with you."

He shrugged. "Why not? You're good and I can—"

She pounded the arm of the chair. "I said no. I've got a good job and my family's support. This is where I belong."

Trey sent a considering look around the room. He seemed to absorb every aspect of the space, from the shape of the wooden desk to the blinds on the window, but one thing he didn't do was look at her before he said, "You don't belong here."

Alicia felt tears build in her eyes. Not from sadness but from rage. Rage she'd been suppressing for the past two months. He wasn't supposed to see that.

She'd been trying—desperately—to fit in. She'd been working her behind off. She'd fallen in line. Done whatever had been asked of her and not gotten one ounce of feedback or praise. She might as well be invisible. Worse, she'd tried to blend in so much she felt like she could stand next to a wall and no one would see her.

She knew she didn't belong, but she didn't need her efforts causally dismissed by this man. She wanted to shout at him. To tell him she wished she'd never seen him again, instead her voice betrayed her and she said, "I'm dying inside."

"I know," Trey said in a soft voice before she could take back her words. He sighed then stood and grabbed one of the bottles of water before he took her elbow and hoisted her to her feet. "Come on."

His grip didn't hurt, but it felt like a vise. He was like a powerful current sweeping her away, it was better to surrender than fight. She let him lead her to the parking lot, where a chilling wind bit at her cheeks. She stopped at the sight of his car. It no longer looked like a maimed silver beast deflated and defeated; it loomed large, its gleaming hubcaps and new black tires ready to claw through any terrain.

Her heart began to pound in relief. This sleek, elegant machine could take her anywhere. Somewhere far away from here. She reached for the door handle as if hypnotized then came to her senses. "I can't just leave."

"Sure you can. It's your lunch break and that can last a little longer than usual."

Alicia shook her head. "No, I have a meeting—"

"At four, I know. I checked. You'll be back in time." He opened the passenger side for her. "It's cold. Get in."

"Where are we going?"

"Does it matter?"

He was right. It didn't.

She cast a wary glance at the office building. She remembered first being introduced to it at six years old and being disappointed. Because her family spoke of it in such reverent tones, she'd expected something magical and enchanting, not a sandy colored brick with windows. Alicia looked at the building now and still didn't see its beauty, but this was her family's pride. She had to claim that pride too.

She sank into the dark interior of the Mercedes and listened to the soft bang as Trey closed the door.

CHAPTER SIXTEEN

*N*ow the shark looked like a hit man.

Alicia had been curious when Trey didn't immediately join her inside the car. He turned on the heat, said, "Give me a minute, feel free to choose something to listen to," and then disappeared to the back of the car. She heard the trunk open.

She looked at his digital console. She didn't trust when people said 'feel free' especially when it came to music. Feel free was usually code for 'feel free to find something I can't use to judge you' or 'feel free to not embarrass yourself by choosing something that I consider low taste and dumb.' With a man like Trey she definitely wouldn't 'feel free' to change the audiobook he was currently listening to, *A Geological History of North America*, to a French hip-hop song by Gims.

A rush of cold air seeped into the car when Trey opened the driver's side door and sat down. He'd put on a black turtleneck and a pair of mirrored sunglasses, making it very hard to read him, which she found both unnerving and thrilling at the same time.

"It's not that bright," she said, "you don't need sunglasses."

"I thought you'd feel more comfortable if—"

"You look menacing, like one of those lifelike robots from a dystopia future where technology has taken over."

He took off the glasses. "When you put it that way..." He set them down then looked at her. "Better?"

Not by much. He still looked menacing. There was just something angular and hard about him, and unlike his car, there was nothing elegant about him, he exuded an intense, coiled power, his presence making the interior of the car feel suddenly miniscule.

Alicia felt a little breathless as if she'd climbed a great height and he was consuming the rest of the thin air. But as unnerving as it was to be pinned under his dark gaze, no matter how briefly, she preferred it to his eyes being hidden. "Yes."

He placed a first aid kit on the dashboard. She stared at it surprised she hadn't noticed it before. "You keep this in your trunk?"

"Never know." He gently turned and tilted her head and checked the wound. "You won't need stitches."

Since she had a hard time looking at his eyes she looked at his lips instead. He had nice soft, full lips. She didn't need a first aid kit, she needed something to calm her down because her heart wouldn't stop beating erratically.

He is not the man for you.

He is not the man for you.

Trey placed some ointment on the wound before he applied a band-aid. She watched that beautiful mouth widened with a smile. "That should do it."

"Thanks."

He kissed her on the forehead. She stared at him stunned. "What did you do that for?"

"It's what you wanted, right?"

She resisted the urge to touch where his soft lips had met her skin and left it aching for more. "Why would you think that?"

"You keep looking at my mouth."

Alicia swallowed, her face burning. "How do you know I was looking at your mouth and not your chin?"

Trey nodded. "Fair point. I guess it was wishful thinking on my part."

She kissed him on the cheek. "How's that for wishful thinking," she said. Or almost said, because his startled brown eyes froze the words in her throat. His gaze met hers and she got to clearly see them, no trick of the light, no guarded emotion, just bare and real and him. And she saw that his eyes were dark brown. The kind of dark brown that reminded her of a teddy bear she'd once owned that she'd held tight at night whenever she felt anxious or lonely. Which had been often.

But as much as she wanted him to be, Trey wasn't a stuffed toy. With him she might not feel anxious, she might felt safe, cared for, less alone, but he was still a stranger. A man she didn't fully know. Unfortunately, she wanted to. That curiosity was a dangerous lure that had gotten her into trouble. She sat back.

"Do you like rescuing people?" she said.

"Is that a trick question?"

"No," she said.

"Do you think I'm rescuing you?"

"Aren't you? You dragged me out of my office."

He faced the windshield and put the car in gear. "You're right." He sighed. "I had to get you out of there. Seeing you in that ugly office hurt. All the light had gone from your eyes. You were like a butterfly trapped in a cage." He nodded. "So I guess you're right. Even before I came today, I wanted to help you."

Alicia folded her arms and frowned as he merged into traffic. "I don't need help. I'm fine."

"You don't like it there."

She hated to admit it but she did. "But I have to go back."

"Why?"

"Because it's my job and I'm determined to be responsible."

"Responsible doesn't have to mean miserable. Why did you quit everything? You could still do something else on the side. Let me hire you."

"What would you have me do?" Before he could reply she held out her hands. "No. Forget I asked. It was a stupid moment of weakness. I'm not interested." She refolded her arms. "I told my family I'd give it at least three years. I've only been there two months."

"I pay really well and it wouldn't take up too much of your time."

Alicia closed her eyes, desperate to not grab hold of the challenge in his voice, the temptation of his offer. "Shut up."

"I will—"

Her eyes flew open. "Take me back right now or stop talking—your choice."

"Okay. You win." Trey slowed the car at a traffic light. "I'll stop, but if you change your mind—"

"I won't." She stared at the red light, its brightness seeming to mock her. Stop. Stop. Stop. Stop wanting more than you have. Stop making the same mistakes.

But another part of her wanted to ignore the warning. It wanted to race ahead—heedlessly, recklessly, wildly. It wanted to hear what Trey had to say. It wanted to know more about him—this strange man who'd come back in her life two days in a row and tilted her dull world.

She watched the light turn green and felt the car shift forward, sensing she was letting a chance slip through her fingers.

CHAPTER SEVENTEEN

She'd probably never see him again.

Alicia tried not to let the thought depress her as she took the elevator to her office. Trey had treated her to a grilled vegetable panini then dropped her back here. He didn't say goodbye or wish her well. He'd just driven off. That was how it was supposed to be. She shouldn't feel as if that lunch had been too short—they'd barely spoken—or that she'd lost a friend—she barely knew him.

She was done taking risks. She was on the regular path now. She couldn't afford to mess up.

Steeled with a new resolve, Alicia walked to her office keenly aware of the stares that greeted her as she walked past the cubicles. She touched the band-aid on her forehead. The stares shouldn't surprise her considering the show Trey had put on only hours before.

Alicia disappeared into her office, cleared her desk of the water bottles—there was enough water to fill a kiddie pool—and turned on her laptop. She began to check her email then paused when the office online forum popped up. People were commenting about something. With a few clicks she got to see what all the fuss was about.

A picture of a shirtless Trey running down the hall filled her screen with a caption that said: Who is Alicia's mystery man?

Alicia quickly discovered who'd instigated it all: Pauline Fox, her sister.

She felt her blood boil as she read the comments.

Bet you he's a bouncer.

Tattooist?

No, not enough tattoos.

I say an out of work musician.

Isn't that phrase redundant?

Think he'd even know what the word 'redundant' means?

Alicia was used to her sister making fun of her, but she wouldn't let anyone make fun of Trey. He deserved better.

Alicia couldn't outmatch her on the platform. That was Pauline's domain, which she ruled with wit and condescension. Anytime Alicia tried to correct her, Pauline always managed to make Alicia's concerns appear childish, pathetic or petty. Fighting her on the online forum was out of the question. She needed a different strategy.

"I'm going to get you back for this," Alicia mumbled to herself as she opened up Photoshop. She took Trey's image and put him in one of their uniforms. Soon she was so focused on making him look good in a pair of grey scrubs that she forgot about her sister and the comments. Not only did Trey look good, he made their clothes look good. Her mind began thinking of a marketing caption.

Across the image she typed: *When you move, we do.*

She chewed her lip. The words didn't seem to work. She needed more. She saved the jpeg file and printed it off then opened another document and began to type.

When you need to move nothing should stop you. Especially not your clothes. Our custom made scrubs are designed with you in mind. You can rest assured that the fabric won't bother your skin, the cut will move with you, not against you. Feel naked without the shame. She deleted the last line and typed: *Feel naked, look fabulous.*

That was a good motto, something marketing could work with. She drafted a few more ideas and put them, as well as the image, in a folder so she could access them later.

Fabian popped his head in the door. "Tiny crisis."

Alicia hit Save then looked at him. "What?"

"One of the factories we use is facing bankruptcy and can't fulfill an order."

"When is the order scheduled to be fulfilled?"

"Two weeks."

She swore. Which meant she needed to find a replacement fast. Not only did they need the uniforms created but distributed as well. She'd have to call the company and see what options they had.

She swore again then quickly compressed her ideas into a zipped folder and emailed them to her brother, Edwin, who was in charge of marketing, as an attachment with a note that said it was something they could discuss later.

She quickly forgot about the online forum, Trey's image or the new marketing campaign idea, and focused on fixing the crisis.

She ignored the jpeg she'd printed out and left on her desk until it came back to haunt her a couple weeks later.

"I LOVE YOUR NEW AD," Deanna told her one Saturday afternoon at lunch. A nice warm bowl of clam chowder was just what Alicia needed that grey day and she savored every bite. Deanna being free to have lunch was an extra bonus and her lunch break may stretch twenty minutes longer than usual, but she felt that she deserved it.

She'd managed to avert disaster with the factory and to dream of Trey only twice. The first time, they escaped prison again, but this time he didn't die. The second time he unlocked the prison door and she ran out before the guards noticed but when she turned to him he'd disappeared.

It felt reminiscent of life. He'd disappeared from her life too. She'd stopped hoping that he'd show up unexpectedly at her office. That he'd pester her to work for him. Part of her wished she'd asked him what he'd hire her for even though she knew she'd say no.

But Trey was gone. Everything was back to normal. And normal meant boring meetings, putting out fires and indulging in lunch with her friend every chance she got.

She took another sip of soup. The last thing she wanted to talk about was work during her break, but Deanna seemed to enjoy it. "New ad?" Alicia said trying to feign interest.

"Yes, it's nothing like the other ads I usually see. It actually made me want to buy one of your uniforms."

Alicia frowned. She hadn't noticed anything special about their ads. "Which one are you talking about?"

Deanna rolled her eyes. "The only one *worth* talking about." She leaned forward and lowered her voice. "You know...the one with the man."

"You'll have to be more specific than that."

Deanna pumped her arms on either side of her body as if she were running.

Alicia's frown deepened. "Still not helping. We've had lots of men in our ads." She paused. "Okay, not lots but a decent amount."

"You've had good looking models who looked like they've been hired before. You've never had someone like this. I even kept it. He gave me great ideas and I matched him with a man on a dirt bike. My story begins with him rushing to the scene because he just discovered that his lover got injured doing one of his dangerous stunts and... you're not interested."

"No."

Deanna pulled out her cell phone. "You will be when you see this." She grinned. "Accept you may wish he was rushing towards you."

Deanna found the image then held it out to her.

Alicia didn't move. Why was Trey's image on Deanna's phone? Why was Trey dressed in a MedForm uniform?

Deanna giggled at Alicia's stunned expression. "I know. That was my first reaction too."

Alicia snatched the phone from her as the icy grip of dread took hold. "No. No. No, this can't be happening." She read the text and felt her heart squeeze so tight it hurt. "This is all wrong."

Deanna's smile faded. "What's wrong?"

"I made it up. This is not supposed to be an ad."

"Why not? It's great. I knew you were talented but this is amazing."

It wasn't supposed to be amazing. It was supposed to be private. Secret. Never seen. "I was doing it as a joke...I mean not the words but the image..." She set the phone down and covered her eyes. "How many people do you think have seen it?" She held up her hand. "No, I don't want to know." She jumped to her feet. "I'll pay you back for lunch but I have to go right now." She grabbed her handbag and coat. "I have to fix this," she said, silently praying that she could.

CHAPTER EIGHTEEN

The moment Alicia walked into the marketing department people started applauding.

Good natured cat calls and 'Way to go' filled the air. Alicia saw her brother's office door open and he appeared in the doorway. Edwin had the kind of face built for sales. His warm brown eyes and welcoming smile made you trust him, although that wasn't always a good thing, but at that moment a rush of relief gripped her. She had to resist the urge to start running towards that smile. She felt like a frightened mouse seeing the safety of a hole in the wall only yards away while a cat bore down on it.

Her brother beamed at her as she took a seat. "Are you coming here to gloat?" He closed the door.

"No. I need you to take the ad down."

He sat behind his desk. He wasn't a tall man but carried himself as if he were. His suit fit due to the care of an eagle eyed tailor and Edwin's own strict instructions. His teeth were as white as his shirt and although his wide grin could be welcoming it could just as easily turn as menacing as a wolf. "Why would I do that?" he said, clasping his hands together. "It's doing even better than I'd hoped. When you sent me what you were working on, I knew it would be big, but not this big."

Alicia groaned. "I said it was something we should discuss."

"Well, there's no need to discuss it now. It's live and—"

"But I was only sending you the words. We can't use the image. I didn't get permission."

His face changed—his eyes turned cold and his teeth glistened with a predatory sheen, but somehow his smile stayed in place. "What did you just say?"

"I'm sorry. I didn't expect this to happen. I was just...I didn't get a model release so—"

"But you sent me a high quality image."

"Because I took it off of someone's phone and enhanced it. That's how I was able to manipulate it. Why didn't you talk to me first?"

"Because I thought it was a done deal. The guy was wearing our uniform. How was I supposed to know you didn't get permission?"

"You could have asked. Isn't that what you usually do?"

Edwin jumped up from his seat and rubbed the back of his neck. "This time was different."

"I sent it only a couple weeks ago, what was the rush? It's not like you to cut corners."

"I had a deadline and no ideas. You don't know how long we were trying to come up with something. It's been months and sales weren't where we wanted them to be. I was desperate and your email came like an answered prayer. Why do you think I gave you the credit? I just needed something...anything to boost sales and this was it. Is it. It's worked." He swore. "I should have known not to trust you. That you'd screw this up for me."

"I didn't screw up anything, you did," she said, but Edwin wasn't listening. He shook his head and said in a bitter voice, "There was a bet going around wondering how long you'd last before you messed something up. Everyone knows you're a walking disaster."

Alicia surged to her feet. They'd been placing bets? They thought of her as a disaster? "All I did was try to help you."

"You sent me the photo without any clarification. It didn't look like a manipulated image."

"I forgot it was in the folder."

"How was I supposed to know that? You had all these ideas and not once did you mention that the image wasn't part of them. You never once told me not to consider it."

He was right, as much as she hated to admit it. She hadn't been more careful, what had started as a petty revenge against her sister now involved the entire company.

A walking disaster.

His words stung. Alicia looked at her brother's tailored suit and felt her throat close. Edwin had never been thought of as anything but ideal. He had the ideal marriage, career, two adorable daughters, as if everything in his life had been as carefully crafted as his suit. She looked at the hem of his trousers and how they perfectly fit over his polished shoes. She'd remembered her sister-in-law telling her how he'd fired a tailor who hadn't been able to get the balance right. He'd fired a barber for the same reason—the man hadn't shaved the back of his head with the precise line Edwin expected.

Edwin wasn't a man to ignore details—ever. So why had he ignored this one? Why hadn't he made sure she'd gotten a model release? Alicia slowly sank back into her seat as another thought struck her. "You knew."

"What?"

She gripped her hands in her lap. "That's why you gave me the credit. It wasn't out of pride or generosity. You knew that if there was any trouble with the photo you could blame me."

"No, that's not it," he said, but his denial held no fire. It had been a game. He could risk giving her credit for the campaign because if it failed he could always blame her. That's how he saw her—a scapegoat. That's how everyone would see her if she didn't do something.

He shrugged and his feigned surprise disappeared. "I'm sorry, I had to do something. I wasn't lying when I said I was desperate."

"So you throw me under the bus for your own survival."

"I've got a family to support and a reputation. You only have one of the two and the latter isn't worth very much. I'll give you credit," he said quickly when she opened her mouth in protest, "you've lasted longer than I thought. I really didn't think you'd last here longer than three weeks. Pauline said one. So we both lost to Fabian."

"If you're looking for an expression of sympathy," Alicia pointed to her face, "this is not it."

Edwin smoothed down his tie. "Listen, as much as it'll hurt, I'll take down the ad. Nothing much has come of it and any notice will soon go away and be forgotten. Fair enough?"

Alicia sighed in relief. Her brother could be a jerk but at least he wasn't heartless. They would both get through this unscathed. "Thank—"

The door burst open.

"Can't you knoc—" Edwin began then stopped when their father entered the room. Like Edwin he wasn't tall, but he didn't have to be, he had what was known as presence. He filled the room with his magnetic command, his trim snowy colored goatee framed a wide smile. "The ad is genius." He grabbed Edwin's hand, joy in his voice. "It's renewed the spirit of our business."

"I didn't do it alone," Edwin said with an awkward smile.

"Of course," their father said, casting a cursory glance at Alicia before looking at his son again. "You're too modest to take all the credit. When the chips are down you're always someone I can depend on."

Edwin had the grace to look embarrassed. "Yes, well—"

"I want more. I don't care how you make it happen." He slapped Edwin on the arm. "I believe in you. We all do."

Their father left the office. He'd offered Alicia no handshake, no pat on the arm, he'd treated her as he always had—the leftover one. Edwin and Pauline embodied what he thought a Fox should be. But Alicia had never lived up to his standards.

"You heard what he said, right?" Edwin said.

Alicia felt her stomach drop. She knew what his words meant. He wouldn't risk taking the ad down, any fallout would be on her—the walking disaster.

They all thought she would quit. They didn't think she had what it took to succeed. She would have to prove them wrong. But first...she had to warn Trey—fast.

CHAPTER NINETEEN

I need to see you.

Trey stared at the text not sure how to process it. If he were an ordinary man, getting a text like that from an attractive woman would have filled him with excitement, anticipation. But Trey knew he was far from ordinary so the sight of those five words caused him to toss the phone on his office desk as if it had turned into a live grey colored animal with fangs, sending his mind spinning.

There were two things he didn't do well—relax in crowds and understand texts.

I need to see you. That was code language. It didn't offer him any input. Without the variance of tone or body language or expression, he could glean nothing from it. Did she need to see him now? Soon? Why did she need to see him?

Did Alicia need to see him in person or did she want

a video chat? Was she angry with him? Concerned? Did she really need to *see* him or did she just want to talk to him? He knew that people sometimes conflated the two.

Should he try to sound urgent or casual? Should he say okay when or should he ask why?

Trey softly swore then did something rare—he acted without thinking. In a moment of panic he became careless, reckless, impulsive. Traits he prided himself on controlling—or not possessing at all. He was a man used to control, but the text had so unnerved him he acted out of character. However, he immediately regretted his action the instant he did it. He knew he'd made a mistake, he'd put his careful plan at risk, but it was too late to do anything so all he could do was wait and face the consequences.

Jacob blamed lack of sleep, too much coffee and the banging from the workers fixing the B&B's roof for the sight of the strange text on his cell phone. Getting the place ready for the spring opening had been more stressful than he'd anticipated—working with the contractor and getting permits. More than once he wondered if he was in over his head. And then there was her...

But he wouldn't think about that right now. He stood in the foyer of the B&B, where he'd been admiring the nice woodwork, and blinked at the screen on his phone. He had to be hallucinating.

But the screaming emoji image was real. No one else sent him that except one person and for one reason: Trey needed help.

He swore, glancing over his shoulder even though he was alone. If anyone saw this it could ruin everything, it wasn't like Trey to ruin one of his crazy plans so that meant it was serious.

Jacob made a wild guess and wondered if it had anything to do with the wedding planner. He sent an image of a woman and then a heart. Anything emotional sent Trey into a tizzy.

Trey sent back two screams.

Jacob swore again and then laughed realizing how much he'd missed his friend. He took a deep breath then texted: *One hour. You know where to meet me.*

The café along the strip mall had an unprepossessing exterior that kept most white collar workers, trendy college students or tourists away. It wasn't hip or part of a chain, just a simple family run business far enough in another county that Jacob and Trey didn't have to fear being spotted together. Jacob had made it his mission to find places where no one knew him. Since he couldn't be invisible in real life, being unknown was the next best thing.

When Jacob walked up to Trey, who waited for him outside the café, there was no ceremony. Trey didn't smile. He didn't wait for them to seek shelter inside the warmth of the café, instead Trey held out his cell phone in a gloved hand, the breath of a bitter wind blowing pass them and whipping a flag into a frenzy, and said, "She sent me this."

Jacob felt his nose going numb, but knew he had to look at the message before he could convince Trey to go inside. He took the phone and read the message. It was as harmless as he'd suspected, but then his heart constricted when he looked at the time. He stared at his friend stunned. "She sent this five hours ago! Why didn't you just reply?"

"I don't know. I froze."

"For five hours?"

"I contacted you."

Jacob ran a hand down his face. "Unbelievable." He scrolled down at the other messages that grew more urgent.

Please get back to me.

This is important.

Please let me know when I can see you.

Trey. This is urgent.

Jacob sighed. All he could do was damage control, but he couldn't do it out here, he'd left his gloves in the car, and his fingers were turning as red as sausages. He walked to the entrance of the café and opened the door, the welcoming scent of chocolate croissants wafted toward him. "I'll get a table. Order for us," Jacob said.

Fortunately, the café wasn't too crowded and Jacob easily found them a seat in the corner. He set the cell phone on the table and rubbed his hands together feeling them stinging back to life as he chewed his lip and thought of the best way to proceed.

He had so many questions. How had Alicia ended up knowing Trey? Why had they been having dinner together? Was this a romantic falling out?

Jacob glanced at Trey as he placed their orders, the barista smiled up at him but also looked mildly confused. He had that affect on people but Jacob couldn't rescue her, he had to figure out what was going on.

Jacob watched Trey nod at something the barista said, noticed him tapping a beat on his leg—Trey rarely did that when he was ordering. That meant he was anxious about something.

The text made him anxious. That meant Trey's relationship with Alicia wasn't romantic. When relationships became too complex, Trey shut down. He wouldn't have sent a screaming emoji, he wouldn't have sent Jacob anything at all. He would have sent a formal reply and that would have ended things. Women tended to find him cold, Jacob knew Trey was protecting himself.

But Trey had panicked. That meant this relationship was new and important to him. Jacob flexed his hands, trying to temper the curiosity swirling in his mind. He'd have to find out how important this new relationship was later, first he had to save it.

"What are you doing?" Trey asked, taking a seat while Jacob typed a message on Trey's cell phone. He set down the coffee in front of Jacob as well as a banana nut muffin.

Jacob sent the message before he took the coffee and indulged in a long sip. He set the cup down then said, "Giving the poor woman a break." He took another sip of the coffee, it tasted better than expected...had a hint of chocolate and peppermint. He looked up at Trey surprised. This was a holiday coffee. They'd stopped making this in January, but it was always his favorite. Jacob now understood the barista's confused expression. "How did you get her to make this?"

Trey ignored the question and said, "What did you say?"

"I apologized for being a complete dick and told her when you want to meet."

Trey shook his head. "No, you didn't."

"I should have." Jacob took another sip of his coffee, briefly closing his eyes, if only life could taste this good. He set the cup down before he sat back and stared at his friend. "What's up with you and Alicia?"

Trey reached for the cell phone. "What did you say to her?"

Jacob moved it out of reach. "Why did you panic?"

Trey held out his hand. "Give me the phone."

The phone alerted them to a reply. "Good, that was fast," Jacob said but Trey grabbed it before Jacob could look at the screen.

He read the message then groaned and squeezed his eyes shut.

"You said we could meet tonight?"

"After the silence you put her through, she deserves that much."

"What if I'm busy?"

"You're not busy and you're not going to avoid this. Now tell me what's going on."

"I don't know." When Jacob looked at him doubtful Trey waved his hands. "I mean it. Truly. I don't know. I wanted to pay her back for ruining her wedding."

Jacob's brows shot up. "You ruined her wedding too?"

"I mean your wedding, but it was the one she organized. She quit after that and I felt bad. I offered to hire her but she turned me down."

"You felt bad because she quit, but you felt fine about embarrassing me, yourself and changing the course of my life?"

Trey stared at him for a long moment. "You look happy."

Jacob felt his chest tighten. Trey knew him too well. There were still things he wanted to tell him but couldn't.

He couldn't tell him that he was happy to see him again. That he'd missed their friendship; that he wished they didn't have to pretend but that he was glad he hadn't gotten married and followed the path his fiancée and family had wanted for him. He couldn't tell him that as much as he'd freed him, he felt like he was trapped in another cage. A cage locked and sealed by lies.

"I should get going."

Jacob bit into his muffin. "You've got time. Tell me more about your relationship."

"There's no relationship. I haven't heard from her in weeks."

"I saw you eating dinner together."

"Okay, I treated her to a couple of meals. As I said, I tried to hire her but she wants nothing to do with me and I can't blame her, especially when I nearly gave her stitches."

"What?"

Trey's gaze fell. "She grabbed me."

Jacob knew how much Trey hated being grabbed and the reason behind it.

"Yeah, it was bad," Trey said.

"Do you think she wants to sue you? Is that why you panicked?"

His eyes shot up. "No, that's not it. I could accept that. She seemed fine after what happened. We even enjoyed a meal together, but...she made it clear she didn't want to see me again so I stayed away. Then she texted me out of the blue. I don't know what's going on."

"Only way to find out is to ask her. In person," Jacob quickly added when Trey lifted his phone.

"I wonder why she needs to see me?"

"You'll find out."

Trey nodded looking grim. "I'm sorry. I shouldn't have sent the message. I wasn't thinking. It was out of habit. I won't do it again."

Jacob drummed his fingers against the coffee cup. "Nobody needs to know about this."

Trey frowned down at the phone. "I wasn't going to tell anyone."

"No, I mean..." Jacob sighed, choosing his words carefully. "No one needs to know we're still friends. We can meet up in secret. I don't mind helping you out. I owe you."

Trey shook his head. "You don't owe me a thing. It's what friends do and I—"

Jacob wasn't in the mood to argue, an idea was forming in his mind. "Are you sure you only wanted to hire her?"

Trey hesitated. "Why?"

Jacob began to grin. "You know why."
"I better go."
"Tell me how it goes."
Trey stood. "Sure."
Jacob's smile widened. "And I expect details."

CHAPTER TWENTY

He didn't know where to rest his eyes. Trey shifted his gaze around the apartment, gripping his hands in his lap. Clutter lay everywhere. He hated clutter.

"Thanks for coming all this way," Alicia said. "I know it's an inconvenience, but I think it's best I tell you in person."

Trey glanced at the turned over sneakers, the scattered stack of magazines on the floor laying beside a tiny pile of clothes, the wig on the back of the chair made him smile, but the half eaten bag of chips on the coffee table made him hurt. He saw a chocolate bar wrapper underneath. He would not close his eyes. That would be rude.

He rubbed his hands together. He would look at her, focus on her. "Okay," he said searching her face. She looked worried. Concerned. Not angry. What did she have to be worried about? And why would anyone as

smart as she was decide to leave one sock—not two, one!
—on the seat of a couch?

"Would you like something to drink?" She started
to stand.

"No," he said so loud he made her jump. He didn't
want her to move, if she left the room he would start to
clean. He motioned to the seat and softened his voice
with regret. She was already worried, he didn't want to
scare her too. "I mean. I'm fine. Tell me what's wrong."

She swallowed. "Are you sure you don't want
anything?"

"Positive." He folded his arms. She was just where he
wanted her, blocking him from the sight of the crooked
blinds. He liked looking at her, liked being with her. He
knew that from the beginning and that feeling hadn't
changed. He'd hoped it would, especially after she'd
turned him down. But that hadn't surprised him, he'd
been turned down plenty of times. Her place itched to be
cared for just like her. He liked the fuzzy blue sweater
she wore and the matching slippers. She looked more like
herself here than in the office, in those suits. He also liked
how her place felt—as much as he wanted to clean it—
desperately, desperately—he felt at home among the
scent of lemon and bubblegum, the soft lamplight and
comfortable sofa. He was sensitive to touch and had to
resist running his hand over the fabric of the sofa that felt
as welcoming as freshly baked bread.

His gaze briefly landed on the crumbs of bread left on
the saucer sitting on the side table that begged him to be
washed and put away.

But he wouldn't touch anything, he'd listen, enjoy

what little time he had with her and then leave. That's all he'd come to do.

He looked at Alicia again and inwardly groaned. He couldn't stare at her too long, when he did that, it usually scared people. He glanced at her hairline, her nose, dipped to her sweater then imagined burying his face in the soft pillows of her chest and quickly shifted his gaze back to her face.

Alicia rubbed her hands together. She couldn't easily read Trey's expression or his mood. He didn't seem irritated, but ready. On edge. And why was he staring at her like that? He usually looked at everything but her, but this time his dark gaze never left her face. And for a moment she forgot why she'd called him over to her place. Everything seemed to fall away—all the fear and anxiety that had gripped her only seconds before seemed to fall away under the gentle pressure of his gaze. How could a shark seem so serene?

She felt that whispering need again...trust me...I won't let you drown. She swallowed again wanting to lean closer to him and inhale the alluring scent of him that had teasingly wafted towards her when he'd entered the apartment. He hadn't taken off his coat. She was sorry she hadn't been able to convince him to, although she already knew what he looked like half-naked.

Like a flash she imagined him sitting in front of her shirtless and suddenly felt too warm. "Are you sure you don't want me to take your coat?"

"I'm fine."

Of course he was, she was the one with the overactive imagination. It was that imagination that had gotten her in trouble in the first place. It was the only reason why he was here—the photo.

She knew he wouldn't want explanations. He'd want the facts. She'd hoped to soothe him with some wine or rum but that plan wouldn't work. She'd have to tell him straight.

"Someone took a picture of you running and then my sister started making comments about it and it annoyed me so I photoshopped you wearing one of our MedForm uniforms and put a caption about how good our product is in times of crisis. I really don't know why I did that," (a complete lie, but he didn't need to know that) "but I did and then I sent it to the marketing department because I liked the caption forgetting about the image and they ran with it and—" She stopped when Trey waved his hand.

"This is too much information. What is the problem? Why did you need to see me?"

"I'm getting to that. I just wanted to give you some background."

Trey frowned. "Why would I need background? Most problems are unnecessarily complicated by extraneous information—"

"Exper—what? No...Never mind," Alicia said before he could give her a detailed description. "The point is, your image has been used with a successful campaign and my father now thinks I'm a genius, well actually he thinks my brother is, but my brother sort of thinks I am and already we've gotten new orders and..." Her voice trailed away as her heart kicked up pace.

She blinked.

She swallowed.

This was too much, holding his gaze had been diffi-cult enough but now a sexy smile had softened his mouth. Not only was the shark smiling, he had dimples. She hadn't noticed he had dimples before and they were adorable.

Alicia shook her head. Wait. This made no sense. He was supposed to be angry. Maybe the smile wasn't real. Maybe he was just showing his teeth as a warning.

"This is great," Trey said.

No, the smile looked too happy to be anything but genuine.

"Great?" Alicia said.

He nodded then stood up before he quickly sat back down and the scent of him embraced her, she had to stop herself from leaning closer. His knee rubbed against hers, a surge of electricity sizzled through her. She licked her lip, knowing she shouldn't be looking at him like this. But he was so close.

"Yes, great," he said. "I helped you, right?"

She could only nod.

"Then why were you worried?"

"B-because I used your image without permission."

"I hurt you. It's the least I could do." He nudged her with his elbow. "You didn't have worry about that. Or worry now." He leaned back and rested his arms the length of the couch. "You were afraid I was going to be angry?"

She nodded.

His grin widened. "That's why you wanted to see me?"

She nodded again. It felt surreal. Perhaps he didn't

understand the gravity of the situation. She pulled out her cell phone. "Do you want to see it?"

"Sure."

She brought up the image and held it out for him to see. Immediately his smile disappeared. He leaned forward and took the phone.

She squeezed her eyes shut. This is what she feared. When he saw the number of views. When he saw the comments. When he saw...

She heard him sigh then swear. She felt the couch shift as he leaned back again, but instead of a causal motion, she sensed tension. Served her right for thinking it would have been this easy. They would remove the ad. Right now they could only see his profile, so it wasn't too identifiable. If she could find someone else, perhaps her brother wouldn't care and...

"I'm sorry," Trey said.

Her eyes flew open. She turned to him and saw an expression she didn't expect to see.

CHAPTER TWENTY-ONE

"What?" Alicia said surprised by the tension in his jaw. His words may have hinted at regret but anger seethed through them. "Why are you apologizing?"

"I thought you said I helped you. But I didn't do anything. This image could have been anyone. You did all the work."

His words made no sense. Didn't he see that the reason the ad was so popular was because of how sexy he looked? He made the uniform look good not vice versa. Didn't he see that he made someone dream, for a moment, that a man like him was coming to their rescue? That anyone who wanted to be a hero could aspire to look like that?

They were selling sex, a fantasy and he was the one who'd helped it come true. But from the frown on Trey's face it was clear he didn't see it at all.

He stood. "You didn't have to ask me to come here to

stroke my ego. I'm not a child." He picked up the empty chocolate wrapper off the ground, the crinkling sound like a silent scream as it disappeared in his fist, and he then went and picked up the saucer on the side table, holding it like a disc he wanted to throw. But he didn't throw anything. Instead he calmly walked to the kitchen. "Sure, you knew I felt bad that I hurt you—"

"You didn't hurt me," Alicia said, hearing him throw the wrapper away and scrape crumbs from the saucer. "I told you that."

He returned to the room as if she hadn't spoken and straightened the blinds. "And I'll admit to being frustrated that you wouldn't let me hire you."

"That's because—"

He picked up the pile of clothes on the floor. "But to lie to me—"

Her brows shot up. "I didn't lie to you."

Trey dumped the clothes on the couch and began to fold them. "You said I helped you."

"You did."

"Really? Did I give you an idea for this campaign? Did it leap from a conversation that we had? Did I research something you didn't know about? Did I offer feedback, insight, anything of remote value? No. You used your design skills and put me in one of your uniforms. You could have put it on anything and gotten the same result."

Alicia watched in silent disbelief as Trey turned her messy pile into a neat stack of clothes as if they'd been delivered—washed and pressed—from a laundry service. What stunned her even more was that he truly was angry. If he hadn't been she would have stopped him from tidying her place. She didn't let anyone do that—her mother and sister tried and she made sure they never tired again. She didn't want order, she liked her things exactly where they were.

But she strangely hadn't stopped Trey. One, because he moved so quickly, before she'd realized what he was doing, he'd cleared her side table and straightened her shoes; second, it hadn't felt intrusive, his behavior felt more mechanical than emotional. He wasn't making a grand show of his efforts as if he knew better, but thirdly —and this was what kept her the most still—he was angry.

She'd never seen him angry before.

Trey angry was more than a little unnerving. His jaw was so tense she feared he'd crack his teeth. He'd impaled her with a fierce dark look before he'd begun folding the clothes, she'd half expected him to tear them to shreds. But he was too controlled for that.

That control scared her too. His eerily cold anger reminded her once again of how dangerous sharks could be.

She'd been prepared for the anger, feared it, but she'd expected him to be angry about the photo not believe that she was lying to him.

She hadn't come up with ways to handle this. It was absurd. But then again this was the same man who'd admitted to sleeping with his friend's fiancée in order to save him.

Alicia ran her finger along the edge of the couch, searching her mind. She wasn't sure how to get him to see how much he had helped her. She delicately cleared her throat. "You realize it's not the uniform people are focusing on, right?"

He set a neatly folded sweater on top of the clothing stack then gathered up the scattered magazines. "That's my point. They are. You were able to highlight the features of your product in a way that turned it into a success. Why are you giving me credit for that?"

"I don't think you understand—"

Trey whacked the magazines down on the coffee table with enough force Alicia feared he'd shatter the glass. "I understand," he said in a soft voice, pinning her with a dark look. Her mouth went dry. "I understand how you see me. You're not the first but..." He paused, a look—pained, vulnerable—passed over his features before it disappeared. "I thought you were different. Doesn't matter. I've been wrong before." He turned towards the door. "Goodbye."

Alicia jumped to her feet. "What? Wait!" she said but he didn't stop walking. She wanted to—had to—stop him, but when her fingers brushed against the sleeve of his coat she remembered she couldn't grab him, and he was too close to the door to jump in front of him so she thought of the next best thing: She kicked him in the back of the knee.

She'd intended to make him stumble forward but she'd hit the back of his knee with such force he completely lost his balance and crashed into the door. It sounded like a bomb blast or perhaps only felt that way because of the terror that surged through her as she cowered back. If Trey had been mad before he'd be furious now.

He slowly straightened, smoothed down his coat, straightened the lapels before resting a large palm against the door. He released a long sigh.

Alicia held her breath.

He didn't move.

"I'm sorry," Alicia finally said, her voice barely a whisper.

Trey didn't look at her. She watched his shoulders rise and fall as he took another breath. "Are you making up for hitting your head on the desk?"

She gasped. "No. I—"

"You kicked me."

"I know."

"Why did you do that?"

Alicia took a hesitant step towards him, wringing her hands. "I didn't want you to go. I couldn't grab you and I couldn't think of another way to stop you."

Trey turned to her. "And why would you want to stop me?"

"Because there's been a misunderstanding. It's my fault for not explaining things better. You really did help me." She rushed over and grabbed the cell phone. She looked down at the image on the screen with both regret and pride. They'd done this together. She remembered how he'd jumped into action after she'd fallen, the feel of his arms around her, the scent of his shirt, the boom of his voice as he demanded assistance.

If he hadn't cared about her so much no one would have been able to capture this image of him running down the hall—for a stuffed toy no less. She'd put the uniform on him but the dynamic power—the image of a man on a mission—had been real. And all him.

The success of the ad belonged to both of them. She wanted him to see that. "I couldn't have made this ad without you and—" She stopped when she felt his hand on her shoulder, the heaviness of his large palm making her sweater feel as thin as tissue paper. That same electric sizzle swept through her, she lifted her gaze to his face, saw the granite jaw and frown, but his gaze had softened a fraction.

"You're very kind," he said. "But you don't have to make up things to make me feel better." He removed his hand and opened the door. "I don't need credit for something you did on your own. You have my permission to use the photo. Don't contact me again."

He walked out the door and this time he didn't say goodbye. He didn't need to. His broad back and assured gait said, 'Don't try to stop me,' forcing Alicia to helplessly watch him walk out of her life.

CHAPTER TWENTY-TWO

He barely remembered how he got there. Trey looked at the quaint little building that would soon be open to visitors in the spring. But presently Jacob's B&B sat among the sparse bushes and leafless trees like a tiny hunched gnome made of red brick, trying to stay warm in the dark evening against the winter chill.

Trey rang the bell.

Once. Twice. Three times.

When he heard no movement he sighed. He took a step back and looked at the faint light from one of the second floor windows. Jacob was home, but he could sleep through an apocalypse. He probably should have called first. Again he'd acted rash and all because of her.

All because he'd thought she was different.

Trey started to turn then paused when he heard the pounding of footsteps before the light above the door came to life in a brilliant yellow haze and then the door swung open.

Jacob stepped out dressed in a thin grey shirt, jeans and his bare feet. He quickly closed the door behind him. He ran a hand through his hair, agitated. "You were supposed to call me."

"I was going to call but—"

Jacob shoved him back with one hand while he gripped the door handle with the other. "Good. Tell me then."

Trey frowned glancing at his friend's reddening nose and bare feet. "What's going on?"

"Just go before she—" The door opened a crack before Jacob closed it again. "Run."

"Why?" Trey briefly closed his eyes as he assessed the situation. The bare feet, the uneasy tone. Jacob was rarely single long. "Damn. You've got a woman in there."

"I wouldn't call her a woman."

"Hey, I heard that," the offended woman said, her voice barely muffled by the wooden door.

Trey froze. The voice sounded familiar. "Is it—?"

"Yes, Maya's here. She dropped by."

"If you don't open this door," Jacob's sister said, "I will smash one of your windows."

Jacob swore.

Trey shook his head. "She doesn't sound like she's joking."

Jacob turned and held the door closed. "She can't see you here," he said in a low voice of panic. "It will ruin everything."

"I won't let her."

Maya raised her voice, pulling at the door again. "I know it's Trey. I saw his car. Now open the door."

Jacob looked at Trey confused. "Why aren't you running?"

"I can handle Maya. I need to show you something."

Jacob tilted his head towards the door indicating his sister. "Something worse than this?"

He nodded.

Jacob sighed and released the door. Maya flung it open then fell back on her bottom with a thud.

She stared at them with wide eyes. "I knew it! I knew something was going on." She pointed at them, swinging her finger back and forth like a pendulum. "You'd better tell me everything or I'll—"

Jacob turned to Trey resigned. "I hope what you have to say is worth it."

"It is." Trey walked into the main sitting room that had a welcoming plush seating arrangement.

Jacob closed the door and followed him.

Maya scrambled to her feet. "I'm not going to let you both ignore me."

But they continued to act as if she wasn't there when Trey pulled out his cell phone and showed Jacob the ad before taking a seat. "This is why she wanted to see me."

"Who wanted to see you?" Maya asked as Jacob stared at the image. "Let me see," she said, pulling at his arm so he could lower it to her level. She gasped.

Jacob laughed.

Trey folded his arms. "You find this funny?"

"You don't?"

"No."

"You're now a model and you don't find that funny?"

"I might have found it funny if she hadn't lied to me."

"She lied?"

"Yes, she wasted my time. She made me think that it was urgent. She had me worried and then she tells me I helped her." Trey pointed to the screen. "That this picture helped her. But I didn't do anything. She could have dressed up a pig and had the same effect."

Jacob sobered, recognizing the pain in his friend's voice and knowing the reason. He shook his head. "It's not the same."

But to Trey it felt the same. The same as when the kids used to joke that there was nothing different between Trey and a rock. That you could put a cardboard cutout of him in class and not know the difference. He endured the teasing, he didn't care that few people under-stood him, but he'd thought— "I thought she really liked me...that she cared about me." The words felt awkward in his mouth, the slow heated rise of embarrassment inched up his neck and burned his face but it felt good to share his senseless emotions. It was good to feel hurt and humil-iation. It was a reminder to stay away, keep himself safe. Jacob was the one person he could trust not to laugh at him. "I thought when she worried about my car and she even put lotion on my hands that she was different. No one has ever done that for me. I was foolish—"

"You weren't foolish."

"Who are you talking about?" Maya said.

Trey sighed. "I thought she saw me as a..." He let his words fall away unwilling to finish his thoughts, ashamed that he'd believed she saw him as an ordinary man like anyone else, that she wouldn't treat him differently. "Then I realized she only pitied me. She thought that I needed my ego stroked."

Jacob sat down beside him, holding his gaze. "Trey, you did help her."

"How? I did nothing. Nothing! Someone took a picture of me and she used it. She could put anyone in a picture. She could have used a mannequin and gotten the same success. Why would she lie and say it was because of me? The ad succeeded because of the caption, the lighting, the quality of the product, the—"

"Sex," Maya said.

The two men turned to her.

"It's true." She walked over and nudged her brother. "Move or I'll sit on your lap."

Jacob scowled and shifted so she could sit down next to Trey. She held up her hand when Jacob opened his mouth to speak. "Right now let me explain to the alien about the human species, you can lecture me later." She turned to Trey. "Sex sells." She pointed to the screen. "This image is all about it. It is climax. It is thrust, pulse, hunger. This is not just a man running. This is about penetration."

Jacob swore. "You're just making this up as you go along."

"No, I'm not," Maya said. "You know he looks sexy in this."

Trey shook his head. "I do not look sexy."

"Yes, you do," Jacob admitted. He held up his hands

in surrender when Trey sent him a dark look. "I'm being honest."

Maya nodded. "See you're not just running, you're—"

"If you use the word penetration again, I'm going to strangle you."

"Taking action," she finished. "Your face is intense, focused."

Trey shrugged. "My face is always like that."

"Give up," Jacob said. "He'll never see it." He looked at Trey. "But she didn't lie to you. She really meant it."

"Who are we talking about?" Maya said.

"She is different," Jacob continued. "And—ow!" he cried when Maya pinched him.

"Who. Is. She?"

"She's Alicia, the wedding planner."

Maya turned to Trey. "The one we saw you eating with?"

He nodded.

"The one wearing a wig and drooling into her pasta?"

Trey frowned. "She wasn't drooling."

"I meant that figuratively. She finds you very attractive."

Trey tapped the tips of his fingers together. "Really?"

Maya smiled and gently patted his cheek. "Yes, my dear adorable alien, and I'll tell you how I know this after you explain what you're doing here."

"I wanted to show..." He stopped when Maya began shaking her head.

"Why are you two still talking to each other when

you should be holding light sabers and trying to annihilate each other?"

Trey rested his elbows on his knees. "How much do you want?"

"I'm not going to blackmail you, I want the truth."

He shook his head. "Can't tell you that. Sorry."

She turned to Jacob. "Then you explain."

"I can't. It was his idea."

Maya let out a cry of frustration. "You two are infuriating."

"You can't tell anyone."

"And if I do?"

"Jacob will lose everything," Trey said.

Maya turned to her brother. "What does he mean by that?"

Jacob stared at the fireplace; Trey remained silent.

Maya sighed in defeat. "Okay, never mind. Don't worry, I won't tell anyone."

Trey pressed a light kiss on her forehead then flashed a sly grin. "I know."

Maya blinked, then feigned fanning herself. "I can't believe you don't know you're sexy."

His grin fell. "I wasn't trying to be sexy."

She kissed him on the cheek. "But you are my little alien."

Jacob shook his head. "I can't believe he lets you get away with calling him that."

She fluttered her lashes. "It's because I'm smart and adorable."

Trey leaned back. "So have you dumped the jerk yet?"

"No," Jacob said, "she's still seeing him."

"Hopefully she'll come to her senses soon."

Maya waved her hands. "Hold up. I'm not going to take relationship advise from a clueless alien who can't tell when a woman has the hots for him or another who stays friends with the very guy who 'supposedly' slept with his fiancée."

"I said I was with her," Trey clarified. "I didn't say I slept with her and what proof do you have that Alicia has the hots for me?"

Maya held up the ad. "This is the proof. She thinks you're so amazing that she truly is giving you all the credit for this ad. She really believes you're the reason it's a success. She knows she played a minor role but doesn't believe in herself. Maybe she's failed a lot in her past and the one time something is a success she attributes it to you. So, she's not lying, it's what she really thinks."

Trey rubbed his chin. "She mentioned something about a brother not expecting much from her."

Maya snapped her fingers. "See? That proves my point."

"So Alicia believed her words even though they weren't true?"

"They're true to her and true to a lot of people. You did help her out. She wasn't trying to stroke your ego. That's not the kind of person she is."

Images began flooding his mind—Alicia staring at him surprised, confused, concerned. He'd thought she'd been surprised by how quickly he'd caught on to her game; confused that he'd still let her use his picture and worried that he might ask for money. But there had been no game. All her words had been genuine. *There's been a misunderstanding.*

She'd said that and he hadn't listened. He hadn't given her a chance. He'd been so certain in his assessment of her. So righteous in his thoughts, filtering them through the funnel of his childhood instead of as the man he was now. He'd never done that before. He prided himself on his ability to compartmentalize things. He could blame the clutter in her apartment or her strange text for his uncharacteristic behavior. But they would be excuses not reasons.

It was him. It was her affect on him. The way she looked at him, spoke to him, touched him. It all boiled down to one simple truth: He found her attractive, even though he really didn't want to. Sometimes he was so smart he was stupid. He pinched the bridge of his nose. "Damn."

"So you finally understand?"

He nodded, grim.

"Then why do you look so depressed?"

"I didn't handle this right." He surged to his feet. "But I can fix this."

Jacob also stood. "What are you going to do?"

Trey walked to the door, feeling suddenly renewed. He hadn't been wrong about her. She was someone he could trust, but first he had to regain her trust in him. He relished the challenge. "I don't know," he said opening the door, inhaling the cold evening air that ordinarily would feel like needles against his skin but tonight it felt like heaven, "but I'll think of something."

CHAPTER TWENTY-THREE

Few things surprised Deanna. Especially when it came to her best friend Alicia. From the first moment she met the blue streaked haired roommate, she anticipated an adventure. She thought nothing Alicia did could really shock her.

Until tonight.

The voice on the phone hadn't sounded panicked, Alicia had called her because she needed help for a situation at work. Deanna loved dealing with work related problems—workflow, inventory management, managerial issues, resource allotment, you name it, she loved it. Aside from writing BL fan fiction her second greatest hobby was compiling spreadsheets—namely addressing the pros and cons of any given situation.

So she raced over to Alicia's apartment ready to figure out the best way to tackle whatever problem her friend had. Although Alicia had vaguely explained it to her—something about a model release from a model who didn't understand—Deanna felt certain that by the end of the evening they'd have a solid plan of action. She'd even stopped by the grocery store to buy some Chunky Monkey ice cream to celebrate.

But when Deanna stepped into Alicia's apartment, the bag of ice cream slipped from her fingers and hit the ground with a thud.

"What happened?"

"What do you mean?"

Deanna took a cautious step forward. "Your apartment...it's c-clean."

"I know. It won't last long but it's nice for now."

Deanna grabbed her friend's hand and searched her eyes. Things must be really grim if Alicia cleaned. Alicia never cleaned. She felt her forehead.

Alicia swatted her hand away and laughed. "I didn't do it. He did."

"Who did?"

"Trey. I told you on the phone."

"I could barely understand what you were saying on the phone. Something about getting a model release but that the model's now angry at you and—"

Alicia picked up the bag Deanna had dropped. She peeked inside and grinned. "Just what I need."

Deanna snatched the bag from her. "That's for later. What's going on?"

"That's the problem. I'm not quite sure." Alicia disappeared into the kitchen then came back with two spoons. She held out her hand.

Deanna made a face then handed her the carton. "What happened?"

Alicia sat down, opened the carton, carelessly tossing the lid on the coffee table, and took a scoop. "I upset him and I don't know why or how or—"

"Wow." Deanna continued to survey the apartment in amazement. "I can't believe you let him clean."

"You're not listening."

Deanna slowly turned in a circle. "I'm trying to get over this miracle."

Alicia pointed her spoon at her. "I'm not that messy."

Deanna sat down beside her and laughed, "Said the woman who just dropped chocolate on her sweater."

Alicia glanced down and scooped it up.

"You know I love you," Deanna said, "but your place usually looks like a tornado and hurricane had just finished making love in it."

"Fine."

"And you *never* let anyone cleanup."

"Not sure I could have stopped him, plus it was oddly comforting to watch him."

Deanna grinned. "I'm sure it was." She took a scoop of ice cream. "But I don't understand the problem. You got permission, right?"

Alicia nodded.

"Does he expect compensation?"

She shook her head.

"Has he specified any conditions?"

She shook her head again. "I know it doesn't make sense. I know that I can probably find another model, come up with other captions and make my father and brother happy it's just...he thinks I lied to him."

"Why would he think that?"

"I don't know! That's what's bothering me."

"I don't think you can worry about that. If he's so thin skinned he's not worth the effort."

That was what truly puzzled her. Alicia knew Trey wasn't a sensitive person, he'd really looked hurt. But for the life of her she couldn't imagine what she'd done or said that had disappointed him. But perhaps Deanna was right, she had to forget him. She was tired of disappointing people. That had been the pattern of her life, a pattern she was determined to change. He'd helped her—whether he wanted to believe it or not—and now she would move forward.

She only wished she didn't miss him. She wished she could pretend that her place hadn't remained clean because she wanted to remember him. Remember the moment that he'd smiled at her and revealed his dimples, the moment his eyes had lit up at the thought that he'd helped her even...even when he'd touched her shoulder before he left.

She felt like she'd lost something important even though she kept trying to push him away. It was for the best. This had to be the last time she saw him because if she did see him again, she likely wouldn't let him go.

CHAPTER TWENTY-FOUR

The man was gone, but the scent of him lingered.

Or perhaps that was just her imagination. Alicia opened up the drawer where she'd stored Trey's shirt. She was glad that he'd forgotten about it. It had become her security blanket. Anytime she felt stressed, anxious or unsure she held it and inhaled his scent and like magic she felt better.

She'd probably never return it to him. She'd used a stain remover, carefully so as not to overpower his scent, to remove the red blemish.

She may not have the man, but this would suit her. At least there was no misunderstanding with a shirt; a shirt couldn't walk out on her or get angry or be disappointed.

This was the kind of relationship she could handle. Trey was too complicated for her. At least he hadn't been angry about the picture. She'd dodged that bullet. Yes, she was glad she'd never see him again.

At least that's what she tried to convince herself the following week as the campaign continued to gain steam.

"Do you think you could get him to do another pose for us?" Edwin said.

He and Pauline stood on either side of her desk peppering her with questions. Alicia could understand why Edwin was there, but not Pauline, except for the fact that she always liked to be involved in anything exciting so that she could get some credit no matter how small. As if she didn't have their father's favor enough she wanted whatever little crumbs Alicia could manage. Pauline, like Edwin, wore tailored suits, kept her immaculately permed hair, a gleaming black curtain that fell past her shoulders, in line with steel clips. She only flashed her straightened white teeth when she wanted something. She smiled now. "Please."

"No, I don't think I can do that."

"How about a video?" Pauline said. "What's his voice like?"

"We don't need a video," Edwin said.

"It's just a suggestion."

Edwin shook his head. "This isn't even your department."

"No need to get huffy, I'm only trying to help."

"Yourself," Edwin said. He turned to Alicia. "I need some new ideas by the end of the day to keep up the momentum. I don't care if it's this guy or someone similar, got it?"

"Yes."

He left her office.

Alicia waited for her sister to leave too, but instead Pauline rested her hip against the corner of the desk. "Poor Edwin must really be in a bad way if he has to depend on you."

"This wouldn't have happened if it weren't for you."

Pauline clicked her tongue. "Only losers blame others for their misfortune. Don't you remember our parents teaching us that or were you napping?"

"Get out of my office."

Her sister sneered. "You're lucky you even have an office. You know the idea was tossed around that you only deserved a cubicle, especially since nobody thought you'd last here long, but for the sake of appearances you ended up here." She folded her arms. "And now you've gotten lucky again. You managed to turn a little office joke into a major win. So you can stop with the befuddled act and tell me who he is."

"And why would I do that?" Alicia said, leaving her office, since her sister wouldn't. She headed for the break room.

"Because if you can't convince him to do more work for us, maybe I can."

She sounded so assured. Pauline was always assured of herself and her capabilities. Perhaps she would have better success with Trey, but Alicia suddenly felt possessive of him.

She stopped and turned to her. "He's not a model, he doesn't want to be a model and—" Her voice fell away when she realized her sister wasn't listening to her anymore. Instead, something near the elevators had caught her attention. For some reason, before Alicia shifted her gaze from her sister, she felt a sense of excitement and dread. She heard the low murmur of his voice but couldn't make out his words.

Alicia turned to him and their eyes met.

Trey didn't smile. He just captured her gaze with his and made everything else fall away. For a moment she could picture him draped in green scrubs with the background hazed out and him the only focus.

He could model a fig leaf and make it sell.

He walked towards her but before she could say anything her sister pounced. Pauline rushed forward with a bright smile. "We can't thank you enough for all that you've done."

He blinked. "But I didn't do anything."

"We'd really like a chance to work with you again if—"

"We're busy," Alicia said, then leaned closer to him and whispered, "I'm grabbing your arm," before she did and led him to her office. She didn't make it there before Edwin, who should have been on a different floor, materialized, his grin even brighter than Pauline's. "It's great to see the man of the hour. What you did was fabulous."

Trey's frown increased. "But I didn't do anything."

"Excuse us," Alicia pushed past him and rushed into her office and closed the door.

She took a deep breath. "I'm sorry about that."

"What is wrong with everyone?"

"I don't—" She paused when someone knocked on her door. "I'm in a meeting."

"This won't take a minute," she heard her father say

before he entered. She knew word travelled fast but this was ridiculous. Her father walked past her as if she were a piece of furniture and held his hand out to Trey as if welcoming a dignitary. "Young man, it's a pleasure to meet you. On behalf of MedForm I wanted to personally thank you."

Trey jumped back from her father's outstretched hand. "What is wrong with you people? I didn't do anything! Alicia did everything. All I did was—"

"He's embarrassed by the praise," Alicia said, hoping to erase the startled surprise on her father's face. "He's very shy and incredibly humble. That's why I didn't tell you about him. Please let me talk to him."

Her father nodded and left.

Alicia closed the door. "Sit down."

"Shy? Humble?" Trey tapped his chest. "Me?"

"Please sit down."

Trey folded his arms. "No. This makes no sense." He rubbed his chin. "Maya was right but it's still nonsense. Why am I being given credit for something I didn't do?"

"You helped me, that's all that matters."

"But I—"

"Please just take credit. It will make things a lot easier for me."

"So the fact that you doctored the image, came up with the caption doesn't matter as much as me *running*?"

Alicia shrugged. "Please. My family doesn't exactly see me as the most reliable one."

"Why not?"

The door burst open and Pauline appeared. "Do you mind if we borrow him for a few minutes?"

"Have you forgotten how to knock?"

Pauline looked at Trey with a predatory grin that could easily be mistaken for charm. "I promise I won't take up too much of your time."

"He doesn't want to model," Alicia said.

Her sister's glance said, 'We'll see about that' while her mouth said, "Do you mind Mr..." She let her words trail off, leaving him to fill in the blank.

"Trey."

"Mr. Trey."

"No, just call me Trey."

"And you can call me Pauline." She reached for his arm.

"Don't touch him," Alicia warned. "He doesn't like to be touched."

Her sister crunched up her face. "Cute."

"She's not joking," Trey said. "What do you want to talk to me about?"

"If you'd just follow me to my office..." Her voice died away.

Trey looked at Alicia and she nodded. There was no use fighting the inevitable. Let her sister have her way.

"Lead the way," Trey said and Alicia watched them leave her office before she closed the door and collapsed in her chair.

Trey was hers and now her sister was trying to take him. That was always the way. Anything Alicia took interest in her sister had to take. But Trey wasn't officially hers. He couldn't be. This was all so wrong.

She wondered why he'd come to see her, but it didn't matter now.

She pulled out his shirt. Just for a minute she could pretend Trey was here with her.

She held the shirt close and inhaled his scent. He was embracing her and telling her that everything was okay. It would be fine. She didn't have to feel as if she were slowly suffocating.

And now she was being overshadowed again. This wasn't a toy being taken or a class project copied and claimed. This was just a simple campaign. Her father was pleased. The company happy, it didn't matter if she got the credit or not.

"I'd wondered what you'd done with it."

Alicia froze at the sound of his voice. She stared down at the shirt. She'd been caught. Perhaps he hadn't seen her sniffing it.

"I knocked," Trey said. "But you didn't hear me."

She squeezed her eyes shut. He was going to think she was crazy. Maybe she was.

"So...Do you prefer the shirt to the man?"

CHAPTER TWENTY-FIVE

"I—" She had nothing to say. Alicia hung her head in shame and held out the shirt. "Here, you can take it, I haven't washed it though, so you just tell me what the dry cleaning bill is—" She stopped when she felt his hand cover hers. Her head shot up. He had closed the distance between them and was pushing her hand down.

Trey came around the desk and sat on the corner of it. The last time they'd been this close he'd been angry with her, but she couldn't sense any anger in his expression. Instead he looked as calm and remote as the first day they'd met. "I think you've misunderstood something."

Alicia swallowed not sure her heart could take anymore misunderstandings between them. "I have?"

He nodded, his gaze falling. "You told your sister I don't like being touched. That's not exactly true." He traced a slow circle on the back of his hand, lowered his voice. "I don't mind being touched," he said in a way that made her gaze stay fixed on his hand, his fingers, the slow way they slid over his skin as if they were sliding over her. Slowly sliding down her arm, making her mouth dry, making her body hot. "What I don't like is being grabbed." He briefly lifted his gaze to hers with the intimacy of a butterfly kiss before it skittered away. "Does that clear up any confusion?"

She was more confused than ever now. How could a man who hadn't touched her, barely looked at her, make her feel as sexy, desirable and treasured as he made her feel at that moment? Instead of making her feel bad about his shirt he'd understood, he was jealous. He was telling her that he wanted more. Her heart began to pound. But more of what exactly?

She heard him clear his throat. "Do I need to—"

"No," she said quickly as he leaned towards her and his irresistibly clean scent urged her to move closer. "No, I'm sorry. I—"

Trey glanced at the shirt. "So if you're using that as a substitute there's no need." He folded his arms. "I'm approachable."

Approachable? Him? Just by folding his arms he looked twice the size, his jaw looked like it could cut steel. He looked as approachable as a metal barracuda covered in spikes.

She laughed. And it felt good to laugh because she'd been a bundle of nerves only moments before. Then she realized he wasn't laughing. Or smiling. Dread crawled over her skin as she realized he was serious. He truly didn't realize how he appeared to others. She noticed he'd stiffened and although she couldn't read his eyes, they didn't stay in one place long enough for her to do so. She sensed she'd hurt him.

She leaned forward, lightly covered his hand with hers. "I'm laughing because you're right. You are. You're one of the most straightforward people I've met. I know where I stand with you. I don't understand you all the time, I admit that, but you're easy to be with. That doesn't happen to me very often."

She saw the shadow of a smile, the wink of a dimple and felt her heart soar then wondered which of her words had appeased him. It took her a moment to notice that his gaze was fixed on something, she followed it and saw that she was gripping his hands. She hadn't even noticed. But he had and it had clearly delighted him. She resisted the urge to yank her hand away, although she felt the need to. He was too alluring. She gently released her grip and leaned back. "How did the meeting go?"

He shook his head. "Wrong question."

"What?"

"Aren't you curious why I came to see you?"

"Yes, but—"

Trey reached inside his coat pocket and placed a chocolate bar on her desk. "I owe you an apology."

"Oh, it's okay."

"Stop saying it's okay when it's not. I shouldn't have treated you like that." He sighed. "I would have come by sooner, but—"

"I'm glad you're here." For some reason his apologies always made her feel uneasy. She wasn't used to it. Usually when people apologized to her it was code for: Sorry I got caught with someone else, or Sorry I took credit for something you did or Sorry you're so sensitive. Never, I'm sorry I hurt you.

Trey's words weren't rote and practiced, they were so genuine that they almost made her want to cry. He truly cared how she felt, he made her feel as if she mattered.

Alicia picked up the chocolate bar and feigned a casual tone. "Now how did the meeting with my sister go?"

"She's your sister? That's why you look alike."

Alicia bristled. Everyone in the family knew Pauline was far better looking than her. "We do not look alike."

"Except for the mouth and the nose and the—"

Alicia gritted her teeth in no mood for his teasing. "What did she say to you?"

Trey rubbed his hands together, avoiding her gaze and her question. "I said I would do only two maybe four more pictures, but I would only work with you."

Alicia set the chocolate bar down and leaned forward sensing he was hiding something. "What did she say?"

He drummed his fingers on his knee. "That it would be fine."

"No, before that."

"Before what?"

"Stop pretending to be dense. What did my sister say to you when she took you to her office?"

Trey stood. "Nothing worth repeating." He walked to the chair facing her desk and sat down as if the conversation was finished. "Now—"

"Did she say something about me?"

Trey looked at her. Implacable and unmoving. Clearly when he found something not worth repeating he meant it. He would never tell her what her sister had said although she could guess it wasn't anything flattering.

Alicia relented. They were semi-strangers again. He'd ignore her embarrassing shirt sniffing habit and the brief moment of intimacy had evaporated, it was best to focus on business. "How much—"

"I don't need the money."

"But—"

"However, I could use a favor."

"A favor?"

He nodded.

"What?"

"I could use a date for a wedding."

Alicia blinked. "*You've* been invited to another wedding?"

"Yes."

"Are you planning to ruin that one too?"

Trey's eyebrows rose in amazement. "How did you guess?"

She waited for him to start laughing or at least smile. But he blinked at her.

Her mouth fell open. "You can't be serious?"

He folded his arms. The action was casual but his quick, dark gaze was sharp. "You don't have to say yes if you don't want to."

Alicia swallowed unsure if it was his look, words or the room that caused her pulse to quicken, for her skin to slowly feel warm. "You can't do this."

"I have to."

She frowned. She couldn't figure him out. He didn't

seem cruel, but this felt wrong. "Are you being paid or something?"

He straightened her glass desktop name plate and shook his head.

She licked her lips, curiosity making her mouth dry.

"What are you planning to do?"

He kept his gaze lowered. "Doesn't matter if you're not coming with me," he said in a soft voice.

A voice so soft it was like the sensation of a breeze on a hot summer day—welcoming and inviting. She shouldn't say yes. She should turn him down. She should tell him that in lieu of payment she'd pay for his dry cleaning for several months. She should keep this strictly professional.

But she wouldn't.

"Fine. I'll do it."

He let his finger trail the length of her name plate. Although he still hadn't lifted his gaze, she felt as if he was studying her, as if she had his full attention. It was both thrilling and unnerving. "Good."

"What are you going to do?"

A brief sexy grin came and went. "Don't worry, you won't get hurt."

"That's not what—"

"Do you have a passport?"

Her eyes widened. "I'll need a passport?"

He nodded then his eyes met hers. "And a dress fit for the beach."

CHAPTER TWENTY-SIX

Belize.

The luxurious beauty of the oceanfront suite which gave her a view of the Caribbean Sea and the large private pool almost made Alicia forget why she was there.

"You can take the master bedroom," Trey said. He gestured to the living area. "I'll stay here."

Full kitchen, private balcony, pool and marble floors. This was nothing like what she was expecting. While her family had several holiday retreats, none were this extravagant.

Alicia chewed her lip caught between excitement and dread. "You cannot ruin a destination wedding."

"I'm only ruining it for one person."

"When is the wedding?"

"In two days. Relax, there's nothing you need to do until then."

"And then what do you want me to do?"

He sent her a quizzical look. "Be my date."

"And that's it?"

He nodded.

"Are you the best man?"

"No."

"But what—"

"It's best you don't know. At least not yet. Just enjoy yourself." He stripped off his shirt.

"What are you doing?" she asked trying not to sound like a prudish virgin.

"Getting ready for a swim." He took off his trousers. "I promised myself that was going to be the first thing I did."

She glanced at his red boxer briefs. "Those don't look like swimming trunks."

"Probably because they're not." He winked. "There's a reason I request a private pool."

"Are you going to swim naked?"

His dimple winked. "Do you want me to?"

Yes. "No. I mean...I wouldn't stop you."

Trey laughed and she felt her face burn. "That's good to know."

She turned away. She heard the sliding glass door open then the splash of water as he entered the pool. She didn't mean to watch him.

She told herself she was just enjoying the view.

She couldn't help if the view happened to include a man's beautiful brown body slicing its way through the pool's light blue waters, or the river of water sliding down his chest when he lifted himself out, droplets sparkling like diamonds in his black hair before he disappeared under the water again.

Alicia watched him so long she didn't notice the sun setting, she forgot that she hadn't unpacked, that she hadn't taken a shower, that she hadn't eaten anything. She watched him with a longing to join him, but also a desire to keep her distance. She would take this as a free vacation. She would enjoy the food and the accommodations—that was all.

He wouldn't tell her what he planned to do and she told herself she no longer cared. He'd gotten her out of a jam—her father told Edwin he was proud, Edwin in thanks sent her a fruit basket with wine and Pauline had stayed away—and if this was the only favor he asked of her who was she to say no?

Trey came out of the water for the final time and Alicia watched him towel himself dry. Oh to be a towel rubbing up and down his legs, thighs, his arms and chest. He wrapped the towel around his shoulders and walked through the balcony door.

She pretended to stare at the horizon.

"If you don't know how to swim," he said, "I'm willing to teach you."

"I know how to swim."

"I hope you'll join me next time." He grabbed his bag and headed to the bathroom.

Alicia sank into the couch. She had to survive a couple days. She hoped she could at least manage that.

CHAPTER TWENTY-SEVEN

"Trey!"

A white woman with luxurious brown hair and more chin than face embraced Trey in a bear hug before flashing a smile as wide as Niagara Falls.

Only hours prior, Alicia had tried to convince Trey that she didn't need to be his date for the rehearsal dinner, especially knowing what he eventually planned to do, but he ignored all her protestations so she found herself wearing a green off-the-shoulder midi dress and matching sandals, standing beside him in the hotel lobby while a woman stared at him as if he'd fallen from the sky.

"I really didn't think you'd come," the woman said. She looked to be in her mid-fifties and had a ease with Trey that surprised her. Alicia never would have imagined anyone wanting to hug Trey with such exuberance, let alone that he would let them. From the quick peck on the cheek to the grin on his face, she could tell this woman was special to him and that made Alicia instantly like her too.

Trey shrugged. "Here I am."

"I heard about you and Jacob. Is it true?"

"Hmm."

"I just can't believe that you'd—"

"What's done is done."

"Right. The past is gone. All that matters now is the present." She looped her arm through his, taking the hint that he didn't want to discuss the topic any further. "Come on."

He gently removed her grip on him and said, "This is Alicia."

The woman jumped, surprised. "You brought someone with you?"

Trey frowned. "The invitation said I could and I made sure to RSVP."

"Yes, of course we... I mean... I didn't think you'd actually do it."

"It's a pleasure to meet you," Alicia said.

"Likewise. I'm sorry, I'm just so surprised to see Trey and he never brings a date to a family function..." She made a dismissive wave of her hand and gave a nervous laugh. "Well... never mind, change is good."

"Hmm." He nodded. "Excuse us."

"When's the ruining part coming?" Alicia asked as they headed to the restaurant.

"Soon."

"Will I need short heels to run?"

"No, I'll carry you if need be."

"Wouldn't that be even more awkward?"

"Awkward?"

"Yes, running while carrying me in your arms."

"In my arms?" He shook his head. "No, I'd just throw you over my shoulder."

"Of course you would," she said in a sour tone. "Because you have the romantic streak of a gnat."

"Gnats are romantic?"

"Shut up."

"Trey?"

He stiffened at the sound of his name. When they turned they saw a beautiful, full figured young woman staring at him—her eyes wide, her face pale. She wore a red sundress, seeming to accent the highlights in her brunette hair. She took one step forward before she began to crumble to the floor.

Trey moved like the wind and grabbed her like a romantic hero Alicia had just claimed he wasn't and held her so tenderly she was strangely jealous. This woman was also someone dear to him.

He took her to one of the lobby couches, whispered something Alicia couldn't hear and the woman's dark lashes prettily fluttered before she opened her eyes. She touched a hand to her head. "I'm sorry."

"It's okay," Trey said in a voice so tender, Alicia could only stare at him. "Sorry I surprised you."

"I never thought you'd come."

"I said I would."

"I thought you were being polite."

"No."

"You'll really do this?"

"Yes."

The woman bit her lip, tears glistened in her brown eyes. "I'm so scared. I don't know if I can go through with it."

"You can. I'll be there with you. Does anyone else know?"

"I hinted at it to Mom, but I wasn't sure you'd agree."

"We can do this." He squeezed her hand before he helped her to her feet. "But only if you still want me to." He paused. "How was the wedding rehearsal?"

She lowered her gaze, looking miserable.

"Okay, then it's settled. I'll see you at the rehearsal dinner."

"Right."

He playfully tweaked her chin. "No more tears. Right, Alicia?"

"Uh, right," Alicia said surprised he'd still remembered she was there.

The woman's eyes widened. "You brought a date?"

Trey shoved his hands in his pockets and rocked on his heels, pleased. "She's the reason I'm here."

Before Alicia could ask him what he meant by that statement the woman enveloped her in a hug and said, "Thank you."

"But I didn't—"

"I'd better go," she said. "I'm so glad you're both here." She hurried away.

"Who was that?"

"Lavinia. The bride."

Alicia folded her arms. "Now can you tell me what you plan to do?"

"I plan to give her away at the ceremony."

"Is that all? That sounds sweet."

"I don't think her father will think so."

"Her father's here?"

"Yes."

"And she doesn't want—"

"No."

"Can I ask why?"

Trey's tone turned hard. "When you meet him I think you'll come to your own conclusions."

CHAPTER TWENTY-EIGHT

ttractive, intelligent, debonair. Those were the three descriptors that came to mind as Alicia's observed Lavinia's father at the restaurant. He had a sprinkling of silver in his black hair, dark brows and long lashes that Lavinia certainly had inherited. He remained cordial to the wait staff, had offered her a kind smile when introduced and kept the conversation flowing with his vast knowledge of economics, technology and gardening. Alicia couldn't see why Lavinia didn't want him to walk her down the aisle. Unless. She grabbed Trey's sleeve and whispered into his ear. "Did he molest her as a child?"

"No."

"Beat her?"

"No."

"Then why?"

"Just wait."

Alicia scowled at her shrimp and conch cervich. She

picked up a fried corn tortilla, reveling in the loud crunch when she bit into it. She was getting tired of waiting. Everything was a puzzle with him. She didn't see things the way he did. She still couldn't understand why he'd humiliate himself and break up a friendship in order to save his friend so she doubted she'd see anything here either. The man was a mystery.

"Are you sure you should be eating that?" a deep voice said.

Alicia bit down hard on another tortilla. What was it with people? If you weren't a size zero people felt they had the right to tell you what to eat—her mother loved to, frequently at that. Sure it was fried, pure carbs but she wanted to enjoy herself, she didn't need anyone being the food police.

Alicia opened her mouth to tell Trey to mind his own business but when she looked at Trey the tortilla became lodged in her throat. His gaze had turned to steel and his jaw clenched—she felt as if the air in the room had lowered ten degrees, triggered by the controlled icy anger that radiated from him. That's when she realized Trey hadn't spoken. Lavinia's father had and he hadn't been talking to her.

"The wedding is tomorrow," he continued, "it would be a shame if you couldn't fit into your dress."

His words were so smoothly spoken they didn't sound like an insult although they certainly felt like one.

Alicia swallowed hard.

Lavinia took another bite of her fried plantain and said nothing.

Alicia silently cheered her. Best to say nothing, sometimes parents said silly things when they cared.

But Alicia soon learned that Lavinia's father only cared about one thing—humiliating his daughter. He jokingly made references at his surprise that anyone would want her, ignoring every effort by his wife to stop him. Nervous laughter skittered around the table in an attempt to lessen the sting of his words. He dramatically thanked Lavinia's fiancé for taking her off his hands. Berated her job, her looks, her friends.

Alicia had a sinking feeling as she realized why Lavinia didn't want this man to be part of her wedding day. She knew and understood and silently applauded her courage.

"There's been a change of plans," Lavinia said. "Last minute."

Her father laughed and turned to the groom. "Don't tell me you've already changed your mind."

"You're not walking me down the aisle. Trey is."

His laughter faded. "What?"

"I'm tired of pretending that you don't hurt me. That it doesn't hurt that you're embarrassed and ashamed of me. You don't have to be anymore. There will be no pictures of us together at my wedding. You can stay and watch or you can leave, but this relationship ends today."

"But I—"

"You have no rights to claim. I made sure to pay for this wedding myself, with some help." She cast a shy, grateful glance at Trey before returning her gaze to her father. "It's my day. Not yours. I made sure that you didn't have to worry about how much extra cloth my dress would cost because of my size: the reference to the size of the church aisles, the seats, my ring. I'm sick of this, Dad. I'm sick of it all. This is a day I want to celebrate with people who truly love me.

"I know you don't. Not as I am and that's a shame because I'm a pretty amazing woman. You just can't see that. Your loss. So if you decide to show up tomorrow fine, if you don't, that's fine too. Because I—" She gulped ominously and turned green. She took a deep breath and tried again. "Because I—" She covered her mouth.

Her father sneered in disgust. "You're going to embarrass me by throwing up? Is that your grand plan?"

Lavinia surged to her feet, tears swimming in her eyes, she opened her mouth and took a step towards him. Alicia gripped her fork half expecting Lavinia to vomit on him, but her face turned pale and she covered her mouth before she raced towards the ladies' room.

When Lavinia's mother stood, a thin, frightened looking woman with big eyes, her husband grabbed her arm and said, "Sit down. If anyone's going to run after her, let it be him." He pointed to the groom. "Go and hold her hair back if you want to. See what you're really getting."

The groom hesitated. "I would but—"

Alicia understood his unease. As much as he'd want to go after Lavinia it would be awkward to enter the ladies' room. Fear shimmered over the table. No one spoke. No one seemed bold enough to move, this man held reign.

Alicia heard Trey sigh, heard the soft scrape of his chair as he pushed it back. He would go after her, but

Alicia knew that could spell disaster. A big black man entering the ladies' room with a face that looked like thunder wouldn't end well. She would have to take action instead. Fortunately, Lavinia's father didn't scare her at all. Her brother Edwin could eat him for breakfast. Her father could eat him as an appetizer.

Alicia lightly touched Trey's arm before she stood. "I'll go see if she's alright."

"I told her she shouldn't have eaten that," she heard Lavinia's father say, but this time only the cold edge of silence followed his words.

CHAPTER TWENTY-NINE

The rush of water being sucked down a toilet bowl assaulted her ears the moment Alicia entered the ladies' room. Thankfully only one stall seemed to be occupied. Alicia crinkled her nose as the faint stench of Lavinia's purged dinner lingered in the air. She heard a faint groan.

"Lavinia? It's me, Alicia."

"I feel like such a fool," she said in a small voice.

"I thought what you did was very brave."

"Is everyone laughing?"

"No."

"I can't stop shaking."

"You were great."

"I was scared."

"You don't have to be scared anymore. You took control. You were fierce."

"Until I got sick."

"He made us all sick."

Lavinia giggle. "No one would ever admit that."

"You made your point."

She sighed then opened the stall door. "You can go, I'm okay now." She washed her hands.

"Um...not an option. Either I leave here with you or Trey's coming to get you. If I didn't know you were getting married, I'd be jealous of your relationship."

Lavinia laughed. She laughed so hard she had to hold her sides. "Trey and me?" She gasped before she laughed harder. Alicia didn't understand why Lavinia found the thought so funny, but she preferred it to seeing her sad.

Lavinia wiped her eyes. "Thank you so much for that." She turned to the mirror and patted her face. "I'm so glad you convinced Trey to come."

Alicia began to shake her head then decided now was not the time to reveal Trey's lie.

"He wanted to be here, he's just using me as an excuse."

"No, that's not Trey at all." Lavinia spun to her and grabbed her hands. "I know my idea was silly and crazy and I should have been strong enough to do it on my own, but just knowing that Trey was there, will be with me at my wedding, gave me the courage I needed to finally stand up to my dad."

"You don't have to explain to me."

"Yes, I do. Trey's always there for others, but he doesn't let people be there for him. The fact that you're here means you're special."

Alicia smiled and accepted the nervous bride's delusions. Special? Her? To Trey of all people? She would laugh if Lavinia didn't look so earnest. "We'd better get back or people will really start worrying."

Fear entered Lavinia's gaze. "Do you think he's still out there?"

Alicia didn't misunderstand her, as powerful as her speech had been, Lavinia's father still had a hold over her. "Yes. But the moment you return to the table you will have won. Don't let him bully you anymore or be ashamed. Your words mattered. He'll expect me to return to the table and tell everyone that you went back to your room to rest. But instead you'll face him. You don't even have to say a word."

Lavinia took a deep breath. "Okay."

"I'm right behind you."

But when they returned to the table Lavinia's father was gone. Lavinia looked relieved as did everyone around her.

Alicia took a seat beside Trey and whispered, "What happened?"

He lifted her hand and kissed the back of it. "Thanks."

The touch of his lips made her skin tingle and for a moment she forgot she'd been in a stinky restroom with a sniffling stranger. She thought of Lavinia's words and gratitude. "Why did you lie about me? I didn't convince you of anything."

"Yes, you did."

"How?"

Trey shrugged then stood. "We should go."

"You just like avoiding my questions."

"No, I really need to sleep if I'm going to be there for Lavinia on her big day."

"You DIDN'T NEED to bring me here," Alicia said as she and Trey rode up the elevator. "You could have done the hero act on your own."

"I'm no hero."

"Giving her the courage to stand up to her father is pretty heroic to me, but you're missing my point. You didn't need a date. You could have come alone."

"I didn't want to."

"Oh, because you didn't have Jacob you needed a new trusty sidekick?"

Trey fell silent and she wondered if she'd said the wrong thing again. Perhaps she shouldn't have mentioned Jacob.

"No," Trey said after a long pause. "I wanted a pretty woman by my side."

"What?"

"Nobody expects me to come with a date. Especially not someone like you. I wanted to surprise them. I may be loyal and dependable but I'm more than people think."

Alicia sniffed. "I think that's pretty clear."

Trey shook his head. "No, it's not."

"Um...after five minutes with you it's easy to see that you might act like a robot but you aren't one." She smiled up at him. "The part about the robot is a joke, you're supposed to laugh."

The elevator doors opened and he stepped out, his jaw twitched. "I wish you wouldn't say things like that."

Alicia hurried after him wondering why he'd started walking so fast. "Why not?"

He stopped at their suite door and unlocked it. "Just because," he said, stepping inside. He turned on the lights. But while it illuminated the suite Alicia still felt hopelessly in the dark about him.

Alicia closed the door behind her and threw up her hands. "What have I done wrong now? I always seem to say the wrong thing to you."

Trey walked over to the balcony window, becoming a shadow that seemed to blend in with the ink black sky beyond, and said in a quiet voice, "That's not true."

Alicia took a cautious step forward. "Then why are you angry at me?"

His voice remained soft. "I'm not angry."

She licked her lip, hesitant. "Why shouldn't I have said what I did?"

He rubbed the back of his neck. "Because you really make me want to do something I shouldn't."

"Like what?"

He turned to her, his gaze heated. "Kiss you."

CHAPTER THIRTY

*A*licia would never remember who moved first—whether Trey closed the distance and pulled her into his arms, or whether she'd run towards him and cupped his face in her hands.

But what she would never forget was the sweet taste of his mouth, the feel of his lips on hers. That intoxicating scent of his encompassing her as his solid arms drew her body closer.

He kissed like a predator—there was an almost savage mastery to him. She felt the same sensation of drowning, of being pulled under to a realm he controlled and dominated.

She surrendered. She couldn't breathe. Her heart raced. It was too much. It was just enough. It was everything she'd ever feared. It was everything she'd ever wanted: A sanctuary and retreat and also—he pulled out something within her. Something dormant and wild. Something dangerous.

She pushed him away.

Trey swallowed hard, stared at her. Only the sound of their breathing filled the room, and the distant laughter of people passing in the hallway. He didn't move. She saw caution in his gaze.

"Tell me one thing," he said. In the quiet of the room his voice sounded deeper.

"What?"

"Are you scared of me now?"

Alicia gripped her hands. She could lie and tell him yes. She could lock herself away in her room and wait until tomorrow. Wait until she could get better control of herself.

He lowered his gaze, taking her silence as concession. "I can get another room," he said in a mild tone as if taking extra care not to frighten her further. "If you want to take an early flight back—"

She gasped in dismay but no words came out.

He lifted his gaze, his eyes searching her face. "You don't want me to go?"

She shook her head.

"Are you sure?"

She nodded.

"Then please don't look at me like that."

The note of pain in his plea unlocked her voice. "I'm not afraid of you, I'm afraid of me."

She took a tentative step towards him, anxiety knotting her stomach. "I have failed at everything. Every business I've tried, every relationship and I don't want..." She took a deep breath. "You're a strange man but I don't care. Does that make any sense? You ruined your best friend's wedding, shouldn't that mean something to me? But it doesn't. You're successful and good looking and don't even realize how appealing you are. You confuse me and—and I like it. I like how you challenge me. I like how you never make me feel dumb.

"I promised myself I would change. I'm supposed to be different now. More responsible. A better person—"

"I think you're great just the way you are."

"You would say that." Alicia rested her hand on his chest, feeling the heat of his body underneath his shirt. "But I have to change."

"No, you don't."

"I want to," she said, gripping the front of his shirt in her fist, a fissure of desperation coursing through her. She glanced towards the window—the darkness peered back at her. If they turned off the lights they could probably see the stars, spot the moonlight on the still waters of the pool and, farther, see the glimmer of the ocean. She loosened her grip on his shirt, feeling a sense of calm and rested her head against his shoulder. "This is just a dream. It won't last."

Trey drew back and lifted her chin, forcing her to face him. "Then let's share this dream together." He kissed her once more slowly, seductively.

"I don't want to ruin this," she breathed against his lips, no longer feeling desperate or calm, only the insistent hunger of desire.

"You won't."

"You don't know that."

"If anything goes wrong, it'll be me." When she

stared at him surprised Trey grinned. "You think you're the only one with failed relationships in that past?"

She lifted an eyebrow in challenge. "Give me one of your worst."

"Dumped by Post-It note."

"No."

He nodded.

"Your ex-girlfriend wrote 'Let's break up?' on a Post-It?"

Trey shook his head. "No, she wrote two letters."

Alicia thought for a moment about the two letters someone could use then gasped. "Noooo."

"Yes. FU. She left it on my fridge and on my computer."

"You were dumped by two Post-Its?"

He nodded. "One was written in black. The other in red."

"Why? Why would she do that?"

He bit his lip, looked embarrassed. "I still don't know."

"You don't know?"

"I came up with about fifteen different reasons, but could never narrow it down to one." He sighed. "I even asked her and she told me that I should know and that's why she never wanted to see me again. That was years ago and I never figured it out. I guess that makes me a pretty bad boyfriend."

Alicia folded her arms. "How about this as a counter story? I fell for a guy who held a surprise party for me and when the cake arrived..." She let her words trail off so he could fill in the blank.

"It was a pie."

"No."

"There was no cake inside."

"No."

"It was a cake for a christening."

Her hands fell to her hips. "No! You really *are* bad at guessing. The cake had another woman's name on it."

Trey looked at her then threw his head back and laughed.

"I was devastated."

"What did you do?"

"Pretended it was my middle name."

"And then you broke up with him."

Alicia hesitated. "I should have, but then he told me he'd been distracted because he was worried about his sick grandmother—"

Trey laughed again this time slapping his thigh.

"And I later learned that his grandmother was never sick...it's not that funny."

Trey waved at her, trying to control his laughter. "No, it's not you. I think I finally figured it out. The Post-It notes."

"What was it?"

"I missed her recital because my grandmother was sick. She really *was* sick, I wasn't lying. I knew the recital was important to her so I sent Jacob there instead." He rubbed his chin, pensive. "I never thought that might have been a reason."

"You trusted Jacob with your girlfriend?"

"I'd trust Jacob with my life."

"And yet you betrayed him."

Trey blinked, all amusement gone from his eyes. "I'll make no apologies for what I've done or who I am. I did what I needed to do for a friend and that's the end of it. Can you accept that?"

Alicia chewed her lip, trying to see Trey as he was. He wasn't bathed under a kaleidoscope of colors or touched by the sun this time, or cloaked in shadow, he stood in front of her cast in the soft lamplight of the room, illuminating the temptation he was—the temptation he had always been—to her.

She now knew what he tasted like, felt like and she wanted more. She wanted more of his laughter, more of his smiles, more of him.

She could manage both worlds. Succumbing to this desire didn't mean she had to give up the life she'd struggled to build over these past several months. Was it wrong to have a little pleasure when her days were set and monitored? Was it wrong to dance with the side of herself that liked a little chaos, a little reckless fun?

Trey took a step back. "We don't have to go any further than this."

"I know." She took a step towards him. "I'm going to grab you now," she said then did, surprising them both with the fierceness of her kiss.

CHAPTER THIRTY-ONE

*T*rey groaned low in his throat and that emboldened her more. Potent pleasure followed as Alicia deepened their kiss. Swimming with a shark would be fun. She had no trouble accepting him, what mattered was would he accept her?

Her dress fell away, along with his shirt. "You don't have to sleep on the couch tonight," she whispered before she took his hand and led him to the main bedroom and turned on the light.

She turned to him when she felt him shudder. "What's wrong?"

His gaze swept over the room in horror. "Nothing."

She looked at the clothes scattered on the bed. "Oh, I can clean it up." She used her foot and lifted her suitcase lid then bent to scoop up the clothes.

"Wait."

She turned to him in question.

"You're not going to just dump them are you?"

"They're in the way." She winked at him. "Unless doing it on a pile of clothes is your thing."

Trey quickly gathered the clothes. "Just give me a minute."

Alicia watched in shock as he began to fold them. "You can't be serious."

"This won't take long."

"Wait...Did you feel that breeze? That was a perfect moment passing us by."

"No it didn't."

Alicia raised her hand then slowly lowered it. "The feeling is falling away. Soon it will disappear."

Trey laid a folded T-shirt on top of a skirt. "Not for me. I'm a patient man."

Alicia sighed, rolled her eyes and mumbled, "But I'm not a patient woman."

"Tonight you will be." Trey placed the folded clothes in the suitcase, paired two wayward socks then held out his arms. "I'm all yours."

"I've changed my mind."

He pulled her down onto the bed. "And I can't change it back?"

She made a face and shook her head. "The mood has passed."

His lips trailed a slow, sensuous path down her neck. "That's too bad," he whispered his breath warm against her skin. He unhooked her bra. "I was looking forward to this."

"You'll have to wait for another time."

His mouth covered one nipple, she felt the warm tip of his tongue. "How long will I have to wait?"

"A long time," she sighed, sinking slowly into the gentle waves of pleasure as his tongue slid a wet, warm path down her stomach.

"Tomorrow maybe?"

She felt the rough texture of his cheek as he placed a kiss inside her thigh.

She closed her eyes. "Perhaps."

He rolled down her panties. "Before or after the wedding?"

"After."

Trey slid his fingers inside her then moved them with masterful ease. "You'll make me wait all day?"

Her body arched, she bit back a moan, she swallowed, feeling her body ready to come. "I thought you were a patient man."

"I am," he said and she heard the satisfaction in his voice and opened her eyes. She faced the flashing grin of a shark and wasn't afraid. Her body didn't fear him and neither did her heart.

"Are you using your fingers because you forgot protection?"

He laughed. "No."

"Then what are you waiting for?"

"I'm waiting for you to come."

"I'm almost there, I'd like you to be there with me."

Trey jumped out of the bed. "I won't be a minute."

Alicia slid under the covers. "The clock starts now."

He managed to be back in seconds, his dark brown eyes heated with passion. He climbed into the bed then shuddered in disgust before he fell on his back. He closed his eyes and pinched the bridge of his nose as if in pain.

Alicia looked at him alarmed. "What's the matter?"

"You eat in bed, don't you?"

"Yeah, why?"

His arm fell to the bed, his eyes remained closed. "Because I feel cookie crumbs."

"Oh, let me see," Alicia said and he let her roll him onto his side. She licked a crumb off his back. "Um...Yes. I knew you'd be delicious but this is even better." She licked another crumb.

"You're planning to eat off me?" Trey said in disbelief.

"I'd hate to see good food go to waste."

He groaned. "My woman, the Hoover vacuum."

She pushed him onto his stomach and sucked up another crumb. "Don't you like this?"

"No."

Her tongue trailed a slow path down his spine. "Not even this?"

"No."

"Really? Not even a little?"

"Not even infinitesimal."

"You're right. It'd be better with some whipped cream." He sent her a look. "I'm only half joking."

"Can I get up now?"

"This isn't fun for you at all?"

He took a deep breath. "This is torture. Please, can I get up now?"

"Yes." She sat up when he began to walk away. "Where are you going?"

"To take a quick shower—"

"Why would you need to take a shower?"

He glared at her, annoyance etched on his face. "Because I'm covered in cookie crumbs."

"That's an exaggeration."

"I have cookie crumbs not only all over my back but on my chest too. They feel like sticky, needles and—" He held up his hand when she opened her mouth. "And if you suggest licking me clean—"

"Actually, I wasn't going to suggest that," she said, brushing the remainder of the crumbs off the bed. "I was wondering if you wanted me to join you."

Trey held his breath. "In the shower?"

Alicia shook the sheet. "Where else?"

He narrowed his eyes. "Promise to be thorough?"

She met his wary gaze and grinned. "When I'm done with you, you'll shine."

Bathing him wasn't as much fun as eating off him, although the view was nice. She liked the shape of his thighs and bottom, the corded muscles in his back, but she didn't get a chance to enjoy the sight in the steam filled room because Trey instructed her every movement. "And don't forget my shoulders."

"I've already done your shoulders twice."

"Are you sure you got everything?" he asked as she lathered his back.

"If I scrub anymore I'll remove your tattoo. Trust me, you're clean."

He held out his hand. "Want me to—"

"No, if we stay in this shower any longer we'll both look like raisins."

"I like raisins."

She shot him a withering glance. "Shut up."

He grinned. "Your turn next time." He turned the shower off. "Thanks."

"Feeling better now?"

He toweled himself dry and released a satisfied sigh. "Much."

She wrapped a towel around herself and yanked off her shower cap. "The mood is definitely gone now."

"Not for me."

She grabbed a bottle of lotion and left the bathroom. "It is for me." She sat on the edge of the bed.

Trey took the bottle from her and squirted some into his palm. "Why?" he asked, smoothing the lotion down her arm before kneeling and applying some to her leg.

Alicia bit her lip, knowing she should pull away. She knew what he was doing but she wanted to stay annoyed with him. She didn't want to enjoy the way his hands made sure, intimate contact with her flesh as if they belonged there. She didn't want to respond to the heat of his palm as it explored the curve of her leg.

"You insulted me."

His hand paused midway up her thigh. He kept his gaze lowered, but his tone became distant. A renewed tension sizzled in the air. "How?"

She lifted his chin. "Look at me."

His gaze shifted to the side, his tone hardened. "Just tell me what I did."

"I will when you look at me."

He sighed. "Alicia."

"Please."

He lifted his gaze and he looked so uncertain that she

almost kissed him to take him out of his misery, but realized how much she enjoyed teasing him.

She cupped his face. "How can I be comfortable with a man who prefers a sponge to my tongue?"

He blinked. "That's why you think I insulted you?"

"Why else? I touch you with my tongue and you have to shower for nearly an hour."

Trey surged to his feet. "That's not it." He sat down beside her. "It's not you. It was the crumbs." He shuddered in remembrance. "I couldn't take the crumbs." He gathered her in his arms then fell back on the bed. "But I love your tongue." He captured her mouth with his. "I adore it." He tugged on her towel and watched it fall away. "I adore everything about you."

"Even my mess?"

He paused. "Maybe we should—"

"Never mind." Alicia wrapped her legs around him. "You leave this bed and you lose your chance."

He licked his lips. "Mind if we don't get under the sheets?"

Alicia felt her patience thinning. Perhaps they weren't a good match. Perhaps he was too much of a mystery for her. He was gorgeous to look at but perhaps too staid for her. "Right now I'm getting cold."

"Let me take care of that," he said then covered her body with his. She thought she knew what his body felt like, she'd seen and touched every inch of it in the shower, but when the length of his form covered hers she thought she'd burst into flames.

His body was more than muscle and flesh it was divine ecstasy. This time when he kissed her she felt like she was being consumed by a river of molten lava, her body melting beneath. There was no beginning or end, their bodies entwined, their breathing in syncopation.

She'd underestimated him. *I'm more than what people think.* That's what he'd told her and she'd made that mistake too, but now in his arms with him inside her, her body no longer felt like her own, her body felt the tiny urgent whisper of his silent plea for understanding and acceptance, an unchecked, fierce hunger and desire that rivaled her own.

She felt renewed, reborn, completely herself. There was no need for apology. He desired her-without question—so with her body she assured him, claimed him, wrapped him in passion in a way he could understand.

To Trey, Alicia was a sun-kissed ocean—vast and beautiful. He rode the waves of her curves, sunk deep into the satin softness of her skin, and explored her tight wet crevices. He inhaled the sweet scent of her papaya scented shampoo, closing his eyes and fighting his need for more. For a moment he danced with the illusion of being in eternity. Time fell away, he floated on the limitless plane of ecstasy. Every part of her was a marvel to him: Her kindness, her strength, her acceptance of him. He took special pleasure when he felt her body shiver in climax, the gasp of delight.

Too soon it was over.

Too soon he was leaving the sacred confines of her body.

For him it could never have been long enough—hours would have felt like minutes. Time was an enemy, there was never enough for him because he was not only a patient man, he was a man who could focus—even obsess a little—on the smallest details. Like the dimples on her thighs, the size of her coffee colored areolas, the shape of her nipples. He'd love to memorize their shape with his hand then his tongue then feel them pressed against his chest...

Trey softly swore, his body responding to his wayward thoughts, before he drew away. He heard her sigh of satisfaction before she drifted off to sleep. He lightly touched her cheek. He didn't want to leave.

He gripped his hand into a fist fighting the urge to gather her close, but he didn't want to wake her. Oh, but how he would like to fall asleep holding her, but it was too soon to ask for that.

She might not be ready. He didn't want to exhaust her—he had a tendency to do that. He could be too intense, his feelings too strong.

Trey slid out of bed, gently pulling the sheet over her to cover her up and tucking her in so she'd stay warm. It was too soon to let her know how dear she was to him.

Space. He had to remember to give her plenty of space. He wouldn't overwhelm her.

He wouldn't ruin this.

CHAPTER THIRTY-TWO

She didn't expect to wake up alone.

Alicia imagined waking up to Trey sleeping beside her, his broad back facing her and she'd lightly bite his shoulder and wake him.

Instead, the space beside her was empty and she'd been rolled up in the sheets like a burrito. How had she managed that? Her cheeks burned in embarrassment. Had she hogged the covers so much she'd forced him to leave?

She heard a soft knock on the door as she tried to untangle herself. Damn. How had she made the sheets so tight? "Come in."

Trey entered and for a moment she wondered if she'd dreamed last night. He didn't look at her with any lingering recognition of what had happened between them. His hard, assessing gaze had returned and it didn't help that he was fully dressed in his dark tux.

Alicia struggled harder. "Are we late? You should have woken me? I—"

"We're not late," he said, tugging the sheet and freeing her. "I have to get there early." He sat down. "I ordered breakfast. You don't have to be there for another hour and a half—"

She barely listened not understanding why Trey was being so formal. She wouldn't have minded getting up early with him, she wouldn't have minded waiting for the guests to arrive.

"Do I need to repeat that?" he said.

She blinked. "What?"

"You're frowning. What's wrong?"

I wish you'd woken me sooner, I would have liked to have spent more time with you. "Nothing. You should go."

He hesitated then kissed the tips of his fingers before placing them against her cheek. "See you later." He headed to the door.

His tender action gave her the boldness she needed. She released a loud, dramatic sigh.

He spun to her. "What's wrong?"

She lay on her side, resting her chin in her hand. "I thought you were planning to return the favor this morning." She slipped her leg out from under the sheets, giving him a full view.

His gaze slowly swept over her thigh as warm as a caress. He swallowed. "Favor?" he said in a deep voice.

"In the shower."

Temptation flared, darkening his eyes. Alicia had to bite her lip to keep from smiling. She now understood his formality, the Trey from last night was still there, but he was keeping him under tight control. "Later."

She sat up, letting the sheet completely fall away. "How about just a sponge bath?"

"No." He backed into the wall with a bang, hitting his head.

"Are you all right?"

"I'm fine." He held out his hand when she crawled towards him like a cat on the sheets. "Stay right there," he said. "You will not make me late for this wedding."

She giggled at his discomfort. "How could I ever do that?"

He inched his way to the door, his eyes watching her as if she were a cobra ready to strike. "I'm leaving now."

She wrapped the sheet around herself. "I won't stop you." She smiled thinking of the bright coral colored dress she planned to wear. He wouldn't be able to miss her. "See you at the wedding."

To ALICIA's relief their actually *was* a wedding on that cloudless day on the beach, even though the day reminded her of all the reasons she hated the beach. Like the sand, which was just dirt's prettier sister, that had made its way into her sandals. The smell of the ocean invaded her nostrils while the sun's rays threatened to scorch her like a hot comb.

The wind blew making her skin feel sticky rather than soothed, but Alicia flashed a genuine smile when she heard the wedding march and saw Lavinia's beaming face. Murmurs of pride and delight followed the bride down the aisle as she clasped the arm of the serious faced man beside her.

Trey looked more like a bodyguard than a replacement for the bride's father; Alicia didn't know how he managed not to melt in the dark tux he wore, the severe cut of which only added an aura of danger. Why hadn't he chosen a lighter color and looser cut?

Behind her, Alicia overheard a worried guest whisper, "Who is that man?" before another guest shushed her.

Alicia wished she had a chance to tell the woman how much Lavinia depended on Trey, that he wasn't as scary as he appeared, but the pastor began to speak.

This time Trey remained silent; this time the only tears that fell were tears of joy as Lavinia joined her life with the man she loved. Her father did not witness that moment and no one seemed to miss him.

The moment the ceremony ended, Alicia lost sight of Trey as she was whisked away with the crowd and led to the main hall for the buffet-style reception. She scanned through the sea of people, who seemed to expand every second as they moved among the circular tables dressed in white accented with tropical flowers.

It didn't get any easier to find him when a tiny crowd of six young ladies, ranging in age from early teens to mid-twenties, circled her and peppered her with questions. She couldn't understand why she'd garnered such interest.

"I can't believe you're here with Trey."

"Trey always brings Jacob. We love Jacob."

"Did you approach him or did he approach you?"

"How long have you been together?"

"How did you convince him to come here?"

"How did you meet?"

Alicia didn't know how to answer their questions and really didn't want to—especially that last one, but it seemed the safest. "At an event we both attended."

"You're a geologist too?" one lady asked in surprise. "Trey rarely attends anything that doesn't have to do with rocks."

"Uh...no," Alicia said, "it was a conservation event." That sounded safe enough.

They nodded.

"Sorry for us crowding you like this," the eldest of the ladies said, "but he never brings anyone with him. This is a first and we want to milk it as much as possible."

"We would ask him."

"But you know Trey."

The six women mimed zipping their lips then made their features perfectly blank. Alicia smiled in under-standing. "Right."

"So, tell us what you can."

Alicia's gaze swept over the eager, interested faces. She wasn't quite sure what they expected from her. It hadn't taken her long to notice that beside two other guests and the Belizean wait staff, she and Trey were the only brown skinned people. That should have made it easier for her to find him, but it hadn't. She also wondered if that had garnered their interest, but she had a sense it was something else.

"I really don't know him very well to be honest,"

Alicia said. "I'm as shocked as you are that he brought me."

"Don't be. We've known him all our lives and he's still a mystery."

"All your life—" Before she could ask more they were called away to take pictures. Trey was liked, that was clear, but there was something more that set him apart.

She tried to renew her search for him, but got caught by a couple who wanted to share about their excursions and then another woman who'd hoped to get lucky that night, but still no Trey.

She began to panic. Where was he? Why wasn't he here with her? He was a tall, black man in a tux who looked like a professional killer. He should stick out. He should be easy to find.

Why couldn't she find him?

What if he wasn't there? What if he never made it to the reception? What if he'd collapsed on the beach from heatstroke?

"If you're looking for the restrooms," a deep voice whispered in her ear. "I can show you where they are."

licia gasped and spun around, tears of relief springing into her eyes. Trey! "I don't need the restrooms, you idiot."

"But you were looking around worried—"

"I'm going to grab you," she said before she hugged him. He was safe. He was here.

Trey wrapped his arms around her, held her tight. "What's wrong?"

"I thought you were hurt."

He started to laugh.

"It's not funny."

"Why would I be hurt?"

"You took a risk coming here and upsetting Lavinia's father. What if he ambushed you, knocked you out—?"

"And tossed my body in the ocean weighted down by cement blocks?" Trey finished.

Alicia drew away and wiped her eyes. "Go ahead and laugh at me."

His smile faded, his voice softened. "No, I'm not laughing at you. I'm sorry." He cupped her face. "You were really worried about me?"

She sniffed. "Yes, I couldn't figure out where you were."

He nodded to a corner. "I was over there."

"Why?"

"Because I wanted you to have a good time."

"How could I have a good time without you?"

He opened his mouth then closed it. He looked confused and that frustrated her more. "What don't you understand?"

He shoved his hands in his pockets and looked down at the ground like a kid in trouble. "Everything." He glanced up at her. "You looked happy chatting with everyone. I didn't want to spoil it for you."

"How could you spoil it?"

"People act different when I'm around. I know I make them uncomfortable." He rubbed the back of his neck. "I'm okay with individuals but I'm terrible with crowds."

"You're pretty terrible with individuals too."

He sighed. "I know." He placed a quick kiss on her cheek. "I'm really sorry." He pressed another kiss on her neck and whispered, "You look stunning by the way."

A rush of pleasure filled her, and her skin tingled from the feel of his warm breath against her skin, but she managed to keep her tone nonchalant. "You owe me two showers now."

He took her hand. "We can start now."

She pulled her hand free. "No. You're staying here

with me a little while longer. I haven't eaten yet and I'm going to punish you for abandoning me."

"I didn't abandon you. I was a few feet away the entire time."

"Blending into the shadows so I couldn't see you. How did you do that?"

"It's not hard. I stand still long enough and people forget I'm there."

"Well now you're with me so you're going to have to put in a little more effort."

He groaned.

"You can try to smile. You look so serious, that's why people don't feel comfortable around you."

Trey shook his head. "No, that doesn't work. I've tried it. Jacob says I look constipated."

"Oh. Can I see?"

A hard expression passed over his face as he widened his lips into a grin.

Alicia waved her hand. "He's right. Don't do that."

His smile fell.

"You can do better than that. I like the way you smile at me."

"I smile at you?"

The fact that he didn't know wasn't good. "Never mind."

"Let's get you something to eat," he said. "I recommend the chicken."

She stared at him stunned. "You've already eaten?"

He shrugged.

"You didn't think I'd want to eat with you?"

His gaze drifted to the far wall. "I thought you were having fun."

Alicia touched her forehead. "I don't believe this. Did last night even happen?" She pressed a finger over his mouth. "That's a rhetorical question." She gripped his shoulders tampering down her annoyance. "How can you be so..." She took a deep breath.

He stared at the ground and mumbled something.

"What?"

"I wanted to give you space," he said just above a whisper.

Her hands fell to her sides. "Why would I need space?"

He flexed his hand before his fingers began tapping a beat against his leg. "Because it's important."

He looked agitated, nervous but she couldn't understand why. His words made no sense to her, but their meaning mattered a lot to him. Why couldn't she fully understand him? She narrowed her eyes as a thought occurred to her.

"Are you—" She stopped wondering the best way to approach it. "Have you been tested for...uh...behavioral differences?"

A quick smile came then went. "You think I'm autistic?"

She nodded.

"I'm not. I'm just weird. That's the diagnosis."

She laughed, relieved he could joke about it.

But he didn't join her. "No, really. I'm serious. That was the official diagnosis. I was tested and they thought I might be on the spectrum but I didn't tick off the right boxes and that was what one of the doctors said, 'He's just weird.' So that's been my diagnosis since nine."

"Well that's irresponsible."

He shrugged.

"Fortunately, I like weird. Actually, I'd prefer to think of you as unique. One of a kind. No test can measure you." She took his hand. "Let's dance."

"I thought you were hungry."

"I'm not anymore. I want to dance."

"I don't dance," he said but let her lead him to the dance floor.

She turned to him and placed his hands on her waist. "But you can swim. It's about the same."

He shook his head. "No, it's not."

"Right now the music is slow. You can do this. Just sway side to side. Like a current."

"A current doesn't sway."

"A wave then. A wave comes and then goes. Right and left."

The first two tries Trey painfully stepped on Alicia's toes then began to get the rhythm of the music and soon she forgot she was the teacher as he took the lead. His body moved in the same mesmerizing way it had in the water the other day. Alicia found herself not only looking at him but being transfixed.

"You sneaky bastard," she said. "You do know how to dance."

The dimple came and went. "I never said I couldn't dance. I only said I didn't."

"Why not when you do it so well?"

He bit his lip. "Maybe I'll tell you one day."

"I think I can already guess. You don't want to make the other men look bad."

He threw his head back and laughed. It was a beautiful sound and turned heads. She caught sight of the bride, who was beaming and mouthed 'thank you' and Alicia nodded, although she couldn't understand what exactly she was thanking her for. But something in the atmosphere seemed to change. The loneliness and isolation that had surrounded him seemed to fall away. He belonged.

In this room with a spattering of curious looks and suspicious glances, he belonged. Alicia felt as if she'd unlocked a key. As if some of the guests were seeing Trey in a new light, a light she'd always seen in him. They all seemed to realize that she was accepting him in a way they couldn't because he was different in ways that couldn't be explained.

"I wasn't trying to be funny," she said in mock hurt.

"I know." The music shifted to an electronic dance beat with a heavy bass that he easily moved to. He released her and moved his body with the smooth, sexy dance moves of a male stripper. He was so magnetic Alicia had to stop herself from shouting "take it off, take it off" and scramble for money to stick into his imaginary G-string. He wiggled his shoulders and motioned her closer. She glanced around, aware of others looking, but Trey was having so much fun she would too. She let loose and matched his movements in a way that made her feel at one with both the music and him. All her worries fell away and she felt powerful and beautiful.

When the song ended and returned to a slow tempo

he pulled her close. His heart pounding as fast as hers. He hesitated. His gaze shifted past her, his voice dropped. "Are you glad you came?"

He said the words so softly that at first she wasn't sure she heard them. As if they were part of her imagination. As if everything about this moment, this man, wasn't real. "Am I glad I came here with you?" she said, wanting to be sure that was what his true question was.

He nodded.

Did he really need to ask that question? Didn't he know what he did to her? She looked at his searching gaze and sighed, clearly he didn't know. She briefly rested her forehead against his shoulder, surprised by how tense he felt. "That's a silly question."

"No, it's not."

"You're holding me this close and you can't tell whether I'm happy or not?" She slid her hand underneath his jacket and rested her hand against his chest. "You danced in a way that made me want to take off my panties and throw them at you." She felt his heart pounding. Pounding so fast it frightened her a little. She lifted her gaze to meet his, but as usual he wasn't looking at her and suddenly he was a stranger to her again. She couldn't tell whether it was desire or fear that caused his body to respond as it had. Her teasing hadn't had the affect she'd hoped for. Maybe it was her, maybe he didn't feel the same as she did.

She'd invited him into a simple dancer's embrace but she was the one who'd crossed the line, who'd pressed her body closer to his. Perhaps he'd danced that way with no expectation from her. Had the panty reference been too coarse for him? Perhaps he was being polite, maybe this wasn't what he wanted. Maybe he was shy about being affectionate in public.

She drew back. "I'm sorry, I shouldn't have—"

She could have sworn she felt a feather light kiss on her forehead before he drew away and said, "No, don't apologize. It's me. It's always me." He flashed a brief grin that somehow eased the tension that had come between them. "So what do you want to do next?"

"Next?" she repeated feeling as if she'd gone through a storm cloud that had suddenly disappeared into a rainbow. It wasn't that he was moody or changeable, it was how he always made her feel safe even when she was confused. That was what unnerved her the most. That as much as he was a mystery to her, she sensed no danger. She never sensed he would intentionally hurt her, which made her question again why he would hurt his friend.

Who are you? She wanted to ask him, but knew Trey would not give her the answer. She wanted to know whether he'd kissed her on the forehead or not (had she imagined it?), wishing he'd touched her lips in the same whisper soft way. Why had he set a barrier between them?

"I don't need space," she said.

"What?"

"I don't need space from you so you don't have to eat breakfast or dinner alone, you don't have to stand alone in a corner. I like being with you, do you understand?"

He nodded. "So what do you want to do next?"

"I want to use your body as a tray and eat off it."

He grinned. "Not going to happen. What else?"

She loved when he grinned like that—playful, sexy, real. Unfortunately, he was asking a question she couldn't readily answer because what she wanted to do next wasn't something she could say aloud. She wanted him to kiss her. To wrap his arms around her and press their bodies close, she wanted him to hold her gaze and watch his eyes heat with desire. She could even imagine suggesting going back to their suite and making use of the private pool. She could pretend to not know how to swim and he could teach her...

Trey took her hand. "You look hungry. Let's get you some food."

"I just thought of an idea."

He winked. "You can tell me later," he said seconds before the ambush.

CHAPTER THIRTY-FOUR

There may have been twelve, but it felt like fifty people suddenly swarmed around them, blocking Alicia's view of the sumptuous food laid out on the buffet table. The crowd drowned them in comments and questions.

"Amazing dance moves Trey."

"I didn't know you could dance like that."

"You two really looked great out there."

"Did Jacob teach you those moves?"

"You're a man of hidden talents."

"Could you teach me?"

The woman with the chin from the other day looped her arm through both of theirs and led them to a table. "You have to tell us what you've been up to."

Alicia's stomach growled as the distance grew between her and the scent of roasted chicken.

"Nothing," Trey said taking a seat. "Really."

"It's true," she said.

The questions started again then fell away when a tall white man built like a lumberjack made an appearance, the crowd moved aside for him. He had a crooked nose and a shock of silver hair. He held his hand out to Alicia. "I'm sorry I didn't have a chance to introduce myself sooner and I know my son won't."

"Your son?" Alicia said confused why the father of the groom would take the time to introduce himself to her. She hadn't seen him at the rehearsal dinner.

"Yes," the man said sending Trey an indulgent look. "He tends to forget the simple niceties so I have to do them for him. Hello, I'm Carl DeVille."

Alicia felt the man's firm grip, saw the twinkle in his green eyes, but had a hard time processing his words. "Mr. DeVille?"

"Yes, Trey's father." He paused. "Did Trey forget to mention something about me?"

"Y-yes, that you're so tall."

Trey's father laughed, his eyes filled with knowing amusement. "I thought as much." He gestured to the woman who'd led them to the table. "I see you've already met my sister."

"Yes."

Everything began to make sense. She'd thought when she'd overheard Trey call the other woman 'Aunt' it had been an affectionate term. She had plenty of 'Aunties' in her life that weren't really family. But this woman really was. Alicia suddenly realized they all were. When the young ladies mentioned knowing Trey all their lives that's what they'd meant. When his aunt had said Trey never invited dates to family functions. The way they interacted with him with affectionate acceptance as you would any strange relative.

"Don't embarrass her," Trey said.

Alicia's stomach growled.

He stood. "That's enough. She needs to get some food."

"That's fine, honey," his aunt said. "You go and make a plate and we'll keep her company."

Trey hesitated.

"It's all right," she continued. "Don't you trust us?"

He sighed conflicted. Alicia looked up at him and smiled.

Trey rested a hand on her shoulder and whispered in her ear, "I'm not abandoning you. I'll be right back." But before she could convince him to take her with him he was gone.

His aunt leaned towards her. "We can't tell you how happy we are to meet you."

The crowd nodded.

"Trey's been a little lost without Jacob," his father said.

"A little?" a pre-teen girl said, rolling her eyes. "More like completely."

"And he won't discuss it," a young man by her side said.

"But with you he's opened up again," his father said.

Alicia waved her hands feeling uneasy. "I'm not sure I should get all the credit."

His father leaned forward and rested his hands on the table, his face growing serious. "Has he told you anything about—"

"Why would she know anything about it?" Trey's aunt interrupted. "That relationship has nothing to do with this one."

"But—"

"Leave it."

He sat back.

"He's not an easy man to know as it is." She patted Alicia's arms. "Don't want to scare her away."

"I don't scare easily," Alicia said.

"Clearly," Trey said, setting a plate down in front of her. "Otherwise these stormtroppers would have had you running."

His aunt gasped dismayed.

"He means the ones from Star Wars not Imperial Germany," the pre-teen explained.

Trey sent the crowd a look. "Now will you let Alicia eat in peace?"

"Can't we just—"

Trey folded his arms.

The crowd dispersed.

Once they were out of hearing, Trey sat back and said, "And they wonder why I don't bring anyone?"

"That's family for you," Alicia said eagerly tucking into her meal. "But you could have told me."

"Would you have come?"

"I'm not sure." She chewed, thoughtful. "Probably." She pointed at him. "But a little hint would have been nice."

"Hint?"

"About your family."

He nodded. "Right, the fact that I was adopted."

She lowered her voice. "The fact that you were adopted by a white couple."

Trey sighed. "I know people tell me it's important but most times I forget. I see my dad. I see my cousin Lavinia. The rest doesn't register. I didn't keep it from you on purpose."

"I know."

He fell silent a moment then said, "Does it make a difference?"

"The fact that your father is built like a Mack truck? No."

He grinned.

"Is your mother around?"

His grin faded but he looked more resigned than sad. "My parents divorced."

"I'm sorry."

"But I still see her when I can."

"Oh."

"Is there a brother or sister you forgot to introduce me to?"

"No." He drummed his fingers on the table with impatience. "After you finish eating, can we please leave?"

"You know we're pretty conspicuous, they'll notice when we're gone."

He blinked, bored. "Do I look like I care?" He pressed his hands together. "Please say yes."

Alicia laughed. "All right. Yes."

Across the room a man watched the happy pair and felt the tension in his heart ease. Carl soaked up the sight of one of his son's rare, genuine smiles. He wondered if Alicia knew how special they were. How special Trey was.

Carl felt a light touch on his arm and glanced at his sister. "Are you still worried about him?" she said.

"He's my son. I thought it was part of the job." He sighed and returned his gaze to the couple. "Besides, I didn't worry enough in the past."

"You can't still blame yourself for—"

"I will always blame myself," he said in a terse voice in no mood for her sympathies or assurances. He was sick of them and didn't deserve them. Although surrounded by buoyant music, happy chatter and laughter, Carl couldn't feel it. A heavy ache still lingered in his chest when it came to Trey. There were so many things he hadn't known, so many ways he'd failed him as a father and yet Trey could still smile.

Carl shifted his assessing gaze to the woman his son stared at so intently. Few could see that Trey's heart was in his eyes, that he was completely taken by her. That she could hurt him more than she knew. Carl knew he'd received forgiveness. Trey loved him and would be surprised by his lingering guilt. But it remained. He didn't know why Trey had pushed Jacob out of his life. Why he kept them all at a polite distance. He'd feared Trey would turn himself into one of the cold, hard rocks he liked to study.

But what he saw now was not a rock, but a man. A man who'd risked letting a woman close, giving Carl a faint hope Alicia would be the one person who could heal Trey of the damage *he* had done.

CHAPTER THIRTY-FIVE

"I have a surprise for you," Alicia announced, opening the door to their hotel suite.

"What?"

She led Trey to the bedroom then gestured to the bed with a flourish. "I had maid service turn down the bed. These are fresh, new sheets. Cookie crumbs-free."

Trey sighed with pleasure, sweeping his hand over the sheets. "Thank you."

She pulled off his jacket. "Get in."

"Now?"

"Yes. Try it out."

He slid under the sheets.

"Nice?"

"Heaven." He gazed up at the ceiling and said in a quiet voice, "Did Lavinia look happy?"

"Over the moon. You were just what she needed today."

Trey sighed again this time in relief. "Good."

"Close your eyes."

He shook his head. "No, I can't."

"Why not?"

"I might fall asleep."

Alicia bent over him and whispered, "I heard that's what beds were made for."

He looked up at her confused. "But I thought—"

"What? That I was going to bring you back to the room, strip you naked and ravish you?"

A faint, tired grin touched his lips. "It's what I was hoping for."

She rested her hands on her hips. "Me too. But you look exhausted. It's been a long day. Especially for you." She placed her hands over her mouth and feigned a look of horror. "All those people," she said referring to the reception they'd just left.

Trey's grin widened with relief that she understood. "You really don't mind?"

She sat on the side of the bed. "No. Now go to sleep."

He started to sit up. "I should change my clothes first."

She gently pushed him back down. "You can change later."

"I won't sleep long."

She rested a hand on his chest. "Close your eyes."

His voice grew soft and heavy with sleep. "Just for a second."

"Of course."

"Because I didn't forget."

Alicia leaned closer barely able to hear him. "Didn't forget what?"

"I didn't forget about the shower," he whispered before he drifted off to sleep.

Trey usually didn't dream or at least didn't remember his dreams, but this time he found himself in paradise. He swam in a crystal clear river surrounded by fruit trees, and pastures bursting with an assortment of melons, which didn't make sense but he didn't question their presence.

Instead, he plucked and squeezed ripe mangoes before inhaling their sweet fragrance. He did the same with the plentiful bounty of fruits like coconuts, watermelons, cantaloupes... He squeezed and ran his hand down a large papaya...

"Watch the hands."

Trey froze. The papaya spoke? He cautiously squeezed it again.

"I mean it."

He dropped the papaya and he didn't hear it fall, which was doubly strange. He touched it with the tip of his foot.

"Trey."

The voice sounded feminine and familiar. His eyes flew open.

The dream scene faded replaced by the sight of the soft morning sun rays touching the light blue walls. Was it morning? How long had he been asleep?

He moved his hand and felt something smooth, soft and warm: A thigh. It wasn't his thigh, but he knew this thigh. He'd kissed this thigh. He'd been between this thigh.

He silently swore. Had he been squeezing Alicia's thigh in his sleep imagining it was a papaya?

He snatched his hand back. "Sorry."

"You certainly are grabby in your sleep," Alicia said.

Trey felt his cheeks burn not wanting to imagine what other parts of her body he'd grabbed. He'd dare not think about what he thought the honeydew really was and he wouldn't even think of how he'd held the mangoes. He should have slept on the couch; she probably wouldn't want to sleep next to him again. "I'm really sorry." He sat up. "Did you get any sleep?"

She flashed a slow smile. "I slept very well."

Trey searched her face. She didn't sound annoyed, or seem like she was lying. That was a good sign.

She pushed back the sheets revealing a cute little nightie with ice cream cones and bunnies on it. "Fortunately, I had something to look forward to."

Trey frowned. "Something to look forward too?"

"Yes." Alicia got out of bed and headed for the bathroom. "You can start with my back."

Trey raced after her needing no further instructions.

CHAPTER THIRTY-SIX

"What do you want to do the next two days?" Trey asked her at breakfast. He indulged in fry jacks with scrambled eggs and beans while she had hers with jam.

"Two?" Alicia said, sucking jam off of her thumb. "I thought we only had one more."

Trey's gaze shifted to his orange juice. "I told your sister we'd extended our stay for business purposes, so there won't be any trouble at work...if you're interested."

"Let me think..." Alicia furrowed her brows in mock confusion. "Stay in the Caribbean or go back to a Virginia winter." She threw up her hands. "It's a hard choice."

Trey clasped his hands together and leaned forward. "Want to list the pros and cons?"

Alicia folded her arms. "I was being sarcastic."

"I wasn't."

She narrowed her eyes. "That's what makes you scary."

He winked. "You mean sexy." He stood and then went over and lounged on the couch. "So Belize is yours. What do you want to do?"

Alicia opened her mouth to reply then became captivated by his pose. He did look sexy, stretched out on the couch. She could picture him wearing one of MedForm's uniforms and a caption could say 'Work or Play. Your body won't notice the difference.'

She grabbed her cell phone and took a picture of him before she said, "Wait a minute." She rushed to her suitcase then returned with a uniform. She'd packed several items with the sole intention of taking pictures of him wearing them. She held it out to him. "Put this on."

"Why?"

"I thought once we got here I could take some photos of you."

He took off his jeans. "You were going to turn this into a business affair?"

She shrugged. "I never thought we'd—"

"It's okay," he said sliding on the trousers. "I don't mind." He tugged on a trouser leg. "This feels really comfortable and the fabric is great."

"Thanks. I thought I'd take pictures of you by the pool."

He changed out of his shirt. "Why not at the beach?"

Alicia groaned. "Ugh, I hate the beach."

He paused with the uniform halfway over his face, his startled eyes met hers. "You do?"

"Yes."

He pulled the top down. "But the picture in your office... I thought—"

"You took notice of that?"

He nodded. "That's why I—" He stopped and tied the string belt on the trousers into a knot.

Alicia studied him and the way he tied then re-tied the trousers. He looked disappointed. She sat down as a realization hit her. "Is that why you invited me here with you?" She placed a hand on her chest touched. "That is so sweet."

"I wasn't trying to be sweet."

She stood. "Come on, let's go."

"Where?"

"To the beach."

"You just told me you hate the beach."

She grinned. "But you started to change my mind."

Alicia spent the next hour and a half taking pictures of him running barefoot in the sand, resting against a palm tree, looking out at the ocean and for the first time she didn't mind being at the beach. It helped that there weren't many people around yet so they could enjoy their surroundings in relative quiet.

As she took pictures, she let herself take pleasure in the early morning haze of the sun, and the breeze sweeping off of the ocean while she listened to the small waves crawling up the bank then receding like a shy visitor.

She posed Trey sitting, resting his hands on his knees looking out at the water. She didn't know what the caption would be but she liked the image. She took several more pictures before Trey put a hand over his face and told her he'd had enough.

She put her phone away and sat down beside him

and took her sandals off. She dug her toes into the sand, letting it seep between them.

"This is nice," she said. "I'm glad you asked me to come." She nudged him with her elbow. "Maybe I don't hate the beach as much as I thought."

"I'm glad."

"Or perhaps you make all the difference."

Trey sent her a sideward glance. "You sound like you mean that."

"Because I do."

"Are you sure you're not trying to get me in the mood to take more pictures?"

"Why would I do that?"

"Because you could take pictures of me at the pool, by the lagoon—"

Her face lit up. "Now that's a good idea."

"I'm done."

"How about a few of you just lying in the sand?"

"No." Trey jumped to his feet. "We should get back."

"Let's stay a little while longer," Alicia said not wanting the moment to end. She grabbed his hand. Too late she realized she hadn't warned him.

Trey yanked his hand free with such violence she cried out in alarm.

Their eyes met. His dark, guarded. Hers wide, uncertain.

Alicia pressed her hands together and said in a rush, "I'm sorry. I forgot to say something first."

Trey turned and faced the ocean. "You shouldn't have to apologize," he said in a hard voice.

"But I—"

"You did nothing wrong." He picked up a sea shell then closed it in his fist, tight, until drops of blood dripped from his hand.

Alicia scrambled to her feet. "No, don't do that." She covered his fist. "Please."

Trey spun away from her and threw the shell in the ocean. "You did nothing wrong," he repeated, this time his voice raw with pain. "It's me. There's something wrong with me." He pounded his chest with his fist. "It makes no sense, but when people grab me it hurts. It shouldn't but it does." He released a shaky breath. "I don't want you to be afraid of me."

"I'm not." She carefully pried his fist open to see the wound. "You startled me, but I recovered." She glanced around before she took off her floral printed blouse.

"What are you doing?"

She wrapped his hand with her blouse. "The same thing you did for me."

"That was different."

She secured her makeshift bandage with a knot then inspected her handiwork. "Not really." She held out her hand. "I'll wear your top back."

Trey stripped out of his top and handed it to her. "You didn't need to—"

"Of course I did." She put his shirt on. "What if the wound gets infected and then the infection spreads and you end up losing your hand or worse you—?"

Trey started to laugh.

"It's not funny. The moment we get back we need to clean—"

He pulled her into his arms. "How come you're always looking out for me?"

Alicia stiffened, not sure how to respond to his question.

"I'm sorry," he said, no humor in his voice. "I'll try harder. Give me time."

She wrapped her arms around him. "Do you know why someone grabbing you hurts?"

He nodded. "But I'm not ready to talk about it."

There were so many things he didn't want to talk about: like Jacob or the wedding and now this. But she wouldn't force him to. He'd asked her to accept him and she would. For now.

"When you're ready will you let me help you?"

He nodded again.

Alicia stepped back and pulled out her cell phone. "And now for some more pictures. This shirtless look is incredible."

He lunged for the phone. "Enough."

She moved the phone out of reach and started to run. "Just a couple more."

"No."

She zigged and zagged out of his reach and ran a few yards before she realized he was no longer behind her. She turned and saw him kneeling on the ground, cradling his hand as if in pain. She rushed towards him. "Are you okay?"

He snatched the phone from her and said with a sly grin, "I am now." He jumped up and ran towards the hotel like a sprinter.

"Why you!" Alicia ran after him, choking on the dust

he left in his wake, knowing there was no way she could catch him. "I'm going to get you for that."

His laughter rang loud and triumphant. He turned and jogged backwards displaying a wide smile.

And at that moment she finally saw the Trey Jacob knew. At first glance people would think they were different. Jacob outgoing, talkative and fun; Trey quiet, reserved, intimidating. But she realized they complemented each other. Just as Trey showed a different side when he allowed her to get close, there were likely sides to Jacob others didn't see. A side perhaps only Trey knew.

I had to save him. That's what Trey had told her. But his words still didn't make sense. What did Jacob need saving from?

Why would Trey risk their friendship for it?

She knew she would have to wait for the answers. Trey would remain a mystery a little while longer.

Fortunately, Jacob's loss was her gain. She glanced at the tattoo on Trey's arm, that he had one still surprised her, before she looked down to his wrapped hand. The pain in his voice only minutes before still shook her. She would be careful not to grab him again. She didn't want to lose him.

She didn't want another failure.

She stopped running and held up her hands in surrender. "Okay, you win. No more pictures of you."

He waved her phone. "Promise?"

"I promise."

He jogged up to her and took her hand. "Great. Now let's have some fun."

CHAPTER THIRTY-SEVEN

They had different ideas of fun.

Alicia enjoyed zip lining and rappelling off a waterfall, Trey preferred looking at the Mayan ruins.

Alicia followed the tour and the enthusiastic guide with polite interest, twice hiding a yawn, while Trey followed along enraptured. She was glad Trey's cut had been superficial and only needed a band-aid.

She attempted to entertain herself by counting the number of red items she could find and had reached twelve before Trey started telling her more about the artifacts. At first he spoke in such a quiet, serious way it was easy to ignore him, but soon she found herself listening and within minutes she became as enraptured as he was.

She discovered he knew as much, if not more, than the tour guide, delighting the guide with pointed questions that also amused the other tourists. He made the history come so alive that even after the tour ended Alicia wanted to know more. She would never have gone on an archeological tour on her own, but Trey had expanded her world.

And his favorite part of the world seemed to be the water. He truly was a shark. He found his way to the water any chance he could. In the morning it was the pool, that afternoon he took her swimming in the caves.

"I see you more wet than dry," she teased him that night in bed. "From showers to the pool and the ocean, not that I'm complaining, you look great both ways, but it's amazing."

He shrugged.

She rested her chin on his chest. "Come on. Tell me the truth. You're part fish."

He nodded looking solemn. "And that's why I don't look like my dad."

Alicia laughed. "That is a terrible joke."

"It's funny. You're laughing, aren't you?"

"Because it's so bad."

"He went fishing one day and plucked me out of the water."

She covered his mouth. "Be quiet. I'm sorry I said anything."

He removed her hand and his voice softened. "My dad's a good man."

"I'm sure he is," Alicia said curious why he'd have to mention that. There was something in his tone that made her know it was important she understand that. "I liked him."

Trey absently stroked her back. "My mother once told me that one night he woke up from a dream and said,

'My son is in Haiti.' Another wife probably would have told him to go back to sleep, but my father is special. He has a certain gift. He saved my grandfather when he told him to delay a trip, helped an aunt avoid a bad marriage and other things. So when he said those words my mother listened."

Trey sighed and flattened his palm on her shoulder. "I wish I could say I remember the first moment I saw my parents. That I looked at them and felt a sense of hope or belonging, but I remember being a little afraid and not knowing why. I remember feeling neither happy nor sad.

I don't know why he chose me, but he's always said the moment he saw me he knew I was his son. That I was special. He worries about me a lot even though I tell him not to, but sometimes he feels things too much."

Alicia lifted herself up to look at his face aware of the precious gift he'd given her by opening up. But she still sensed there was something he wasn't telling her so she chose her words carefully. "Are you happy he chose you?"

Trey fell quiet for a moment, his gaze straying everywhere but her face before he said, "Yes." His unguarded eyes met hers and his mouth curved into a smile. "Always."

Alicia smiled relieved. It was at that moment she realized how much she wanted him to be happy. She lay on her back and groaned. "You may have been your father's dream come true, but I'm my father's nightmare."

"I don't believe that."

"It's true. I've been a big disappointment to him." She blinked back the gathering of tears. She envied Trey a little. Her family never considered her something special. "But now it's going to change. It's already changed with your help."

"I still wish you wouldn't give me so much credit."

She reflected on their past two days. How they'd sat at a table under a thatched roof on the beach, gazing over the lagoon while the Maya mountains rose in the distance.

She enjoyed corn and beans wrapped in a plantain leaf, pita bread stuffed with beans and curry vegetables while Trey enjoyed baked snapper stuffed with vegetables and lime. For dessert there was coconut pie and cinnamon spice bread pudding.

She gazed at Trey, feeling warm and safe beside him, dreading the life that faced her back in Virginia. The role she had to play. But she had him now. That would make a difference, right? Or was this all just a dream? Could their relationship stand the realities of life? Would she fail again?

Trey sat up. "What's wrong?"

Alicia didn't realize she was crying until she felt the tears fall down her cheeks. She wiped her eyes. She couldn't tell him she didn't want to go back. How much she felt she was hiding her true self back at home. But as long as she had him she'd be all right. "I-I'm happy. I'm glad you asked me for this favor."

He cupped the side of her face. "I'm glad you said yes." He kissed her. "You'd better get some sleep, we have an early flight."

"Could you hold me for a little while?" Alicia said, hoping she didn't sound as miserable as she felt.

Trey drew her into the circle of his arms. "I can hold you all night if you want me to," he said his voice low and smooth.

"I do." She sank into the warmth of his embrace.

She closed her eyes but didn't sleep. The longer she stayed awake the longer the dream of being here with him would last. Once she closed her eyes the dream would be over.

CHAPTER THIRTY-EIGHT

So this was what envy felt like.

Jacob stared at the picture Trey had sent him of Lavinia proudly walking down the aisle beside him on her wedding day. She'd finally stood up to her father, cutting him out of her life. She was free.

He wished he could have been there. But someone else had been there in his place. Someone else had witnessed Lavinia taking a stand.

But as much as Jacob envied her, he knew her battle was different than his. Easier. She didn't have to stand up against her entire family, years of expectations and the constant threat of shame. He hadn't been able to risk that. And Trey had paid the price.

But now Trey had Alicia.

Jacob closed the image when he heard the heavy footsteps of boots coming down the hall before a woman appeared in the entry way of his office. His contractor, Sandra Park, stopped and folded her arms before she said, "You look like someone chopped off your balls and fed them to a lion."

Jacob scowled and put his cell phone away. "What is wrong with you?"

She shrugged unfazed by his tone. "It sounds better than saying 'You look upset,' don't you think?"

"No, I don't." He wasn't in the mood for her today. He was never in the mood for her. The sight of her usually made his mood dip further for a number of reasons. One being he found her annoying and the second being he thought she was sexy as hell.

Not that he'd ever thought he'd go for a woman who could rock a tool belt. He liked her pixie hair cut, wide hips and full lips. She was beautiful and strong and more than once he'd imagined her riding him like a jackhammer. She could pound him into the ground and he'd enjoy every minute of it, which really got to him. Quitting his job to restore and run a B&B was one thing, getting involved with a woman like Sandra was completely insane.

Unfortunately, he was feeling more than a little crazy whenever she was around. "What do you want?"

"Do you want the good news or the bad news? No, scratch that, there's no good news. Only bad news and worse news."

He sighed. "Just tell me."

"Remember when you said you'd take care of the materials and all you wanted me to do was put the gazebo together?"

He nodded. It seemed simple enough.

"You ordered the wrong wood."

He froze. He took a deep breath. He wouldn't panic. "Okay, what's the bad news?"

"That's the bad news the worse news is that some of them are measured wrong."

Jacob jumped up from his chair and swore. He rushed outside, the chill of winter not cooling his heated skin. Anger and humiliation threatened to burn him as he stared at the delivered material resting in the center of the bare garden. Some of the material sat in neat packs while others were laid out on the ground. They looked fine to him. They looked like they'd fit together.

But they wouldn't. They were wrong.

"If there were longer pieces I could saw them down," Sandra said, "and work with them, but many are too short."

He'd tried to save money but he'd end up spending more. Because he was an idiot. Because he didn't have Trey to cover up his mistakes for him. The gazebo had been Trey's idea. He'd said it would be a nice addition to the garden. Give people a place to sit and enjoy the foliage of the Shenandoah Valley in the fall and the lush sights in the summer.

His heart twisted. He missed his friend. He missed the life he thought he would once lead. He missed not feeling like he had a threatening storm cloud over his head, threatening to soak him in regret.

But this was bad. He'd exposed himself to a person like Sandra. She saw a side to him he'd never wanted her to see. Now she knew he was stupid. That he was terrible with numbers. Always had been.

After years of thinking he was an idiot he'd finally

gotten a diagnosis in college but that hadn't made life any easier. His parents had expected even more.

As if having a learning disability were to make you a genius in some other way. They expected him to be the next Richard Branson, but he'd proven himself to be ordinary. No hidden genius. Still an idiot.

Just one with a diagnosis.

"I'm sorry." He ran a hand through his hair. He'd wasted not only his money, but her time. She'd have to fix his mistake and she had another job scheduled. Maybe he should quit. Maybe he was in over his head. Maybe...

"So this is what we're going to do."

She was talking. Talking as if this wasn't a catastrophe, as if the guy who'd hired her wasn't a complete fool. "What?"

"We can work with what we have. It will take some creativity, but it will be manageable. So you can stop looking like someone torched your Porsche."

He glared at her. "Stop saying things like that."

"But it's true. This isn't a big deal."

It *was* a big deal. She was lying to help him save face but it didn't change the fact that he'd done a major mess up. "I'm sorry."

"So what happened?"

He stared at the material on the ground. "I'm just stupid, that's all. I'll compensate you for your extra time."

"You're not stupid. I said the material was wrong, but I didn't say it was bad. Actually it may even turn out better than I'd planned."

He spun to her. "Really?"

"Yes, really. So what made you choose this kind of wood?"

"My choice really was a mistake. I must have entered the wrong item code or something. I'm...I'm really bad with numbers."

"You can't be that bad, your cheques never bounce. You pay on time."

"Money's different."

"How about cooking?" She made a face. "Do you know how many pints go into a gallon? Or how about 'For each pound of roast beef cook at X temperature.'"

He laughed. "Can I assume cooking isn't your strong point?"

"That's putting it mildly. I can manage the basics like boiled water and instant noodles, but beyond that I'm lost."

"Cooking is actually something I'm good at." He clasped his hands behind his back and flashed a satisfied smile, glad he had something to brag about. "The next time you need help in the kitchen, give me a call."

She blinked, parting her lips in surprise. And the cold air tainted them red. Kissably red.

Jacob felt his face heat again, but not from embarrassment. He liked surprising her and leaving her speechless. He took a step back and cleared his throat. Flirting with his contractor was not smart. He pointed to the items on the ground. "Are you sure this mess won't put you behind schedule?"

"I'll talk to my boss." Sandra pulled out her cell phone, pretended to dial it before she placed it by her ear and said, "Hi, Sandra? Yes. I've got a situation here that's going to take time. It's the Jacob Kim project. No, not that one. We've already finished most of the work inside, it's the gazebo. Uh...huh. There's a little trouble," her eyes slowly measured him from head to toe like he was a project she was getting ready to work on, "but you know I like a challenge." Jacob swallowed, her assessing eyes felt like a hot caress. He shifted his gaze to her grey Ford truck. "Uh...huh," she continued. "He even said he'll cover for our time. Right. Right. Okay, I'll tell him." She put her phone away. "She must like you because she said it's fine. On one condition."

"What's that?"

"You cook me dinner. I want to find out more about these skills of yours."

He winked and said in a smooth voice, "With one bite you'll know."

She cocked her head to the side. "Do we have a deal?"

She was crazy, but his mood hadn't dipped. In fact, for some reason he felt better than he had in a long time. "Yeah. It's a deal."

CHAPTER THIRTY-NINE

She'd been summoned.

Her father wanted to see her.

Alicia looked at the message on her cell phone and resisted the urged to bang her head on her office desk.

It had been almost four months since Belize and she still hadn't fully adapted to the dull days at the office. Every day she found herself gazing at the beach scene on the wall wondering when her next vacation day could be. The last thing she wanted to do was add another boring meeting to the drudgery of her current life, but she had no choice.

Her father welcomed her into his spacious office, motioning her to sit down on one of the chairs facing his desk. The fact that the meeting wasn't in the conference room was a good sign. That meant it wasn't too formal. She sat down beside her stiff-faced mother, dressed head to toe in Chanel, her light brown hair in a French knot updo, and saw a light sheen in her eyes. Oh no. Were they tears? She hoped not. Tears were not a good thing. Alicia frantically wondered what her father was going to say, what she'd done wrong.

Her father sat behind his desk, clasped his hands together and flashed a wide smile. "You're a natural."

Alicia gripped her hands in her lap. Something was very wrong. She'd *never* seen her father smile at her like this before. "I'm sorry?"

"I'll admit I was hesitant at first but you've proven yourself beyond all our expectations. You're a true Fox."

Alicia turned when she heard her mother sniff and watched her dab her eyes with a handkerchief. Her mother *was* crying. This *was* bad. "Somehow in my heart I knew not to give up on you," she said.

Alicia looked at her parents confused. "I-I don't understand."

He spun his computer screen to her. "Our sales have increased three hundredfold thanks to your inventive marketing. Three hundred percent! Numbers like that are unheard of in an industry like ours. Especially with a business as old as ours. But that's not all, thanks to some of your insights our distribution system has improved and there's a renewed sense of purpose and energy you've brought to the business. In several years I see you running the business and I'll happily step down knowing it's in good hands."

Alicia rested a hand on her chest. "Me? Run MedForm? Are you mad?"

Her parents laughed. "The thought surprised us both," he said.

"Never in a million years would we have ever considered it," her mother added.

"But we can't ignore what you've managed to do in
less than a year. As they say, The proof is in the profit."

Alicia doubted anyone said that. It was likely a saying
her father made up. She licked her lip. "I'm not sure—"

"There's no need to be humble and I'm sure you're
concerned that this is an anomaly. But it's not. If it had
only been one ad I would have conceded, but you've
done seven. All successful. It's not a fluke."

"But the ads feature—"

"A very attractive man," her mother said, "but you
were able to make it about the clothes and our brand.
That takes skill."

"Plus, as we mentioned, the other divisions like
working with you, your ideas for fulfillment and software
upgrades have been sound. We can't stay stagnant. The
future of this company depends on you."

Her mother nodded. "Absolutely."

Alicia moved to sit on the edge of her seat eager to get
them to understand the mistake they were making. She'd
been able to make certain suggestions only because of all
the different types of businesses she'd worked in and the
one she'd tried to run. She wasn't a natural at anything.
She'd gotten lucky. "But Pauline and Edwin—"

"Will support you."

Alicia scoffed. "Not bloody likely."

"We understand that Pauline may be a little disappointed—"

Alicia's voice cracked at the understatement. "A little

disappointed? That's like calling a bullet wound a little cut."

"But once she understands it's our decision," her father continued, "she'll recognize that our decision is what's best for the company. And what's best for the company is best for all of us."

Anxiety quickened her pulse. "But I don't want—" She stopped. She couldn't tell them what her heart was screaming. *I don't want to run the business. I don't want to be here!* "I don't want to let you down."

"You won't. You'll have plenty of time to grow into your new role. I don't plan to go anywhere for a long while. We just want you to keep it up."

Her mother covered her hand. "I don't know why you stayed away so long when this is where you belong."

ALICIA WALKED BACK to her office in a stunned haze. Where she belonged? This boring place? This place where she had to drink copious amounts of coffee and use the thought of being with Trey at night and on the weekends just to keep going? She'd never seen her father so proud, her mother so relieved.

This is where you belong. Shouldn't she be happy? Thrilled? Instead she felt depressed. How could this place, a place that felt so ill-suited, be the right place for her?

How could she be succeeding at something she found so tedious?

Why had none of her other ideas worked when she'd been on her own? Was this really her destiny?

Alicia walked into her office and collapsed behind her desk. She opened a desk drawer and lifted the gemstone Trey had chosen for her.

He was still her secret. Her family didn't know about Trey and she wasn't sure when she'd tell them.

She wanted this part of her life untouched by their critical eye. She could just imagine Pauline's smug grin silently saying 'Oh so that's how you got him to do so many poses.' They'd naturally want to know how they met (she'd lie) and how long they'd been dating (she'd lie about that too) and then they'd silently wonder what he was doing with her.

At first glance Trey was the perfect example of the kind of man they'd want her to be with. He fit in perfectly with the image they wanted her to have. He was stable, dependable, employed. But then they'd find out he was the adopted son of a white man named Carl who supposedly had 'the gift' and that he had a hard time relating to people.

Alicia held the gemstone so that it could catch the light and remembered the spring evening when Trey had gifted it to her and had shown her another side of himself that not only shocked her but left her in awe...

CHAPTER FORTY

"I think I'm lost," Alicia said into her cell phone as she surveyed her surroundings. She was in one of Virginia's moneyed zip codes, having passed a country club, golf course and private academy (that had been her school's rival) as a not so subtle hint of where she was, but she now saw nothing. "Yep, I'm definitely lost." She'd parked her car on a narrow road after driving what seemed like miles. Her cell phone kept telling her 'You have arrived' but all she saw were lush manicured grounds and a winding pea gravel drive that stretched on with no houses in sight.

She really hadn't wanted to be late for her first luncheon at his house. They'd eaten out and at her place plenty of times (she'd even hired a housekeeper for Trey's sake), but this was the first time she'd see his place and now she couldn't even find it. She felt like an idiot.

"You're not lost," Trey said. "Keep driving."

"But—"

"Trust me. See you soon."

Alicia scowled at the disconnected phone. He had higher hopes than she did. She got back in her car and continued along the pea gravel path that eventually curved in front of a soaring building with large windows.

The front door opened and Trey met her with a grin. "I told you you weren't lost."

She stared up at the house. "I didn't know a geological consultant made this much."

"Well, it's more like my company makes the money," he said in a dismissive tone. He held up his hand. "Don't ask, you've never heard of the company and that's fine with me as long as it does what it's supposed to." He took her hand. "Come inside."

She hurried after him, half afraid she'd get lost, as he led her through the formal reception area to the family room where French doors welcomed them to a covered veranda and outdoor stone fireplace. He gestured to a small dining table covered in peach colored linen and an elegant table setting. In the distance she heard a frog before she saw a robin fly over a tranquil private pond.

His personal chef (he had a chef?!) served them *poulet aux noix* a Haitian dish of well-spiced chicken and cashews, its golden brown sauce heightened the bright red of the diced tomatoes, purple onions, served next to a bed of white rice and green peas.

She knew Trey had money, (the suite in Belize had been a clue, however she'd suspected he'd gotten a wedding party discount). She had never realized he had this much money. Enough for a house staff, garden crew and acres of land and now she knew he wasn't just a consultant he owned his own company. He was a self-made man.

While she'd had everything handed to her in life.

Instead of enjoying herself Alicia felt small and insignificant.

Suddenly the golden yellow maxi dress she wore felt garish, her shoes too showy, as well as the glitter nail polish she wore. She was whisked back to the numerous awkward family dinners full of proper etiquette and decorum. She'd always managed to mess up somehow—whether it was her clothes, food selection or behavior.

She didn't feel worthy of the magnificent house, picture perfect landscape, the delicious food or the handsome, successful man sitting across from her. A seize of insecurities (this will never last, you don't belong, you're so stupid, how could you have not known he was this rich? This was the guy whose dry cleaning you'd offered to pay for?), made her eager to run.

It felt like the only place she felt she could be completely herself with him was on holiday or in her comfortable, cluttered apartment.

Not here.

So to combat those feelings she did what she did best. She pretended she felt the complete opposite.

Similar to how she pretended at work that she wasn't silently dying every day, here she'd be happier than ever. She'd be even bubblier, brighter than she'd ever been before. She wanted to make him laugh and smile, she wanted him to remember this time with her as one of the best he'd ever had.

But her efforts didn't seem to be working because

Trey would only briefly look at her before his eyes shifted to gaze at the late afternoon rays melting into the still waters of the pond.

"Am I boring you?" Alicia said, trying not to sound hurt.

Trey glanced down at his plate then looked at her. "Bored?"

"Yes, sometimes you look bored. You look like you want to be somewhere else."

He shook his head. "That couldn't be further from the truth."

"Then why don't you look at me when I'm speaking?"

"I look at you."

"Not always. Definitely not now. You seem to find the pond more interesting. I can see why. It's certainly more beautiful."

"Don't do that," Trey said in a quiet voice. "It hurts me when you put yourself down. It's like you're making fun of me."

Alicia blinked surprised by that conclusion. "How does that make any sense?"

"Isn't making fun of something or someone I care about making fun of me too?"

Alicia forced a laugh, uneasy. "I was just kidding."

Trey didn't smile. "No you weren't."

Alicia swallowed, feeling exposed and ashamed of herself. She'd fallen prey to her own insecurities and hurt him. It wasn't his fault that she felt out of place; he'd done and said nothing to make her feel that way. At times she still had a hard time accepting that he liked her as she was. Flaws and all. She still had a fear that she'd mess up somehow. That's she'd fall short of what he wanted.

He leaned forward and looked at her half eaten meal. "At least tell me you like the food."

She gasped surprised he could ask her that. "I *love* the food. This is the best I've tasted in a long time."

Trey nodded pleased and leaned back relieved. "Giles is excellent, but if you want a real treat you should see Jacob in the kitchen. He can—" He stopped, sighed, suddenly remembering himself. "Never mind. Just tell me what I've done wrong."

"I didn't say you did anything wrong."

"You didn't have to. I can tell I've upset you." He waved his hand when she opened her mouth. "I've told you, if I've done something wrong, I need you to tell me." He narrowed his gaze and his voice hardened with the soft threat of warning. "Don't talk in riddles."

CHAPTER FORTY-ONE

The desire to run gripped her even more. He was right. It wasn't his job to try and read her mind. He'd offered her this wonderful afternoon and she was ruining it. "It's not you," she said ashamed of herself. "It's me. This place is so beautiful and I feel so..." She took a deep breath and tried again. "When I was talking to you just a few minutes ago you seemed distracted. I want you to look at me when I'm talking so that I feel like I matter to you.

"It's not the first time you've done it. You don't mean to but when you look away at almost everything but me it makes me feel insignificant. You've accomplished so much and I'm still just...me."

"I like looking at you, but," Trey released a heavy sighed, looked up at the sky, "people say I can be a little too intense. They say it's off-putting. So I try to be casual by shifting my gaze."

"But I want you to look at me."

His eyes captured hers with such startling swiftness she flinched.

He pointed at her. "See?"

"Okay, okay they're right," Alicia admitted, resisting the urge to shiver. "You can be a little intense and it's unnerving, but only because right now I don't know what you're thinking. It's intimidating."

"You want to know what I'm thinking right now?"

Alicia felt her courage waning. "I'm not sure anymore."

"Too late," Trey said with a tiny grin. "I'll tell you. I'm thinking that I like studying your face so much I could stare at it for hours. If I had to choose between an international treasure and you, there'd be no contest on what would fascinate me more."

Alicia rolled her eyes and laughed embarrassed by his praise. "Until you get bored of it."

"I doubt that will happen." He pulled out a stone from his pocket. An opal with a pale blue shade, like the sea had been locked inside it and at any moment could burst into life, soaking them both in water and the fresh scent of tropical fruit. It also had a feeling of peace and harmony. "I like to look at this too," he said. "It's a rare gemstone. Every day I find something new and remarkable about it."

Alicia peered at it in awe. "How long have you had it?"

"Ten years."

She stared at him startled. "You're joking."

"No, I'm not. It cost a lot and was worth every cent. It gives me immense satisfaction." Trey tilted it and peered closer. "So many shapes and shadows, it constantly astonishes me." He shifted his gaze to her, his voice soft as velvet. "I don't get bored easily."

Alicia lowered her gaze, feeling ashamed that at that moment she did find his gaze too much to take in. It wasn't just an intense stare; she finally saw something in his gaze close to wonder. He made her feel as if she were as beautiful and thrilling as a galaxy and it filled her with so much joy she feared she'd burst into tears.

"Told you so," Trey said in a knowing voice.

She briefly closed her eyes and steadied her voice. "No, it's not—" She bit her lip and opened her eyes. She wasn't used to this kind of attention, but she wanted to be. She wanted to be the kind of women who didn't shy away from compliments but embraced them. Let him believe her to be beautiful and exciting because, like a hypnotist, his compelling gaze made her believe it too.

"I like how you look at me," she said. "Don't stop."

Trey playfully narrowed his eyes. "I take challenges like that very seriously."

"Good."

"Hold out your hand." When she did, he placed the rock in it. It felt warm from his touch; intimate somehow that he would let her hold something so dear to him.

"I shouldn't—"

"Look at it."

She did and for an instant she didn't see the complex beauty of the stone instead she saw the mystery of him. Like the water he loved so much he was adaptable, changeable, something hard to grasp; there were so many different aspects to uncover and explore. How was he able to still say Jacob's name with such fondness and yet talk about his company with all the enthusiasm of someone mentioning they owned a used car? Why did being grabbed hurt him so much? Why had his family been so surprised he'd brought a woman with him to the wedding? Why had she been so drawn to him that day in the cathedral? Even more...what had drawn him to her?

Alicia looked up and saw Trey looking at her and felt her face grow warm.

"Would you like one of your own?" he asked.

She opened her mouth then closed it.

"No need to answer." He took the stone from her and put it back in his pocket. "I already know." His eyes swept over her, lingering as it slowly made a path down her dress before it lifted again and rested on her face then dipped down once more. It felt as intimate as a caress.

"Wha-what are you doing?"

"You said I could look at you."

"You're not just looking you're studying me."

"I'm doing more than that." Trey abruptly stood and said, "Wait here," before she could reply. He disappeared into the house then emerged minutes later and placed a stone on the table. "This is for you."

Alicia stared at the rare gemstone that looked like he'd captured sun burnt clouds inside of glass. It was like he'd seized the desires of her soul desperate to break free. Gazing at the stone made her feel like she wasn't locked into a life of duty. That she could soar above it; bathe in the sunlight of a distant sky no matter how dark she felt at times.

She lifted the stone. It felt as precious as a pearl or a diamond.

"Tell me about it," Alicia said then listened as Trey told her about the sunset fire-opal and other gemstones.

"I'm glad you like it," Trey said, "but you don't have to worry. This isn't all I will offer you."

Alicia frowned. "Offer me?"

He cleared his throat. "I know that offering stones are unorthodox so you can be reassured the next gift will be jewelry instead."

She sensed a story there. She could imagine Trey attempting to give a stone to someone else and them wanting it in a necklace or earrings or such. But then they didn't realize the beauty. They didn't understand him. She sighed feeling the residual knot of anxiety unravel and release her. There was nothing to be afraid of. No reason to pretend. She did belong here, because *he* was here. She enjoyed him and he enjoyed her and that was all that mattered.

She stood and walked over to him. She placed a hand on his shoulder. "I'm sorry. I forgot."

He looked up at her, his dark gaze uncertain. "Forgot what?"

She placed a light kiss on the cheek then whispered in his ear, "That you're wonderfully strange."

He rose to his feet this time forcing her to look up at him. He held her gaze. "And you like strange," he said more as a statement than a question.

Alicia's face relaxed into a smile. "I love strange."

He hesitated, his expression serious and still.

She playfully tweaked his chin. "In case you think I'm talking in riddles, the fact that I love strange things is a good thing."

He nodded, coming to a decision. "Then I want to show you something."

CHAPTER FORTY-TWO

The sight of the door at the end of the long hallway half excited and half terrified her.

After following Trey into the heart of the magnificent house then entering a door that revealed a narrow staircase, which descended down to the basement, Alicia half expected to hear strange sounds coming from a locked room. What did he want to show her? Why did she get the sense that they were teetering on the edge of one of his secrets?

A secret just beyond an ordinary looking wooden door. Trey turned the handle and opened the door.

"Go on," he said.

Alicia blinked. For some reason she'd anticipated him taking out a key and unlocking the door, she hadn't expected it to turn so easily in his grip. Maybe it wasn't as important as she'd thought.

She pushed away her disappointment and stepped into the room.

Except it wasn't just a room. It was Ali Baba's cave of wonders.

She took a few cautious steps forward as if afraid if she moved too fast it would disappear like an apparition.

Glass shelves and cages lined three of the four walls featuring rows of stones—some glittering like diamonds, some as dull as a pebble, encased inside. On the far left sat a black couch and coffee table, to the right, a large wooden easel with a half painted watercolor of the small path leading to the pond with patches of snow melting under sunlight, straight ahead a long wood table stretched out covered in sketches and paintings neatly fashioned next to each other so she could see them all clearly. One illustration that caught her attention was of a lizard sunning on a rock. The intricate details reminded her of something—his tattoo.

"Do you have a special fondness for reptiles?" she said.

"Not really. Just one."

Alicia turned to ask him what he meant then jumped back when she noticed a small white lizard with black spots sitting on his shoulder.

Trey noticed her reaction and grinned. "She's a leopard gecko. Her name is Liz. She likes to keep me company."

Alicia had been so in awe of the artwork and display cases that she hadn't even noticed the large cage in the corner.

"You don't have to be afraid," Trey said.

"I'm not afraid, just surprised. I never pictured you owning a pet."

Trey shook his head. "Liz is not a pet. She's my friend going on ten years now. One of the longest relationships I've ever had. Do you want to touch her?"

"Not really." Alicia folded her arms. "She's cuter at a distance."

Trey laughed. "Probably best you didn't. I once had a girlfriend who decided to place Liz on her head because she thought it'd be a cute picture."

"And was it?"

"The picture was fine but Liz nearly died from strangulation when she got caught in the woman's hair. Don't put a lizard on your head." Trey looked at Alicia's braided hairstyle in consideration. "But you might be okay."

Alicia held up her hands. "Not going to happen."

Trey placed the lizard back in the large terrarium. "Give me a minute to wash my hands," he said before he disappeared into the attached bathroom.

Alicia walked up to Liz's enormous cage designed with lots of surface space, three hiding places and fake plants for decoration. She bent down and peered through the glass at the lizard in fascination. "You've been with him ten years, huh? And he's got you tattooed on his arm. I can't believe my competition is a lizard, but I have to admit you are attractive. Any tips you wanna give me about this guy?"

The gecko blinked.

"I'll take that as a 'no'."

Alicia straightened and noticed a journal on a side table with Liz's name written on the front in Trey's bold handwriting. She lifted the journal, opened it and saw he'd kept track of Liz's eating habits and weight, even her mood. He even monitored the weekly cleaning of her cage, the temperatures of the hot and cold sides of the terrarium and how often he changed her water. She also noticed bottles of calcium and D3 supplements.

When Trey returned to the room, Alicia held up the journal and D3 supplements. "Are you conducting an experiment or something?"

"No, most lizards need supplements, which I dust on her food, and I use the journal for basic maintenance so I can monitor her weight weekly to make sure she's healthy and so I can spot any health issues. With lizards, the moment you see something is wrong, it's usually too late to fix it."

Alicia set the journal and bottle down. "Sounds like a lot of work."

"Not to me," Trey said with affection. "Observing and caring for her is a joy not a chore. Even when I travel I monitor her by video and have strict instructions about her care."

Alicia pointed at him. "I knew it. For the longest time, I've suspected you've been hiding something from me."

An expression of shock and guilt crossed his face. "Hiding?"

Alicia laughed at his expression. She knew he didn't understand her teasing and decided to let him in on the joke.

"I'm talking about Liz."

He glanced away, but she caught a flash of relief. "Right. Of course. Liz."

Before she could ask him about his odd response he motioned towards the couch. "Want to watch anything?"

Alicia looked around the room confused. "On what? I'm really not into watching shows on my phone. I like it big."

"I can do big."

"But you don't have a TV."

Trey pointed towards the sitting area. "I have a flat screen that descends from the ceiling."

Of course he did, but Alicia wasn't as interested in the different hidden technology in the room as much as what she could see. They revealed a lot more about him than any show could. "We can do that another time. I want to see more of your work." She returned to the long table and lifted up a paper with several sketches of a gazebo with different structures. "What's this? A design?"

Trey casually took the paper from her and handed her a watercolor instead. "It's nothing," he said. "What do you think of this?"

Alicia watched him hide the gazebo sketches under another and wondered why he'd wanted to divert her attention from it but decided not to ask.

Instead she looked at the watercolor of gemstones under a lake, she felt as if she could see the wind moving the current and rippling the water. "You could make money doing this."

Trey shrugged. "Why? I have plenty of money." He followed her as she walked to one of the glass cases. "I like doing it for fun."

Alicia stared down at the array of stones and rocks, some beautiful in their ugliness. "You're like them."

She sensed him stiffen and realized she'd said something wrong. He took a step back.

She turned to him. "I hurt you."

He shook his head, shoving his hands in his pockets. "No, you didn't."

"Just a few minutes ago you told me not to lie, don't do the same."

"I can't be upset with you for telling the truth." He hung his head, his voice growing soft. "I know I'm like a rock. I know that's how people see me. Hard, cold with no feeling."

"No," Alicia said firmly. She lifted his head, forcing him to look at her. "That's not what I meant at all. To me rocks are beautiful and strong, durable and full of mystery." She kissed him. "But not so much a mystery anymore. This room tells me so much about you." She rested her hands on her hips. "However, something bothers me."

"What?"

"Your security."

A smile ruffled his mouth. "My security?"

"Yes, it needs to be better."

Trey threw his head back and laughed.

Alicia folded her arms. "It's not funny. This room is filled with priceless objects and anyone can enter. To get into this room you didn't use a key or a keypad or biometrics or...will you stop laughing?"

Trey bent forward, resting his hands on his thighs, weak with laughter. "I-I'm sorry."

"I'm serious."

He took a deep breath and straightened. "I know you are," he said in a low voice, his fingers sliding sensuously over her bare arm causing her skin to tingle. "That's what I like best about you." He closed his fingers around her arm, pulled her close and brushed his lips against hers before he said, "You're always looking out for me."

The sweetness of his kiss helped to assuage the annoyance of his laughter. "So you'll do it?"

"Alicia," Trey said, flashing a ruthless, sharklike grin, again reminding her that he was more predator than prey, "there's security everywhere and anyone who got this deep inside my house would have a hell of a time getting out of it. I'll bore you with the logistics later. For now, I want to show you one more thing." He walked to another door that she'd assumed was a closet, instead the scent of chlorine hit her first before he turned on the lights and illuminated a large underground pool.

Alicia smiled. "Somehow I'm not surprised."

Trey glanced at his watch. "It's been an hour since we've eaten. Want to go for a swim?"

"I don't have a swimsuit."

Trey winked. "You don't need one."

And when he convinced her to spend the night, she didn't need pajamas either. Trey made sure to be the only heat she needed. In the luxury of his king sized bed Alicia felt transported back to the elegant suite in Belize.

This time amid the soft whisper of sheets, the scent of his skin, the warm, hard length of his body against hers, a sensation both strange and exquisite coursed through her. She'd seen him naked, showered with him, been in bed with him but this moment was something new. Something more intimate than before. Another fissure of doubt died, he was right for her. She belonged with him.

Before Trey drifted off to sleep she tapped his arm and said, "I'll never look at your tattoo the same way again."

She heard him laugh. "Don't worry." He gathered her close. "Liz likes you."

Alicia smiled, knowing Trey liked her very much too and that she could be assured in the knowledge she was special to him.

But it would take weeks, in spite of Trey's coaching, before Alicia felt brave enough to touch Liz's soft leathery skin. Fortunately, Liz, being Liz, didn't hold Alicia's skittishness against her.

ALICIA SIGHED in happy remembrance of that night and the months that followed. She cradled the stone in her hand and took a deep breath. Trey kept her strong.

Alicia tucked the stone away and closed the drawer as she thought of her parents words again. *This is where you belong.*

She looked around the office, feeling the walls closing in on her, the sight of the beach scene only a reminder of the life she kept hidden from view.

There was nowhere else to go. MedForm had to be her home now. Her family needed her.

They'd never needed her before. No one had. She

now had value. She had a place: A place above Pauline and Edwin. She couldn't give that up.

But there was also something else about Trey that had crept into her thoughts the last couple months, a growing whisper of questions that demanded answers she was afraid to seek.

That uneasiness, about their relationship, made her feel that she had to hold onto this chance to please her family even more than before.

As much as the thought made her want to weep.

rey: <two screaming emojis>
Jacob: *What's wrong?*

Trey: *I took Alicia to the Cave. She saw my hobby and met Liz.*

Jacob: *She freak out?*

Trey: *No. It went well. Too well.*

Jacob: *Bro, you're not making sense. What's the problem?*

Trey: *She's been back a couple times now. She really likes it. I've charted the progress of our relationship.*

Jacob: <hand to face image> *I told you not to do that.*

Trey: *Couldn't help it.*

Jacob: *Stop it now.*

Trey: <thumbs up> *I'll send a screenshot.*

Jacob: *I don't need a *&$! screenshot. Tell me what's wrong.*

Trey: *I love her.*

Jacob: *It's too soon to know that.*

Trey: *Not for me. According to the progression of the chart we're at a crucial stage.*

Jacob: *Have you told her?*

Trey: *She doesn't know about the chart.*

Jacob: *Never tell her about the chart! Forget the chart! Did you tell her you love her?*

Trey: *No.*

Jacob: *Good. Wait a little longer.*

Trey: *How much longer?*

Jacob: *Another month or two.*

Trey: *Okay, but can I buy her an engagement ring?*

Jacob: *It's too soon for an engagement ring.*

Trey: *How about a car?*

Jacob: *Do not buy her a car! Nothing extravagant. Don't overdo it.*

Trey: *I'll scare her away?*

Jacob: *Yes. Calm down. Wait a couple more months. Trust me.*

Trey: <okay hand signal>

TEN MINUTES later

Trey: *What should I do with the chart?*

Jacob: *<pointing finger, flame> Burn it. NOW.*

CHAPTER FORTY-FOUR

Deanna frowned. "What's wrong? We should be celebrating. This is great news. Your family's impressed, you beat your sister at something, business is good, and you've found something you excel at. You should be floating on cloud nine."

Alicia leaned back in her chair and gazed out at the traffic driving past their table outside the restaurant. A large umbrella protected them from the sun, but Alicia felt that no amount of shade could damper the seething heat of frustration roiling within her.

"Are we even having the same conversation? My parents have lost their minds. There's no way I can run MedForm."

"Not right now, but in a few years—"

"I don't *ever* want to run it." Alicia paused. "And there's something I need to tell you."

"What?"

"I've been seeing someone."

"That's great! What does he do? When can I meet him?"

"I'm not sure you'll ever meet him."

"Why not?"

"Because..." Alicia's words trailed off, the sting of tears touching her eyes.

Deanna's voice softened. "Because what?"

Alicia swallowed ready to admit the real reason she'd invited her friend for a Saturday lunch. She hadn't called Deanna to moan or sound ungrateful about the status of career or talk about her love life. Her relationship with Trey was special and amazing, but there had been moments that had her question his strange response when she'd teased him about hiding something.

She'd brushed it off, but couldn't deny it any longer. Weeks after their time in his amazing room, she'd come to a horrible conclusion: He was definitely seeing someone else.

She'd pretended not to notice his strange behavior. She didn't want to see the signs, but the subtle clues were there. He wasn't completely hers. It had been too good to be true.

Twice when they'd been in the middle of playing her favorite prison game on the flat screen TV, he'd answer his cell phone and leave the room. He'd also done the same when they were eating dinner. At first she assumed it was so he wouldn't bother her, but another time she'd overheard him speaking in the hallway in a low and indulgent tone she hadn't heard before.

She'd also caught him texting someone then quickly putting his cell phone away when he noticed her.

What didn't he want her to see? What didn't he want her to hear? It felt as if by introducing her to Liz and showing her his gemstones and artwork he'd opened one door to her and closed another.

The secrets were killing her.

Alicia bit her lip. "I feel like he's hiding something from me."

Deanna's voice sharpened as did her gaze. She put her fork down and leaned forward. "Hiding something or some*one*?"

"Someone." Alicia shook her head. "I knew he was too good to be true."

"You don't know anything for sure yet. Have you asked him?"

"No, I'd hate to confront him and then be wrong."

"Do you think you're wrong?"

She shook her head again. "No, but I want clear evidence."

Deanna sighed. "If that's the case, do what any sensible woman would do in this situation."

"What?"

"Follow him."

CHAPTER FORTY-FIVE

Alicia tracked his car not having the boldness to track his cell phone. She followed him one humid Sunday afternoon to a park in the adjoining county: A county known for lush landscapes, picturesque small towns and tourists' attractions. Was he seeing someone from out of state?

Alicia told herself she was being crazy as she followed behind his car. She told herself it was a waste of time when she pulled into the park and watched Trey exit his Mercedes and head down one of the winding tree lined paths.

She was going to hurt herself by uncovering the truth. He was meeting someone, his footsteps were too eager. She'd been cheated on before. She knew the signs.

She gripped the steering wheel. She didn't want to know. Let him lie to her a little longer, let her lie to herself.

But something else whispered to her to face the truth.

She had to endure this. She jumped out of her car and hurried after him before she lost sight of him.

The path ended at a clearing where people lazed on the grass, some tossed a freebie, others kicked a ball.

She jumped behind a tree when she saw Jacob's sister, Maya.

Wait. Maya?

Trey was seeing Maya??

Alicia rested her head against the tree and looked up at the sky, her heart aching with both humiliation and defeat.

Alicia peered from behind the tree, expecting to see them kissing or embracing. But she didn't see that. Instead she saw Jacob jogging up to Trey with a big smile on his face.

What. The. Hell?

The two men did the typical one arm hug, patting each other on the back, but it was Maya's response that caught Alicia's interest. Maya cupped her face and mimicked making kissy faces. Jacob playfully shoved her away; Trey didn't seem to respond.

The teasing didn't bother him.

Alicia grabbed the front of her shirt as her world tilted.

Trey was seeing Jacob? The man whose wedding day he'd destroyed? And Jacob was smiling at him? Why was Jacob smiling? What was going on? Shouldn't they be enemies?

Maya said something and Trey laughed. He draped his arm around Jacob's shoulders and said something in his ear, making Jacob laugh.

Jacob said something back to Trey and the two men laughed together.

The sound of their laughter should have hurt, angered her, but it was filled with such spirited, loving joy it was as beautiful as a piano concerto ringing in the cathedral of trees.

Maya raced on ahead of them and Jacob pointed to a spot where three towels lay stretched out next to a picnic basket. The two men took their time walking. Jacob gestured and talked while Trey silently listened, his hands in his pockets, his leisurely gait in step with Jacob's.

A true pair.

Alicia crouched closer and watched them sit down. Fortunately, their backs were to her so she could inch closer without them seeing her.

Alicia pulled out her camera and took a picture. Here was her proof. Trey wouldn't be able to deny this.

But it wasn't enough.

She had to hear what they were saying. Was Trey congratulating himself on how much he'd fooled her? And why had Maya gotten herself involved in the sham?

The pieces came together. Trey's affectionate tone whenever he mentioned Jacob. The lack of regret for what he'd done. *I had to save him.*

Alicia now remembered Trey's words with a bitter irony.

By saving Jacob he'd been saving himself and what they shared.

He loved him.

She no longer cared what they had to say. It wouldn't

change anything. Trey liked her but as nothing more than a diversion. Alicia took a step back to retreat, but her action came too late.

Jacob saw her first. Alicia had a wayward bee to blame for her foiled escape. He'd been shooing it away and glanced over his shoulder.

The smile froze on his face.

Maya turned next. Shock became etched on hers.

Then Trey turned. He didn't register shock or surprise instead his eyes narrowed in careful consideration.

He said something to Jacob before he surged to his feet. Jacob reached to stop him but wisely held back before he grabbed him.

Trey stopped a foot away from her. "Alicia," he said his voice holding no regret or remorse but a desperate urgency. His tone surprised her but it was the words that followed her name that froze her broken heart. His eyes darkened with a plea. "You can't tell anyone about this."

CHAPTER FORTY-SIX

Alicia couldn't remember when she started running or why. She remembered her sandals slipping in the soft grass, she remembered hearing someone shouting her name, but all she could think of was how to escape. She didn't want what she'd seen to be true. Trey and Jacob had fooled everyone but most of all they'd fooled her. Or perhaps she'd fooled herself.

"Alicia, wait." She felt the warmth of his large hand grip her wrist before Trey spun her around to face him.

She closed her eyes unable to look at him. "It's okay, I won't say anything," she said then opened her eyes and regretted it because he was too close and smelled so good and she wanted him far away. "There's no one to tell anyway, not that I would."

"I'm sorry I brought you into this."

"Let her go," she heard Jacob say. "Can't you see you're scaring her?"

"I am?" Trey looked at her baffled. "Am I?"

She wanted to nod, but she remained frozen looking into his eyes. Eyes, which at that moment, she wanted to let herself melt into.

He cupped the side of her cheek and she wondered how such tender hands could break her heart, how his gentle gaze made her feel as if he were breaking her in two. She hadn't broken the curse. She was still falling for the wrong kind of man. This time it was someone who could never belong to her. "You were never supposed to see us," Trey said. "We—"

Maya slapped her forehead and groaned. "Trey, you're making it worse."

His eyes didn't leave Alicia's face. "I need her to understand. Please understand."

"It's okay." Alicia yanked herself free. "You don't have to explain anything to me," she said with a shaky laugh. Yes, she'd treat it lightheartedly. Laugh at the fool she'd been. Laugh that she'd thought she'd ever have a chance with him. Heartbreak and failure that was what she was used to.

"I should have known that you wouldn't do anything less for someone you love. You'd sacrifice anything for them."

Trey nodded. "Yes."

"No," Jacob said.

Trey turned to him. "Yes, I would."

"Not the way she thinks."

"What do you mean?"

Jacob ran a hand down his face. "This is when you frustrate me. Look at her face Trey. Really look at it."

Alicia folded her arms. She didn't know why Jacob

was being cruel. It was enough that he had won, did he have to taunt her? Wasn't it enough that Trey had used her?

Alicia felt a light hand on her shoulder and turned to Maya. The younger woman's look of pity hurt even more. "It's not what you think." She waved her hands. "I mean, *really* it's not even close."

Alicia turned. "I should go."

"We're not a couple, Alicia," Jacob said.

"Why would she think we're a couple?" she heard Trey ask. Maya shushed him then whispered, "Be quiet my sweet alien," before Jacob said to Alicia, "We have the loving bond of brothers. Nothing more. Nothing less."

Alicia slowly turned to him her heart lifting with hope. "You mean you're not—?"

"No."

Trey frowned. "We're not what?"

"Lovers," Maya said.

"Why would she think we were lovers?" Trey looked at Alicia confused. "Why would you think—?"

"Shut up, Trey," Maya and Jacob said in unison. Jacob held up his hand before Trey could argue. "I'll explain later. I promise."

Alicia took a deep breath, trying to calm her racing mind. She folded her arms. "So you're telling me that Trey didn't make a scene at the wedding so you two could be together?"

"No." Jacob pointed at Trey without looking at him. "Open your mouth and die."

Trey threw his hands in the air. "But she's not making any sense!" He pounded his chest. "This is important to me. *She's* important to me. I need to understand." He turned to Alicia and gripped her shoulders. "No, don't look at me like that. I don't mean to frighten you. I'd never hurt you. I just don't understand...please explain it to me. Tell me what's going on." He pressed a trembling hand against her cheek. "I know I should have told you about Jacob. You have every right to be angry with me about that—"

"I thought you were cheating on me."

His voice deepened. "Why would you think that?"

She couldn't tell whether he was angry or annoyed. Neither mattered to her, she was finally facing her fears. "Because of the private phone calls and texts." She wiped away a tear. "It's happened to me before. I knew that you were hiding something. I knew there was someone else more important to you than me."

"Important yes. Not more so. Please, don't cry. I'm so sorry. I didn't mean." He took a deep breath. "The truth is I—"

Jacob fastened his hand on the back of Trey's neck and said in a low warning, "Now is not the time."

"I think—"

"You want to risk losing her?"

Trey sent him a cutting glare.

"Then you'll have to trust me."

Trey continued to glare at him; unfazed Jacob stared back.

Alicia looked at the two men in confusion. "What is going on? What are you talking about?"

"Don't try to understand," Maya said with a dismissive wave of the hand. "This is how they are." She lowered her voice. "This staring match used to always crack me up as a kid. Believe it or not they're communicating right now in their own secret code. It'll end in a minute. Don't worry, you'll get used to it. Trey usually breaks first."

As if on cue, Trey made a low growl in his throat and turned away. Jacob smiled.

Maya clapped her hands and said in an exaggerated snotty tone. "Another riveting performance by my stupid brother and his alien friend," she dropped the affected tone and motioned to Alicia, "now will one of you explain a few things to my dear friend here?"

"I'm sorry Alicia," Jacob said.

"Can you forgive me?" Trey said.

Alicia looked at the two men. She scratched her head. "Right now I'm not even sure what to forgive you for. I mean, if you're not lovers, what are you two hiding? Why are you meeting in secret? What was the wedding fiasco about?"

Trey's shoulders sagged. "I can't tell you that."

"But I can." Jacob rested his hands on his hips and released a long, tired sigh. "I think you deserve the full story."

CHAPTER FORTY-SEVEN

A YEAR AGO

It was still hard to say it out loud. The humiliation still burned.

"What happened?" Trey asked Jacob as they walked around Trey's pond enjoying the tranquil peace of a late summer evening. Walking was good. Jacob needed something else to do as he spoke about the pain that still lingered. He couldn't face his friend's too clear gaze right now. Trey always saw more than Jacob wanted him to.

But still Jacob had to tell Trey the truth even though he'd never tell anyone else.

He looked down at his sneakers and told Trey about a couple whose room had been double booked at the hotel where he worked. Jacob had taken the time to get them an even more expensive suite in another hotel only two buildings away, which had been no small feat and the man turned to him and...

Trey stopped walking. He gripped Jacob's arm, forcing him to stop walking too. "What. Happened?"

Jacob took a deep breath, swallowed tears. "He spat on me. A big, fat wad."

He could still feel the sensation of it sliding down his cheek before he wiped it off.

Trey released his grip but didn't move. He didn't say anything, but Jacob wasn't disappointed by that. His friend's stunned, angry silence was more comforting than any words could have been.

Jacob started to walk.

"You have their information, right? Things can be done. If you want them to face a non-fatal accident, it's possible. Both here and abroad."

Jacob couldn't help a smile. Although he knew Trey wasn't joking, it felt good to have someone on his side. "I wouldn't think of it."

"You wouldn't have to, I would. With pleasure and no remorse."

"It's over now." Jacob glanced up at the sky. "I want to quit. I don't want to wait the five years Beth wants me to."

"Did you tell her what happened?"

"I can't." He didn't feel safe being that vulnerable with her. One day he may tell her and make a joke of it, never allowing her to see how deeply he'd been wounded.

"Yes, you can."

"I won't. She doesn't need to know." Jacob pulled out his phone and showed Trey a picture of a brick structure.

"My only regret is not being able to snap up this beauty when it had gone on sale. It used to be a B&B and needs some repairs but I could have done so much with it."

"You should quit your job and—"

Jacob shook his head. "Beth would not be happy with that. Not to mention my family. Leave a prestigious position to run some small B&B? No way."

"It's what you want to do. You're not happy."

Jacob sighed. "Doesn't matter. You can't always be happy."

Trey fell silent for a moment before he said, "You can't marry her."

It was something Trey'd been saying for months. "It's too late. The wedding's just around the corner. There's no way I can back out now."

"But you're not happy."

Jacob hit Trey in the arm annoyed. "What are you a kid? Life isn't about happiness. It's about expectations and promises and pride. I've got my pride. I'm not going to hurt or shame anyone. Besides, Beth didn't say 'never' about me owning a B&B. She's just not ready now." He didn't have grandiose dreams of making a lot of money and climbing a corporate ladder and he needed to give her time to adjust to that.

"She's wrong for you and you know it. Instead—"

"Don't say it."

But even in the sudden silence between them Sandra's name and face came to Jacob's mind. She was completely wrong for him, but he was strangely drawn to her. Someone completely unsuitable. Someone loud, reckless and totally irresistible.

He'd first met her at a garden party Trey had hosted in celebration of Jacob's birthday. Trey didn't host garden parties, or any parties for that matter, that should have been Jacob's first sign that something was amiss, but Beth had been so excited and his parents happy, that Jacob hadn't paid attention to his friend's uncharacteristic behavior.

Beth stood with her parents on the veranda looking over the expansive view while Jacob stood a few yards away, watching Trey staring at something in the pond, lost in thought. He was terrible at parties.

Jacob saw Maya creeping over to Trey with a mischievous grin and headed over to him in order to save his friend, but before Jacob could reach him someone said, "So who took a buzz saw to your hair?"

He turned around to the low smoky voice and met the eyes of a mischievous imp in the form of an Asian woman dressed in jeans and a leather jacket zipped up to her neck. Her hair had been longer then and she'd outlined her eyes in Kohl black.

"Do you know how much this cut cost?"

"You should get a refund."

"You should mind your own business."

"Right now you are my business."

"What?"

She held out her hand. "I'm Sandra Park."

Jacob ignored her outstretched hand wondering if somehow she'd snuck onto the property without anyone knowing. "And that matters because…"

"I'll hopefully be working on a renovation project for Trey. He said if you like me, I'm in." She handed Jacob a card. "You can find out more on my website, but I can tell you—"

"Say no more," Jacob said, wanting her to leave him alone. It wasn't like Trey to ask him about workers, but perhaps it was because Jacob felt more comfortable around women than Trey did. He tucked her card in his pocket. "You're fine. But you'll have to decide whether you want to work with Trey, rather than vice versa. He's different."

Sandra laughed. "I know, I like that."

Her laughter and words filled Jacob's heart with a warm glow and he found himself staring at her with new eyes.

She liked Trey. It was the first time in his life to hear someone say that to him. Even Beth had taken time to warm up to his best friend.

Sandra liked Trey. Understood him. They'd have fun on a renovation project Trey hadn't even told Jacob about yet. The brief surge of jealousy surprised him.

Jacob mentally shook his head. It didn't matter. "So you're an interior designer?"

"I'm a contractor. Says so on my card. Trey didn't tell you anything about me? We've been talking for weeks."

Weeks? Trey had known this woman for weeks? That didn't sound right.

Sandra waved her hand in his face. "Do you need to be plugged in or something?"

"Excuse me for a moment." He didn't give her a chance to say anything, which really wasn't like him because manners were usually very important to him, except when his best friend sidelined him with a woman like that.

Jacob marched up to Trey, who was ignoring whatever Maya was saying, and said to her, "Disappear."

She made a face and said, "Only because it's your birthday," before she stomped off.

Once she was out of hearing, Jacob said, "You could have warned me."

Trey blinked. "Warned you about what? You knew I was having a party for you."

"The contractor."

Trey frowned. "What warning would you need?"

There were times that his friend's obtuseness was exhausting. "Why did you tell her to talk to me?"

"I wanted you to meet her. What did you think?"

It was just like Trey to hire a contractor who went against stereotype. But he couldn't tell him that in his mind he'd thought his contractor should be some burly guy not a woman who could elicit certain thoughts. "She's loud."

Trey nodded in understanding. "Yes, but she's good. No, that's an understatement. She's excellent. I'm lucky she's willing to work with me."

"What's this project anyway?"

A sexy feminine voice interrupted Trey's reply. "Have you gotten over the shock yet?"

Jacob inwardly groaned.

Trey frowned. "Shock?"

"Yes," Sandra said. "You didn't tell him that I was a Korean-American woman with small tits and big ass for one thing." She paused. "Or is it big tits and a small ass?" She winked. "I haven't had that verified in a while."

Trey gave her body the once over. "I'd say you have both equally measured."

"That's what I thought."

Jacob frowned. "You could get in trouble for that."

Trey blinked. "She mentioned it first."

"Relax," Sandra said. "This is a party and I wouldn't file a complaint anyway." She winked at him. And he should be offended, disgusted, instead he felt heat in his cheeks. He noticed she'd opened her leather jacket and wore a T-shirt that said: With the right tools...

He leaned closer trying to figure out what the rest of the message said.

"Are you staring at my tits?"

Jacob jerked back. "No, no absolutely not. I was trying to read your shirt."

Sandra laughed. "I'm just teasing. I know you weren't. And the T-shirt reads: With the right tools...I can make magic."

"That doesn't make any sense," Trey said.

"Depends on the tools."

She wasn't just loud, she had a dirty mind too. Jacob loved a dirty mind. But Trey? How could Trey think he could work with her?

Trey looked at her thoughtful. "What kind of magic are you talking about?"

"The best kind," Sandra said.

But Trey completely missed the innuendo and said, "Can you be more specific?"

"I can be very specific."

Jacob shook his head. "This conversation shouldn't be happening."

"Why not?" Trey asked.

Sandra smiled. "Is he really this sweetly naïve?"

Jacob nearly laughed at that. Nobody had ever referred to Trey as sweet before. But before he could answer her question, Beth called him over to join her and soon he forget about Trey's new contractor.

Except moments like now when he stood at the same spot where she'd teased his friend. Trey didn't tell him about the renovation project and Jacob didn't ask. Although on more than one occasion Trey had mentioned how much fun Sandra was.

Jacob couldn't have fun. Not any longer. A woman like Sandra, a dream like owning a B&B were out of reach.

Although he felt his life closing in on him, he didn't know a way out.

Until Trey gave him one by ruining his wedding. But Jacob later learned Trey'd been planning Jacob's escape even longer than that.

A week after the wedding, he got a package in the mail with the deed for the B&B he'd told Trey about and paperwork that listed a certain entity as a silent partner. Jacob instantly knew it was Trey's doing. Jacob also learned the B&B was the renovation project Trey had hired Sandra for...

∼

"So it was all a lie?" Alicia asked Trey after Jacob finished his story. "You made it all up?"

"No, I was with Beth the night before the wedding," Trey said. "But it was to convince her to go along with my plan."

"How did you do that?"

For a moment Trey looked uncharacteristically ashamed. "This is where I *did* lie. I said I was worried about her not knowing the truth about Jacob. I told her that after their honeymoon Jacob planned to quit his job and open a B&B. I showed her the building I'd bought and convinced her how miserable she'd be living there. It hadn't been hard.

"Once I promised to pay for everything she was onboard. Hinting that I seduced her seemed the best way to make me the villain."

"I'm still amazed you were able to pull it off," Alicia said.

Trey shrugged. "I had to."

"I really didn't think he'd do something like that," Jacob said, "but I didn't try to stop him either. I could have said I'd marry her anyway, but I didn't. I let Beth and Trey take the blame so I could be free because I wasn't ready to let my family know the truth." Jacob ran a hand through his hair. "All this doesn't put me in a very good light, does it?"

"No," Alicia said. "But I know what family pressure's like, so I'm not one to judge."

"I'll tell them the truth one day when the business is on better footing. It's too soon now."

Trey took Alicia's hand. "So can you forgive me now?"

"Walk me back to my car and I'll think about it." She turned to Jacob. "Don't worry, your secret's safe with me." She waved goodbye to him and Maya then headed to the parking lot.

She and Trey walked in silence a few yards before Trey said, "I'm a little disappointed in you."

Alicia stared at him wide-eyed. "Disappointed in *me*?"

He nodded. "Why would you think I was cheating? You're usually more imaginative than that. Why didn't you think I was being stalked or on a special assignment?"

She hung her head and lowered her voice. "I told you...it's happened to me before."

"It won't happen with me." He squeezed her hand. "Besides, I can only manage one woman at a time."

Her head snapped up. She glared at him. "That's supposed to assure me?"

He laughed. "Doesn't it?"

It did, but she didn't want to admit it. "I haven't said I've completely forgiven you yet."

"What do you want me to do?"

She stopped walking and faced him. "I want you to tell me the truth about your night with Beth."

He stilled. "I did tell you the truth. Nothing happened."

"I believe that." She clasped her hands behind her back and headed to her car. "What I don't believe is that you only used money to convince her to follow your plan."

Trey fell in step beside her. "Interesting. Go on."

"I think you worked on Beth a lot longer than anyone would ever suspect. I know you're not as naïve as people think. I saw how she looked at you and how you looked at her. Now that I've gotten to know you a little better I can interpret that look. It was calculating."

"Perhaps."

"Working with her, I got a sense Beth was more in love with the idea of getting married than with Jacob. You felt the same way, didn't you?"

Trey sent her a sideward glance. She could imagine him considering his response. Trey was protecting his friend from the truth.

Alicia decided to probe further. "Or maybe you sensed that she wasn't as devoted to your friend as she should be."

A long silence passed before a quick sharklike grin came and went. "Let me feed that imagination of yours a little," Trey finally said. "Perhaps Beth thought I was interested in her in a way that I wasn't and *maybe* because of that misunderstanding she got the idea to send me pictures and a text. Maybe one night she went too far and I decided to blackmail her with them."

"What do you mean by too far? Did she try to kiss you? Did she stop by your house wearing a raincoat and nothing else? Did she grab your—" Trey's cold, cutting look stopped her words. He found no amusement in her questions and Alicia immediately felt ashamed. Trey wasn't sharing some story plot but the actions of his best friend's fiancée. It must have pained him. "Sorry, I got carried away. Never mind. Do you still have the photos? Were they really explicit?"

Trey hung his head and said in a quizzical tone. "Photos?" Trey looked at her blank. "What photos? I don't know what you're talking about."

Alicia narrowed her eyes at him. "You just said—"

"I gave you a possible scenario and that's all." He grinned. "Let your imagination run wild as it tends to." He stared straight ahead and his voice grew soft. "But there are some things you and Jacob never need to know."

CHAPTER FORTY-EIGHT

"*Trust me.*"

Trey submerged himself under the water of the pool, letting silence embrace him as Jacob's words echoed in his mind.

The watery silence helped stop the sound of crying.

The unbidden auditory memory of someone crying always shook him. He didn't know the source (whether it had been an adult or a child) or the reason. He couldn't remember whether he'd first heard the sound while in Haiti or in the US. He didn't know exactly how old he was when it imprinted in his mind, perhaps four or maybe six, but it had never left him. He remembered lying on something that felt both hard and soft, in a room that smelled of vinegar and bleach with a hint of lemon.

The crying started as a whimper, carrying the incessant misery of a wounded animal, before it dissolved into the deep sound of sorrow.

Sorrow he could do nothing about. He could only listen.

It had been a month since Alicia had discovered the truth about him and Jacob. Only a day since he'd held her in his arms and heard her whisper his name before she fell asleep.

He had saved Jacob but sensed Alicia was in danger now. He sensed that heavy, unspoken misery Jacob had once had. Trey had listened carefully as Alicia told him how happy she was that her parents trusted her. That she was getting used to her role at the company. That she had ideas for another campaign.

But her eyes didn't shine. Her voice was flat. The Alicia he loved was slipping away from him.

His mind began to spin. Alicia needed rescuing.

He remembered his father crying when his business failed; his mother crying when she filed for divorce. His grandmother crying when she'd briefly been forced to look after Trey while his parents fought for custody, he even remembered his aunt and Lavinia crying when his uncle had been particularly cruel.

Trey weathered it all.

His biggest fear was drowning under the weight of someone's tears.

Alicia was crying inside. Hurting. But she wouldn't let him close to her pain.

Trey emerged from the water and took a deep breath. He must not drown. He must keep moving.

He began to swim, struggling to fight back the pain seeping into his heart. He couldn't tell Alicia how much it hurt that she wanted to keep their relationship a secret.

She didn't want to introduce him to her family or friends. Was she ashamed? Afraid he'd act too strange?

"Trust me."

Jacob's words rang in his mind. He was the one person Trey could trust. His friend wanted the best for him and he understood women.

Trey had to be patient, not overeager.

He couldn't reveal his true feelings yet, not until Alicia was ready. She was too fragile now. He didn't want to scare her away and he knew the force of his feelings would do exactly that.

CHAPTER FORTY-NINE

"Trey doesn't know I'm here."

Those were not the words Alicia had expected from the tall bearded man standing on her doorstep. The scent of autumn leaves and wood smoke clung to Carl DeVille's flannel shirt as he passed her and entered without invitation.

Alicia forced a laugh and closed the door behind him. "I'm glad you're telling me that otherwise I'd have to kill Trey for this surprise visit."

The visit was more than a surprise. It was a mini disaster. Her apartment was in no state to host Trey's father. Her housekeeper wasn't scheduled until next week. Alicia frantically scanned her messy living room and quickly picked up the large bags of shrimp crackers and seaweed crisps Trey and Jacob had gotten her addicted to from H Mart, the bags crossed each other like deflated balloons on her coffee table next to a bottle of ginger beer.

She pulled a wayward sweatshirt from the back of the couch, a sock that had found its way on a side table and a pair of jeans left in front of the TV. She dumped them in the closet and closed the door before she motioned Carl to take a seat.

"This won't take long," he said.

"Sounds serious," Alicia said with creeping unease. She'd met Carl three more times since Belize and he'd always been smiling. She wasn't used to seeing him serious like this. "Am I in trouble?"

"Don't know yet."

She rubbed her hands together. "Would you like something to drink?"

He shook his head. "Sit down please."

Alicia did, clasping her hands together.

"If Trey still had his friend Jacob I wouldn't feel the need to be here. My ex and I could always trust Jacob to look out for him but...he's on his own now with no one to look after him so here I am."

If only you knew. "I don't think Trey's on his own. He's got me."

"Hmm."

"Are you sure you don't want something to drink?" Alicia said when Carl fell silent.

"Trey tells me he hasn't met your family yet. Why is that?"

Alicia opened her mouth then closed it, not knowing how to respond. "Is Trey using you to get me to change my mind about that? I told him—"

"Trey isn't using me for anything. I told you he doesn't know I'm here. He'd be angry if he did know, but

I don't care. In a casual conversation I asked what he thought about your family and he told me he hasn't met them yet. None of your friends either. It's been several months now. I want to know why."

Alicia swallowed, Carl's gaze was just as intense as his son. Perhaps even more so because she sensed he didn't trust her. "It's complicated." She stood. "And really none of your business."

Carl stroked his beard. "You're right. My sister was right. This was a waste of time." He stood. "I'd overestimated you."

"Overestimated?"

"I thought Trey had found someone who was proud of him. Proud to have him at their side."

"I am."

Carl walked to the door. "Don't string him along too much longer if you're planning to cut him loose."

"I won't."

"You will. You have no guts."

She rested her hands on her hips. "Say that to my face."

Carl slowly turned to her and she felt her courage ebb. He was protecting his son that made him a fierce opponent.

"Am I wrong?"

Alicia felt her temper flare at the tone of his soft challenge. He didn't repeat his words, he didn't need to. He was waiting for her to prove him wrong. She planned to. "I'm not ashamed of Trey. I never have been. I'm protecting him. My family can be suffocating."

"And you don't think they'll like him?"

"I don't care about that."

"I think you do. I think their opinion matters more than you're willing to admit."

She hated how true that was. Her hands fell to her sides. "That has nothing to do with Trey."

"It has everything to do with him. The problem with Trey is that people think he doesn't feel the way the rest of us do, but he does. Sometimes more than you can imagine."

Alicia returned to her couch and sat down, feeling more worn than angry. "I know that."

Carl sat in front of her. "Really?"

"Yes, I know how caring he is. How wonderful he is."

Carl nodded. "Okay."

She gripped her hand into a fist. "I won't give him up."

"I'm not asking you to. I'm asking you to be fair to him." He sighed and leaned forward, resting his arms on his knees. "Has he told you anything about me?"

Alicia hesitated. "He said you have a special gift."

Carl nodded again, this time more slowly, his green eyes never leaving her face. "Is that all he said?"

"Uh...just how happy he is that you're his dad."

Carl leaned back and folded his arms. "So he didn't tell you I'm the reason he doesn't like being grabbed?"

CHAPTER FIFTY

Wordlessly, Alicia shook her head.

A grim smile touched his lips. "Somehow I didn't think so." Carl stroked his beard. "I probably married too young. I was painting dorm rooms at the height of summer in New Orleans when I met my ex. Not only did she offer me cold pressed apple juice that humid day she offered me a chance at being normal. Something I never felt at the time I could be. My gift made that hard.

"I'd gotten a degree but didn't see myself in an office or working for anyone so went from one menial job to the next. I didn't have much going for me but getting married at twenty-three seemed like a good idea at the time.

"My ex gave me some stability and I even started a moving and storage business when we moved to Virginia. When I had that dream about Trey I was twenty-seven years old. It felt right.

"But I didn't realize my business and my marriage

were already in trouble by the time we adopted him. My gift didn't help me see that. It was as if I could see everyone else's life clearer than my own.

"I loved being a dad." Carl voice softened with wistfulness. "I remember Trey's first Christmas with us and his serious little face when I handed him a present. A medium sized box with green wrapping paper and a red ribbon and a bow. Trey's eyes widened and he held it.

"He held it so long that my ex and I assumed he didn't know what to do next, so I took the present from him and began to tear the wrapping paper and he started to cry. When I asked him why he was crying he said I was 'breaking' his gift. I tried to explain to him that the *real* gift was inside. But he didn't care. He wouldn't stop crying until I fixed his gift.

"I had to get masking tape and everything and make it look like new. I actually ended up having to buy a second gift 'unwrapped' so that he'd accept the original toy we'd bought for him." Carl shook his head and laughed. "He was an odd one even back then and I loved him so much, but I didn't handle the stress of my struggling business and rocky marriage well. I wanted to be numb.

"Drink seemed the best way to do that. Just a few sips here and there to take off the edge of life. I didn't realize I had a problem until it was a lifestyle.

"I was numb but one thing that still managed to reach my heart, still made me feel and mattered to me more than anything was Trey."

Carl briefly closed his eyes, furrowed his brow. "I was supposed to be his protector. But one night, with my business facing bankruptcy, I got into an argument with my ex. I don't even know what triggered it. Anything could trigger me in those days. But this time she told me she was leaving me and taking Trey with her.

"I was not having that. Trey was the reason I existed. He was *my* son. Mine. No one could have him.

"She called Trey to the living room and told him they were leaving. She took one little hand in hers. I grabbed the other. She tugged. I tugged. She pulled.

"I pulled harder. So hard I heard a pop before Trey screamed. I'd dislocated his shoulder.

"I still remember letting him go and seeing the sight of his arm dangling at an odd angle beside his little body. I felt sick.

"Thank God the doctors were able to put it back in place. He didn't suffer any torn ligaments or permanent damage." Carl let his arms fall to his side. "But the worst part was that I was sober that night. It was a rare moment, but a real one. I had nothing and nobody to blame but myself. It could have been easy to blame my temper on one too many beers. But I hadn't even had a drop of whiskey." He smiled without humor. "That would come later." He shook his head in regret. "I saw my life slipping from my fingers and let myself get drunk on rage and it blinded me.

"In that moment I forgot Trey was a child, an individual separate from me. He became a possession, a symbol of who I was as a man.

"I worked hard to turn my life around and make it up to him. Make up for my failures. I haven't touched a drop in nearly thirty years. I eventually got custody of him. I determined he'd get the best of everything—from schooling to vacations. I know my best wasn't always good enough, things that he experienced as a black boy that I didn't see or understand. Things that my love couldn't shield him from.

"But every day I remember how I failed him that night. He's forgiven me, but I haven't forgiven myself."

Carl stood. "Trey's easy to use. He will be there for you. But if you can't do the same for him, it's best to let him go now. I've already left him with emotional scars, I'm not going to stand by and watch you leave fresh ones."

Alicia followed him. "I won't."

Carl opened the door then turned to her. "Like I said, the problem with my gift is I might miss things about myself, but I can see other people clearly." He measured her in one sweeping glance. "And right now I see a woman who tells herself she's protecting Trey, but is really protecting herself. I hope I'm wrong." He walked out and closed the door.

Alicia told herself Carl was wrong. She told herself he was wrong for the next six months as fall turned to winter then spring. Trey showered her with gifts—pink gold dangling earrings, a trip to Hawaii, a dark blue silk dress. She kept him to herself even more. She avoided seeing Carl again, coming up with excuses so that Trey wouldn't suspect anything different about her.

She didn't want Carl to see the truth-that Trey was her anchor. Trey kept her from drowning.

But she wasn't using him. She loved him.

Her love for him helped her through her many crying

fits sitting alone in an empty parking lot. As she ate her way through her misery of each passing day, gaining fifteen pounds until she didn't want to look at herself in the mirror anymore. Her parents continued to praise her. Edwin and Pauline no longer could put her down.

Trey continued to make her feel beautiful and smart.

Even as her heart continued to break.

CHAPTER FIFTY-ONE

A broken bed.

The irony wasn't lost on him. Jacob remembered teasing Beth about breaking the headboard after one energetic encounter. If his life had turned out differently he would have celebrated his one year anniversary. Instead he was trying to fix a four poster bed at three in the morning because two over exuberant honeymooners had broken it.

But at least he had customers. Business was slow but steadily growing.

The newlyweds had apologized and Jacob had assured them it was fine although it really wasn't. His patchwork lasted until the couple left, but without professional intervention the bed would break again. Unfortunately, a new bed was going to cost him even more than repairing it.

The following evening, when his remaining guests were safely asleep in their rooms, he called Sandra.

He'd grown dependent on her, especially after she'd saved his gazebo and turned it into a bench with a lattice canopy; she'd even gotten a landscaper friend to twine ivy around it. Jacob had already prepared three dinners and two lunches for her, but breakfast seemed a long way off. He was biding his time. She was smart, attractive and he liked any excuse to see her again but he didn't want to ruin what they had.

When Sandra arrived Jacob led her straight to the bedroom and nodded to the bed. "What do you think? Can it be saved?"

"Yes, but with help. Shame. It's a beautiful bed." She checked underneath then stood. "What did they do to it?"

"I'd rather not know."

Sandra sent him a sly grin. "Really?"

"Perhaps I should just get a new bed."

"Okay, I'll stop teasing you."

But it wasn't her teasing that bothered him. It was the crazy thought that had slipped into his mind. He knew several ways the couple have broken the bed and briefly he'd thought of Sandra doing two of them—naked except for her tool belt. He even imagined testing it out together to see if it could hold them and—

"Jacob?"

He blinked. "Huh?"

Sandra sat on the bed and patted the space beside her. "Sit down."

"Why?"

"Earth to Jacob I told you why. I want to see if it creaks with our weight."

"I'll just get another bed."

"Relax I won't jump you." She grabbed the front of his shirt and pulled him forward. If he'd known what she was about to do he would have been prepared to stop her, instead he was caught off-guard and fell forward right on top of her.

For a brief moment he didn't move. He was afraid to because any movement would put him in even deeper contact with her soft body.

"Well, that's a success," Sandra said with a laugh. "Looks like it can hold us."

Jacob rolled away and stared up at the ceiling. "Sorry about that."

"I didn't expect you to try to replicate the honeymooners."

"I wasn't. I tripped because—"

"I know," Sandra said with a sad laugh. "I was just teasing you again. I know you'd never—"

He turned sharply to her. "I'd never what?"

"Nothing."

"No, finish what you were going to say."

"I don't want to." She stood. "The good new is you don't have to get a new bed. I know how to fix it." She opened the door. "I'll just—"

Jacob slammed the door shut.

"Careful or we'll have to repair that too."

"Tell me what you were going to say."

Sandra sent him a strange look. "You really don't know?"

Jacob didn't move.

"Fine. I know you'd never sully your pristine reputation with someone like me. I'm a buddy, a friend. Someone to pass the time with when you're bored and nothing more. Happy now?"

"You're wrong."

"About what?"

"Everything. About me. About you." His voice deepened. "Definitely what I think about you." He covered her mouth with his, her lips as soft and inviting as he'd imagined.

He felt her tremble before she deepened the kiss and he felt her hands sliding up his back.

Jacob drew away before he lost control and shook his head. "Nooo. Nope. I can't do this. I have my limits."

Sandra looked at him hurt but hid it behind a smile. "Right. I should—"

"Rooms designated for the guests are sacred." He took her hand. "But my room isn't." He led her to his room. She stopped in the doorway and stared.

He looked at her uncertain. "What is it?"

"I forgot to dream about this part."

Jacob pulled off his shirt and flexed his muscles, pleased when he saw the hunger in her eyes. "For some reason ladies like dreaming about me."

Sandra made a face. "In my dreams, you didn't speak."

He winked. "So you dreamed about me more than once?"

She rested her hands on her hips. "They were short."

"Mine weren't." He grinned at the surprise on her face. "You were always holding a tool."

Her gaze dipped to the front of his trousers. "Was I

ever holding you?" She laughed pleased she'd shocked him into silence. She slowly walked towards him. "Want to compare notes?" She slid her hand down his bare chest. "Because I can recall each one in detail."

"I'd rather you show me."

Sandra took off her T-shirt. "I'll do my best, but I always pictured you in your office. I never imagined you in a bed like this."

Jacob didn't need to look at his bed to imagine her impression of it.

The massive iron framed bed and arched headboard was nearly swallowed by a navy blue oversized duvet covet set and four pillows. One of the few luxuries he'd allowed himself. Not only was it comfortable and suited him he felt it was somewhere he could hide.

He wasn't sure if Sandra was pleased or horrified by the sight of it, but he didn't care. He drew her close and unhooked her bra. "The good thing is," he said, leaning back on the bed and pulling her down with him. "I don't see this bed breaking."

"But if it does," Sandra whispered against his lips, her husky tone making his skin tingle. "I know how to put it back together."

CHAPTER FIFTY-TWO

*J*acob: *Maya finally dumped Grayson.*
Trey: *I know.*
Jacob: *How?*
Trey: *I made sure.*
Jacob: *How'd you do that?*
Trey: *Ask Maya.*

Four hours later
Jacob: *You threatened Grayson?*
Trey: *Define threaten.*
Jacob: *No. Did you threaten him?*
Trey: *What did Maya tell you?*
Jacob: *That you scared him so bad that he wet himself.*

Two minutes later
Jacob: *Is that true?*

Trey: *He made her cry. I stopped it. She dumped him. The end.*

Jacob: *Thanks.*

THREE DAYS later

Jacob: *I'm seeing Sandra now.*

Trey: *Good.*

Jacob: *Have you told Alicia you love her yet?*

Trey: *No.*

Jacob: *You can tell her you love her now.*

Trey: *Not going to.*

Jacob: *Why not?*

Trey: *Won't make a difference.*

Jacob: *What do you mean?*

A MINUTE later

Jacob: *Trey? Come on.*

THIRTY SECONDS later

Jacob: *What's going on? Did you panic? Did she freak out?*

Jacob: *Tell me what's going on. Are you okay?*

Jacob: *Do you need me to talk to her?*

Jacob: *Fine. I won't push. You don't have to tell me anything just let me know you're okay.*

Trey: <okay hand signal>

Jacob stared at the text image barely feeling the spring breeze as he stood in his garden. It was a unique quiet moment before he had to clean a bedroom and prepare for dinner. He'd given his guests information about an exhibit they might enjoy in town before he'd texted his friend.

Trey may say he was okay, but Jacob sensed he was far from it. Trey wasn't going to tell Alicia he loved her? That didn't sound like Trey at all. By now he'd expected Trey to have bought her an engagement ring, planned their wedding, honeymoon and the first five years of their married life.

But he hadn't. Even when Jacob had had a chance to talk to him Trey rarely talked about Alicia.

Trey was hiding something from him; few things frightened Jacob more than that. Trey only pulled away when he was in pain.

Jacob paced the garden grounds trying to figure out what to do. Trey was the reason Jacob's life had turned around. But he couldn't be happy with his business and girlfriend when his friend was hurting.

Jacob had to figure out what was going on.

However, when he spoke to Alicia she seemed distracted and didn't sense that anything was wrong with Trey. She seemed to care about him just as much as she always did. That was a relief. But not enough.

That night before bed he sent Trey another text.

Jacob: *Can we meet?*

Trey: *I'm traveling soon.*

Jacob: *Business?*

Trey: *Yes.*

Jacob: *How soon?*

Trey: *Soon. Look after Alicia for me.*

Jacob: <smile> *You want me to juggle two women?*
Trey: *I trust you.*
Jacob: *Enough to tell me what's wrong?*

Minute later

Jacob: *You know I love you, right? I'm there for you. You're sure you're okay?*

Trey: *I'm fine. I'm glad you got Sandra.*

Jacob set his cell phone down on his side table, a chill sweeping over him. Trey's text was ominous instead of reassuring. He was definitely pulling away. Jacob always had plenty of friends. Trey never worried about him being alone, but this time it was like he was pushing Sandra forward as a replacement.

But nobody could replace Trey.

Jacob didn't send anymore texts but he knew sleep wouldn't come easy that night.

Something was wrong with Trey.

He had to find out what.

CHAPTER FIFTY-THREE

Thud!

Trey awoke to darkness and felt the empty space beside him. Alicia should have been lying there. He'd spent the weekend at her place before he was off to a dig in Argentina.

He left the bedroom and found Alicia in the kitchen holding a pint of ice cream. He glanced at the microwave clock.

He rubbed his eyes. "It's three thirty-seven in the morning. What are you doing?"

A sheepish smile touched her lips. "I'm sorry. I didn't mean to wake you. I opened the freezer and it fell out."

That didn't surprise Trey. Recently he wondered how Alicia managed to close the freezer since she'd stuffed it with so many popsicles, custards and ice cream cartons he half feared she'd be knocked out by a frozen projectile.

His eyes swept over the once clean living room now

littered with snack bags and ginger beer, a pile of cloth samples under the side table and three yellow pads scattered on the coffee table. When they'd gone to bed together only four hours ago the living room had been clean—he'd made sure.

"How long have you been up?" he asked her.

"I don't know," she said with a nervous laugh. She put the ice cream carton on the counter. "Is today Sunday?"

He nodded.

"Right. Tomorrow's Monday. I have a meeting on Monday. Two I think and then another on Thursday."

"Alicia."

"I really hate meetings. I don't even know why we have them."

"Alicia."

"But my family seems to love them." Another nervous laugh. "So I'll learn to love them too," she said between sharp, quick breaths. "And they're proud of me. They respect me. I'm doing a good job. So good that R&D wants my feedback on a new fabric they're developing and our designer is considering a new line and also wants my input. I'm succeeding. I have to keep succeeding."

Trey grabbed her shoulders when she gripped the front of her nightshirt and began gulping for air. "Alicia, what's wrong?"

"I...can't...breathe."

He rested a hand on her chest, his voice firm. "You can breathe. You're going to be okay. Start small and slow.

One breath. Two breaths. Three...yes, that's it. I've got you."

Alicia squeezed her eyes shut. "It's too much. I don't know how I can keep going. I don't want—"

"Shh." Trey held her close for a moment then led her to the couch. "Sit down. I'll be right back." He grabbed the cover from the bed and wrapped it snugly around her. "When I was a kid, this would make me feel safe. I know it's not much."

Alicia flashed a watery smile. "It's perfect."

Trey looked around the living room wondering where he should clean first. He had to create order. But did he start with the coffee table or the floor?

"I wish I could be normal," Alicia said in a small voice.

He sat down beside her. "I wish I could be normal too. Whatever that is." He cupped the side of her face. "But you shouldn't think you need to be anyone else but you."

Alicia rested her cheek against his palm. "I can do this. This job, anything. I can make this work as long as I have you."

His gaze shifted, he let his hand fall. "Alicia—"

"I love being with you. Especially at times like this. You don't judge me. As long as you're with me you make everything bearable. I treasure all the nights and week-ends we get to be together."

"Yet you're still unhappy." Trey turned away from her and said in a soft voice, "I'm not enough."

She stared at him. "Yes, you are."

He shook his head.

Alicia stared at him for a long, tense moment. "What are you trying to say? Are you going to leave me?"

Trey leaned forward, looking down at his hands.

"I don't blame you. You've gotten tired of me, right? Why would a man like you want a pathetic, sloppy, fat, ugly girlfriend?"

Trey closed his eyes, his brows drew together in pain and Alicia knew she was hurting him (*It hurts me when you put yourself down*) but couldn't seem to stop herself. Even though she knew her words weren't true, they were how she felt.

She hated who she'd become. She could hardly recognize herself anymore when she looked in the mirror. She hated buying larger sized clothes in styles she didn't like. She hated the heavily painted face due to the foundation she'd used to hide the dark circles under her eyes because of sleepless nights. Sometimes, she even hated when Trey held her close and she felt his firm, healthy body. He felt so vibrantly alive when she felt like the living dead.

She didn't want to hurt him.

But rage felt better than sadness.

"Are you going to do to me what you did with Jacob? Are you going to come up with some elaborate scheme and then leave me? Do you think you know what's best for everyone else?"

His jaw twitched.

"It must be nice to be so superior, the all knowing observer. Jacob and I are like Liz to you, right? Do you have a little journal about me where you monitor my eating habits and mood?"

She saw a tear fall and the sight nearly broke her. She

closed her eyes. *You have no guts,* that's what Carl had said. *I already left scars I don't want you to leave new ones.*

She hated proving him right. "I don't need this. I already got a lecture from your father."

Trey turned sharply to her. "You spoke to my father?"

Alicia silently swore. She hadn't meant for him to find out about that. "It was nothing."

"What did he say?"

"Nothing."

Trey froze her with a dark look. "What did he say?"

Alicia looked down unable to face him. "He basically said I didn't deserve you and maybe he's right." She met his gaze. "No, he *is* right. I'm a coward. A gutless coward. I can't stand up to my family—"

"Let me help you."

She struggled out of the blanket. "No. I have to do this on my own."

"Alicia, if I can't help you then I'm no use to you."

"Don't you get it? I don't need your help. I don't need you telling me how to live my life. I don't need to be rescued. Because if you do then I have to admit that I'm a failure. That I can't stand on my own. And I can't be that again.

"My life isn't perfect, but you already knew that. I'm asking you to accept me as I am. You just said I shouldn't have to be anybody else but me." She pounded her chest. "Well, this is me. Flaws and all. I need your support. I need you to support me no matter what and...Stop shaking your head like that."

"I can't do what you're asking me to. Not anymore. Not when I see you so unhappy. Let me—"

"You won't accept me as I am?"

Trey covered his eyes and groaned. "That's not what I'm saying."

Alicia took his hands in hers, hope in her eyes and voice. "Then let's not argue. Let's forget about tonight and go back to bed."

Trey pulled his hands away and sighed, frustrated. "Alicia—"

A coldness crept over her heart. "You *are* thinking of leaving me."

He lowered his gaze.

"If that's what you want, then go I won't stop you."

He didn't move.

She pushed him. "Just go. If you're going to leave anyway you might as well go now." She pushed him hard. "Go." In her heart she screamed 'See Carl I do love him. I love him so much I'm pushing him off this sinking ship of my life. I'm freeing him to find someone else, someone better.'

She would drive Trey away with all the love she could muster. She wouldn't use him anymore.

Alicia shoved him a third time, but he still wouldn't move. "I said go!"

"Is that really what you want?" Trey asked, his tone flat and courteous like a waiter at a high end restaurant.

They were already becoming strangers. "Yes."

"That will make you happy?"

She wanted to say yes, but couldn't take her lie that far. She'd miss him so much, the thought of losing him turned her stomach into knots. But she couldn't relent. Trey had suffered enough misery in his life, she didn't need to add to it. Letting him go would be the bravest thing she ever did.

She wrapped the blanket tight around herself and closed her eyes. "I'm tired. Turn off the lights when you go." She felt the weight of the couch shift as he stood, heard him shuffling around in the kitchen before he headed to the bedroom. She fell asleep, exhausted by regret and sorrow, before she heard him leave.

She might have dreamed she felt the soft touch of his hand against her cheek and neck, the featherlike touch of his lips against hers. When Alicia opened her eyes the next morning to a cleaned living room—Trey had cleared all the snack bags, stacked the yellow pads, organized the cloth samples and placed them on the coffee table—she laughed before she broke down and cried.

CHAPTER FIFTY-FOUR

It wasn't an exaggeration to say that Carl *knew* Trey was coming for him. He'd opened the Falls Church antiques store early that Monday morning ready for a showdown and he wasn't disappointed.

Trey walked through the front door of the medium sized brick faced building bringing in the ice cold breeze with him and sent Carl a look as ominous as the glint of a pistol.

The clerk and stock manager froze in fear near the display of dish ware. Their expressions should have bothered Carl. It usually irked him when people looked at his son with fear and suspicion first, especially when Trey just walked into a room and wasn't doing anything, but at that moment, when Trey filled the entryway with silent determination Carl couldn't blame them.

Trey looked menacing.

Carl smiled at his staff and told them about the special on stuffed toys (he'd gotten a bit too many from an estate sale) before he motioned Trey to his back office—safe and out of sight.

"You had no right," Trey finally said once they were alone in Carl's cramped, windowless office. It still had the faint scent of stale cigars from the previous owner.

Carl sat behind his oak desk. One with silver handles and three drawers Trey had helped him pick out. He opened the top drawer and pulled out a pack of mint flavored gum. "To do what?"

Trey remained standing with his arms folded. "The names you called Alicia—"

Carl's brows shot up. He took a stick of gum from the pack. "She told you I called her names?"

"Was she lying?"

Carl folded the gum in his mouth then began to chew. "Depends on what she said."

Trey twisted his lips as if he'd tasted something foul. "You said she was gutless and that she didn't deserve me."

Carl chewed for a few seconds before he nodded. "No, she wasn't lying."

"You had no right to say those things."

Carl tossed the gum pack back in the drawer and slowly closed it, keeping a reign on his temper. He and Trey could disagree about a number of things, but one thing Carl never wanted to get between them was a woman. "I had every right. Do you think I'd stand around and watch a woman use you?"

"She wasn't using me."

"She hasn't introduce you to anybody she knows. She kept you a secret. If she's hiding you from them, what could she be hiding from *you*?"

"She's not like that."

"How do you know?"

"I know her. She's got a good heart, she's just unhappy."

Carl pointed at him. "And that's the problem. You care about everyone else's happiness above your own."

"That's not true."

"What happened between you and Jacob?"

Trey let his arms fall to his side. "I didn't come here about that."

"I don't care."

Trey turned. "I'm done talking."

Carl came around the desk and grabbed Trey's arm before he reached the door. Because he knew what to expect he was prepared for Trey to violently pull away, but Carl didn't give him the chance. He held Trey tight then pulled him close into a one arm hug.

Trey struggled to free himself and growled. Carl knew his son's pain was both physical and emotional. He still didn't let go.

"Listen to me," Carl said in an urgent voice. "Your mother and I did a piss poor job of raising you if you think you deserve to be mistreated like this."

Trey gritted his teeth. "Alicia cares about me."

"Then why are you here? Why didn't Alicia tell you the full reason I spoke to her instead of just the parts she knew would hurt you?"

Trey shook his head. "No, it's not like that. She has a lot to think about. She didn't want me—"

"I didn't raise my son to be somebody's secret! She needs to earn the right to be with you." Carl choked back tears. "I'm sorry I didn't give you the childhood you deserved. I'm sorry I hurt you the way I did."

"I'm tired of being the constant source of your guilt."

"No," Carl said with feeling. "No, that's not it. Don't you see? You're the source of my strength. There's a reason I have a picture of you on my desk. Because I'm proud of my son and I'm not afraid to show it. Every chance I get I talk about you. Do you know the one thing your mother and I can talk about without fighting? You. How much we love you.

"Having you in my life is the greatest gift I could ever have hoped for. I will fight for you. I will make sure you're never alone. You are not a rock to be kept in someone's pocket hidden from view. You deserve the light. You are worthy of so much love. As long as I have breath I will stand by your side. You call and I will be there for you. Anyone else who loves you, truly loves you, will feel and do the same."

Carl felt the tension in Trey's body ease and closed his eyes against tears as his son finally heard and felt his words. "I wasn't enough," Trey said in a quiet, broken voice.

"You're more than enough," Carl said, holding him tight. "Always will be."

Trey hugged his father back although his body still ached and the emotional pain stayed fresh. He needed something to hold onto since he couldn't disappear under the waves.

The audio memory of someone crying roared to life: Louder and more insistent this time. He feared drowning; his father's embrace the only thing keeping him afloat.

The sound of whimpering grew and in a flash it all became clear. He remembered.

He remembered the sound of sorrow hadn't belonged to someone else. It had belonged to him.

He'd been hiding under his grandmother's kitchen sink, wrapped in a green cotton blanket, crying. He'd been about five years old remembering his time at the orphanage when a soft brown hand and a voice like music had told him he was a lucky boy. "You've been chosen. You're going to make your new parents very happy." But hidden in his grandmother's kitchen Trey realized he hadn't made anybody happy. His parents were so sad. That made him sad too.

He couldn't block the memory out now. The pain cut deep.

All these years he hadn't feared the tears of others, but the well of sorrow that lived within him. He held onto his father.

He thought of Alicia. He understood her pain but she wouldn't let him help her. The thought of her suffering alone nearly ripped him apart. She'd pushed him away, but he couldn't stay gone.

"I have to save her." Trey drew back and stared at his father. "Even if she doesn't love me, even if I can never be what she needs. I know I'm not making any sense and I know what you think of her. But she's different."

He dug into his trouser pocket and pulled out a folded Post-It. He unfolded it and revealed a smiley face. "She leaves these notes around for me to find—on fridge doors, on table tops, in my pockets. They make me happy. She cares about me in her own way."

"You're worth fighting for."

He put the note away. "Fighting tends to end with winners and losers. I don't want that. I've never had someone like her in my life before. I'm used to being pushed away and I don't care anymore. I will not rest until I see a smile on her face again."

Carl sighed. "And I know I can't stop you."

"I'm off to Argentina for a week." He was helping a local company with their surveying equipment as they mapped out new energy resources. "I'll start on my plan when I return."

"She's lucky to have you."

Carl walked Trey to the front exit and waved as he got into his car but before he turned a feeling of dread gripped him.

A fear he'd never see Trey again.

CHAPTER FIFTY-FIVE

*J*acob nearly buckled under a wave of nausea as he changed the bedsheets in one of the unbooked guest rooms.

Something was wrong, he felt a wave of loss, but he couldn't pinpoint what or why.

Seconds later he received a call from Maya.

He stared at her phone number. It wasn't like her to call.

"What?"

"Did you hear about the avalanche?"

"Avalanche? What avalanche?"

"In Argentina." She shared the location. "A bunch of people are missing. Didn't you tell me Trey was going there?"

"Uh...I'll get back to you."

With cold fingers Jacob dialed Trey's phone. The call didn't go through. He thought of calling Alicia but didn't want to worry her any more than necessary. What if it was nothing?

But what if it was? What was this strange feeling of loss?

Trey had to be okay. He couldn't be dead.

But knowing Trey, he'd laugh at the irony of being crushed underneath the rocks he loved so much.

Trey wouldn't even face death the ordinary way.

Dead. Trey couldn't be dead.

A roiling nausea swept through him again and he made it to the bathroom just in time.

He flushed the toilet and washed his face with hot water. He began to shake. He felt so cold.

So damn cold.

Trey couldn't be dead.

Jacob closed his eyes as he remembered one hot summer when he was about eleven. Trey had come over to play at Jacob's house. That day the house smelled like fried fish and fermented bean paste. Maya played alone in her bedroom, Yong sat at the dinner table studying, ever the dutiful student even on summer break, while he and Trey sat watching a movie from the seventies with Jacob's parents.

At that time Jacob loved any movie featuring sports so *Brian's Song* seemed a safe bet even if it was old. He'd thought it was about football but it was really about the friendship of Brian Piccolo and Gale Sayers.

Jacob remembered his mother tearing up when Brian got sick and the hospital bed scene even choked his father a little and Jacob would never admit his eyes had watered too.

But Trey stared transfixed and as his family held back tears at the ending, Trey smiled and said, "That's us."

Jacob remembered being annoyed with Trey. Jacob didn't like anything to do with death or dying. Even Halloween scared him—all those skeletons and zombies.

But Trey had only noticed Brian and Gale's love for each other.

Too late Jacob feared Trey knew something that he never had: That their friendship was not something to take for granted. That he might lose him forever one day.

Jacob gripped the sink bowl and stared at his reflection. All that he had achieved now—a new girlfriend who understood him, a new business that suited him, a life he loved—he had one person to thank.

Trey had risked not only their friendship but his reputation for Jacob to be free.

But Jacob could never be free if his friend was buried under the weight of a lie.

The world needed to know who Trey really was.

Jacob's heart pounded with renewed purpose. He thought of the kid he'd once been who'd wanted a superpower. He now realized all a superhero really needed was courage and the willingness to act.

He wouldn't hide anymore.

He would reclaim his life and live it boldly without shame and guilt.

He'd be happy.

Because Trey would have wanted that.

CHAPTER FIFTY-SIX

Lawrence Bae had harbored a guy crush on Jacob Kim since Lawrence was twelve years old. It hadn't ebbed in the thirteen years since. Although Jacob was considered the dumb but handsome one of his family, Lawrence admired Jacob's charm, his way with the ladies and easygoing manner with everyone around him.

Jacob hadn't come to church in years, but today…

"Ya!" Lawrence's mother cried, hitting him hard on the shoulder. "Are you trying to kill us?"

Lawrence ducked his head in apology and focused back on the road to make sure the family Hyundai didn't drift into another lane and get side swiped by the truck barreling down beside them.

He glanced at his father who pretended to be sleeping. His father always pretended to be tired after church, leaving Lawrence the one to drive the family back home under his mother's watchful eye.

She was always an extra vigilant backseat driver on Sundays as if she expected God to be ever eager to take them to heaven. Lawrence looked in the rearview mirror. His younger brother kept his gaze glued to the game on his cell phone while his sister bobbed her head to a song only she could hear from her earbuds.

Lawrence slowed at a traffic light—the red light reminding him of the sight of Jacob's red socks as he walked up to the stage. The choir had finished singing and Lawrence remained on the stage sitting at the piano when Jacob had whispered something to the pastor.

Jacob walked across the stage and stood behind the podium like a rock star dressed in black trousers, black shirt and black jacket. His thick black hair sleeked back only emphasizing his angular jaw and handsome face. "I have a confession to make," he said.

"We're not Catholics," someone shouted from the upper balcony making everyone laugh.

"True," Jacob said with a smile, "but I still owe you all the truth." He took a deep breath. "I quit my job and started a B&B not because of my ruined wedding but because it was something I'd always wanted to do. But I didn't have to courage so my best friend, Trey DeVille, forced my hand. He lied about being with the bride." He looked around the church. "My ruined wedding last year was all staged."

A collective gasp swept through the congregation.

"My best friend, Trey DeVille, came up with a plan so that I could be free." Jacob turned to his stunned family. "I didn't want to disappoint you. I'm sorry. But I don't want to live a lie anymore.

"Right now Trey's missing. I can't reach him. No one can. I ask for you to pray for him. Pray that they find him. I need to see him again even if it's for one last time."

Jacob left the podium and walked out of the church, for a brief moment just a silhouette in the doorway outlined by the light glow of a winter sun, leaving a stunned silence behind him.

Lawrence had sighed in amazement and admiration, resisting the urge to put his hands on the piano keys and play Handel's Hallelujah.

Jacob would forever be his hero.

He'd given Lawrence courage he hadn't known he needed. He was finishing up his second master's degree but didn't really care about it. He hadn't cared about much except being the dutiful eldest son. He'd been studying corporate law but music law really fascinated him.

Something else fascinated him too.

Jacob's sister, Maya. He'd seen her on campus a couple of times and hadn't had the courage to approach her.

The next chance he got.

He'd seize it.

CHAPTER FIFTY-SEVEN

He's alive.

Alicia looked at the text from Jacob and thought it was a joke she couldn't figure out. She took a sip of her extra sweetened coffee (she desperately needed both the sugar and caffeine) before she sat back in her office chair and replied.

Alicia: *Who's alive?*

Jacob: *Trey.*

Alicia: *Why wouldn't Trey be alive?*

When Jacob didn't immediately respond she called him. "What's going on?"

Jacob swore. "Sorry, I thought you already knew."

"About what?"

"The avalanche."

Her heart began to race. *Avalanche? What avalanche? Trey had been involved in an avalanche!!* "I've been busy at work," she lied not wanting Jacob to know she and Trey had broken up.

"Right," Jacob said in understanding. "It happened so fast but felt like forever. Maya sent me a text and we'd both tried to reach him for nearly a day. We just learned that he hadn't even been there because his father warned him it was dangerous, so he'd been at another remote location and couldn't receive cell phone service. He's fine and didn't even understand why we were worried." He laughed. "Again, sorry. I didn't mean to bother you."

"No, I'm glad you told me. He's still gone for about a week, right?"

"Right."

"Jacob—"

"Sorry, Alicia, I gotta go prepare two rooms before guests arrive this evening."

"Okay, bye."

Alicia set down her cell phone, her mind spinning. All of a sudden the meetings, her parent's praise, beating her siblings at something, the profit and loss, didn't mean anything to her anymore.

If Trey had died her family would never have known what a wonderful person he was and how much he'd meant to her. He'd been more than a face for MedForm, he'd been her inspiration and love.

If Trey had died she'd never have gotten the chance to introduce him to Deanna.

If Trey had died her last words to him would have been... No she didn't want to remember them.

If Trey had died her last memory of him would be the pain on his face before she closed her eyes and told him to go.

Alicia opened her desk drawer and pulled out the

stone Trey'd given her. If Trey had died this would be one of the few things left to remember him by.

But Trey hadn't died. He was still alive in this world and that meant she had a second chance.

Alicia surged to her feet. Trey was alive!

She could be alive too. She could shine bright again like the sunlight that seemed caught in the stone.

She didn't care what her family thought of her. She didn't care if she let them down again. She didn't care about failure or success.

She cared about Trey. She cared about being brave enough to be the woman he deserved. She cared about loving him—and herself—again.

No more lies.

Alicia grabbed her coat and left her office. "I'm out for the rest of the day," she told Fabian.

Fabian stared at her open-mouthed. "But you have a meeting—"

"Tell them it's an emergency."

"They won't be happy about that."

"I know." Alicia smiled feeling a powerful relief. Trey was alive and for the first time in months she felt fully alive too. "I'll deal with them later."

First she had to get Trey back.

CHAPTER FIFTY-EIGHT

He must hate her.

Alicia walked down the hall to her office feeling deflated. It had been a week since Trey's return from Argentina and five days since she'd sent him a crucial text.

A text that should have changed everything between them.

But he hadn't replied.

Perhaps he never would.

Perhaps she'd been a bit too confident that he'd give her a second chance. She probably shouldn't have bought a new bedroom set, cleaned up her apartment and added new pillows, bought another hiding place for Liz's terrarium and a special gift she'd hoped Trey would treasure.

She walked past Fabian's desk and muttered a cursory greeting before she turned to her office door.

"Alicia, you have—," Fabian began but Alicia waved

him away. "Yeah, a meeting. I know." Her parents had given her a proper scolding for missing the last one. Not that she'd listened. She still had to figure out what to do with their plans for her but didn't want to deal with two major changes at once.

She chewed her lip as she absently walked inside her office.

What if Trey was still angry at her? Or worse, felt nothing?

She'd have to figure out how to win him back.

She didn't want to imagine a life without him in it.

She took off her coat and casually hung it up on the freestanding coat rack. She turned to her desk then paused.

Wait...she *still* didn't have a coat rack.

She spun around and gasped. Trey!

She stood frozen, her eyes hungrily taking in every inch of him before she lunged at him.

She hit him in the chest both pleased and enraged to see him standing there. "Why are you hiding behind a door?"

"I wasn't hiding. I was—"

She waved her hands, her heart and mind racing too fast for her to take in any explanations. "Never mind." She took a deep breath. "Did you get my text?"

Trey folded her coat over the chair before he held out a sheet of paper. "Yes."

She frowned. "You printed it out?"

"Only the image. I wanted to study it."

Alicia closed her eyes in frustration. "There's nothing to study. It's a pros and cons chart for giving me a second chance. I thought you liked charts. Jacob said so."

Trey nodded. "I do."

She'd worked so hard on it. She'd wanted to impress him, but instead he looked bored. She rubbed her hands together. At least he was here, that was a start. "Well... then what did you think?"

Trey lowered his gaze, carefully folded the paper and shoved it in his pocket before he met her eyes. "I think that no chart can measure how much I love you."

Alicia felt her knees give way. She grabbed the back of the chair for support. "I thought you hated me."

He frowned. "Why would you think that?"

"Because you took nearly a week to reply."

"Sorry about that. I was sick when I got back and was knocked out for a couple days. I didn't want to bother you."

Alicia's gaze sharpened. He did look a little off-color. Why hadn't she noticed that before? She touched his forehead. "Are you okay now? Do you need to sit down? You look like you've lost weight. Did you drink plenty of fluids? When did you last eat something?"

Trey gently removed her hand from his forehead; his mouth twitched with amusement.

Alicia caught the expression and frowned. "It's not funny. I'm serious. What if you caught a rare disease?"

Trey laughed. Filling the room with a deep, rich laughter that reminded her of why her life had felt empty without him. "Don't be mad at me," he said, drawing her into his arms. "This is one of the reasons I love you so much. You're always looking out for me."

She wrapped her arms around him and held him tight, inhaling his scent, feeling his heartbeat. "I missed you. I'm sorry I pushed you away."

Her cell phone rang.

Trey released her. "I should go. I know you're busy." He brushed his lips against hers, leaving them aching for more. "We can talk more later."

"Wait," she said when he turned to the door. She grabbed his hand, too late forgetting not to, but this time he didn't violently pull away. He winced. She began to loosen her grip when he said, "No, don't let go." His dark eyes met hers in a silent plea. "Hold on to me."

Alicia tightened her hold and pulled him towards her desk. "I have something for you." She opened her top drawer and pulled out a ring box.

"What is this?" he asked in a harsh whisper.

Only a year ago that voice would have filled her with unease, but as she lifted his hand then slid the Damascus steel ring with blue opal inlay on his finger, she felt only a glorious joy. "This is my declaration of love."

Trey stared down at the ring for so long she began to worry a little. "You don't like it? Is it the wrong stone?"

He reached inside his coat pocket and pulled out a ring box. He opened it and revealed an oval-shaped blue opal rose gold ring, accented with diamonds.

She held out her hand and let him slide the ring on her finger before she held her ringed hand beside his.

The stones they'd chosen were nearly identical.

They were of the same heart and mind.

Alicia cupped Trey's face and kissed him before she

dashed behind her desk and called Fabian on the phone. "I need you to organize a meeting," she told him.

"But you hate meetings."

"Not this one." She smiled, looking over at Trey. "I want the family to officially meet the man I'm going to marry."

CHAPTER FIFTY-NINE

*A*licia ended up planning a double wedding: One for her and Trey and Jacob and Sandra. It wasn't easy to create a Haitian-Jamaican-Korean-American wedding but the ceremony was memorable for all the right reasons.

She finally formally met Trey's mother, she'd seen her in the past through video chat where she'd shared about her life living as a potter in New York, but seeing the heavy set woman with punk rock hair, reminiscent of the eighties, in person was extra special.

To her relief, Trey allowed her to host the reception on his property where she'd hired a crew to erect large white tents and three different catering crews to host a variety of foods.

She'd gotten Trey to promise to heighten security to protect his private room and Liz from wandering and/or nosy guests.

At the reception, while Lavinia and Trey's cousins

surrounded Alicia and peppered her with questions about her planned honeymoon, her friend Deanna grabbed the chance to get to know Trey and Jacob better.

"I'd love to get a picture of the two grooms," Deanna told them. She took a quick picture on her cell phone then said, "Could I get another with you two back to back? Yes, good and how about one with Trey's arm around Jacob's shoulder and Jacob looking back at Trey—"

Alicia jumped in front of her friend, having escaped her other guests. "That's enough." She turned to Jacob and Trey. "For the rest of the evening ignore her."

Trey furrowed his brows. "But she was just—"

"I mean it. Ignore her." Alicia took Deanna's arm and dragged her away, briefly waving at Maya and her lanky, shaggy haired new boyfriend, Lawrence. When they were far enough away, Alicia stopped and turned to her friend. "Behave."

Deanna gazed down in awe at the picture she'd taken of the two men. "I couldn't help myself. They're gorgeous. Together they're so beautiful. Do you think you could get Jacob to rest his head on Trey's shoulder?"

She looked at Trey who was smiling at something Sandra was saying to Jacob. Jacob sent Trey a pained expression before the two men laughed. Jacob looked jubilant and carefree; Trey coolly content. The bonds of their friendship stronger than ever. "No."

Deanna made a face. "No wonder you kept them to yourself all this time. Your descriptions of them didn't even tell half the story. I mean Trey is—"

"Careful, you're talking about my husband now."

"Trey may be your husband but Tristan and Jace are my creations. My fans will love them and I just got a great idea." Deanna dashed into a corner and started typing on her cell phone.

Carl approached Alicia with a smile. "Congratulations. I didn't see this wedding coming."

Alicia narrowed her eyes. "Somehow I don't believe you."

He laughed. "That's fine by me."

"I really do love your son."

"I always knew that. I just needed to see how much."

With Trey's help Alicia had also seen a lot more about herself. She hadn't needed to quit her job. Instead she'd found a way to make it suit her. By using Trey's pros and cons chart, she learned she enjoyed coming up with ideas and working with the different departments, but hated going to the office every day and the endless meetings.

So his solution was to have her work from home. She managed to convince her family that she could be just as productive working in a home office. She also let them know she wanted to work as a consultant on a project by project basis—that would allow her the freedom to try different things. She also let them know she had no intention of running the company one day, but would happily support whoever did.

Her parents had reluctantly agreed.

Trey walked over to Carl and Alicia, his gaze suspicious. "What are you two talking about?"

Carl patted him on the back. "Relax, we're all family now. I can't scare Alicia away."

"No," Alicia said turning to Trey with a happy grin. "Nothing can scare me now." She wrapped her arms around his neck and gazed at him with eyes of love. "I am so happy." She never wanted him to feel uncertain again. He was her rock, she'd be the same for him. "You never have to fear losing me," she said with a kiss. "I plan to stay by your side. For now. For always."

ABOUT THE AUTHOR

Dara Girard, an award-winning, national bestselling author of more than forty novels, from romance to suspense, loves telling stories.

Born in the US to immigrant parents, Dara enjoys pulling from her Jamaican, British, Nigerian heritage and exposure to various cultures to bring what reviewers and fans call "vivid emotional stories" to life. She is best known for her popular Henson Series, the mysterious Clifton Sisters, and the fun Black Stockings Society.

You can write her at:
contactdara@daragirard.com
or
P.O. Box 10345
Silver Spring, MD 20914
If you'd like to receive a reply, please send a self-addressed stamped envelope.

Visit her website to sign up for her newsletter and get sneak peeks, monthly updates on new releases, and special offers.

For more information visit
www.daragirard.com

www.ingramcontent.com/pod-product-compliance
Lightning Source LLC
Chambersburg PA
CBHW030711190726
48286CB00001B/269